# THE
# UNSTOPPABLE
# WASP

## BUILT ON HOPE

### SAM MAGGS

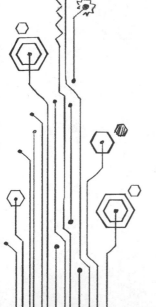

AUTUMN
PUBLISHING

# AUTUMN
## PUBLISHING

Published in 2021
First published in the UK by Autumn Publishing
An imprint of Igloo Books Ltd
Cottage Farm, NN6 0BJ, UK
Owned by Bonnier Books
Sveavägen 56, Stockholm, Sweden
www.igloobooks.com

© 2021 MARVEL

0621 001
2 4 6 8 10 9 7 5 3 1
ISBN 978-1-80022-160-4

Printed and manufactured in Italy

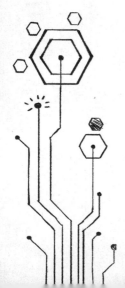

*To all the girls sick of waiting for a seat at the table.*
*We're making our own tables from here on out.*

# CHAPTER 1
## NADIA MEANS 'HOPE'

She was going to force Nadia to hurt her, and Nadia *hated* when people forced her to hurt them.

Nadia didn't like hurting people. Nadia liked science and her friends and her stepmum and those amazing sambusas from that Ethiopian place in the West Village that Shay ordered from for dinner every day for almost three months straight.

She liked Dazzler's second album and podcasts about history and the way her brain felt when she finally cracked a problem she'd been trying to solve for months. She even liked her driving instructor. Really, there were very few things in the world that Nadia *didn't* like.

It was kind of her thing.

But hurting people? That would never sit right with Nadia, no matter how many times she had to do it.

And as an Avenger, it turns out you actually have to do it a whole lot.

Nadia took a moment to assess her current situation. She was about fifty feet in the air, her biosynthetic wings beating fast enough to keep her aloft. She had made some adjustments to her father's original designs — after lengthy experimentation involving several online mattress orders (did you know people will just bring mattresses to your door in a box? Amazing), Nadia had come to the conclusion that the ideal number of beats per second for her wings was one hundred and twenty-five.

The ideal number of times to land on an internet mattress after jumping off your own roof? Still zero.

Below her, a large and terrifying tower sprouted from the middle of a previously sleepy Brooklyn street. It looked kind of like a regular electrical transmission tower, except this one had what appeared to be a UFO on top of it, and it was bursting through the pavement in front of a Korean place that made top-notch kimchi aioli and definitely deserved way better. Huge arcs of electricity streaked from the top of the tower, striking at random as the ominous crackle of uncontrolled energy tore through the air. Nadia knew exactly what she was looking at, and she had to be careful to stay out of its danger zone as she determined her next move.

"Monica," Nadia called out from behind her mask, "I liked the death ray much better when it was just a theory!"

"You know it's called a *Teleforce!*" Monica Rappaccini shouted back from the base of the tower. Monica wasn't a particularly flashy Super Villain, but she was familiar. Nadia had run into her a few times, and the encounters were never pleasant. A genius who had an unfortunate predilection for evil, Monica made up for a lack of super-powers with a bevy of truly horrific technological creations.

Nadia sighed. Clearly Monica had been busy since escaping S.H.I.E.L.D. custody. A death ray wasn't exactly a one-day project.

In another universe, one where Monica wasn't totally evil, Nadia might've *wanted* to meet Monica and maybe become friends, and then after that maybe even ask her to join G.I.R.L. (that's Genius In action Research Labs), the all-girls science lab Nadia ran out of Pym Laboratories to try to get S.H.I.E.L.D. (Strategic Homeland Intervention, Enforcement and Logistics Division) to invest in more up-and-coming women in science.

But noooooooo. Instead, Monica had to go and join A.I.M. (that's Advanced Idea Mechanics) – a group that also did science, but to overthrow governments and for various other nefarious purposes.

Nadia hated when people used science for evil. Science is inherently morally neutral; it just *is*. It's *people* who choose whether to use science for good or for evil. Nadia was raised by people who chose the latter. She, personally, chose the former.

And Monica was alone, here. Nadia wasn't.

"Sit rep?" Nadia asked. The headset in her helmet picked up her query and transmitted it back to G.I.R.L.

"No other A.I.M. agents on the scene," reported Taina. "Kind of hilarious, actually."

"Teleporter set for your quick exit, and it's not even malfunctioning today!" added Shay.

Nadia was always happy to hear that. "Backup?"

"Ready and extremely cute," joked Priya.

"In position," Ying clarified. She wasn't much of a talker, but that was all Nadia needed to hear. Her team had her back, and when they were working together, Nadia felt invincible.

She turned her focus back to Monica. "Why are you doing this?" Nadia yelled at the woman, zipping to the other side of the tower. "I'm pretty sure this isn't what Tesla had in mind!"

Monica was right: the death ray was, in fact, more properly called a Teleforce. It had come from the mind of Nikola Tesla, an electrical engineer in the early twentieth century who we mostly have to thank for modern electricity in our walls (big win for humanity). Nadia liked Tesla because he was a Serbian American scientist and she was a Hungarian-and-kind-of-Russian American scientist and that, she felt, made them kind of similar, in a way.

Tesla also, in the 1930s, invented a death ray (less of a win for humanity).

Or, sorry, the *Teleforce*. Tesla never actually built one (or if he did, no one ever saw it), but he *did* describe his plans for a charged particle-beam superweapon in great detail in a treatise called *The New Art of Projecting Concentrated Non-Dispersive Energy through Natural Media*, which is a very scientist way of saying *I Figured Out How to Make a Death Ray*.

It was designed to exude a massive electrical force that could shoot out microscopic particles at high speed. Kind of like a giant death torch–slash–Van de Graaff generator,* except if you touched this one, instead of making your hair

*A really cool electrostatic generator that uses static electricity to make your hair stick straight out from your head. Looks like a big lowercase *i*.

stand on end, it would probably explode your hair out of your scalp with the force of ten thousand suns. When focused into a beam, that force could disrupt the very atoms of whatever creature or machine had the misfortune of being on the receiving end of the death ray.

Teleforce.

No matter what you called it, it was a real day-ruiner, even for someone with as generally sunny a disposition as Nadia.

Still waiting for Monica's response, Nadia scrutinised the tower. It was definitely not a true Teleforce. There was probably no way to make one of those for real, though she wouldn't put it past Tony Stark to try. But it definitely *was* a huge and dangerous electrical generator.

So still a big problem for the people just trying to enjoy their bibimbap.

"Why am I doing this?!" Monica parroted back at Nadia. She was manipulating a control panel at the tower's base – probably Nadia's best bet at disrupting the circuitry powering the generator. "Why *wouldn't* I do this?!"

"Isn't that what I asked?" English wasn't Nadia's first language, but she was pretty sure she'd been crystal clear there. Nadia tucked her arms into her sides and sped down towards Monica – and the control panel. She landed an arm's length away from her one-time-potential-future-friend-and-lab-partner-now-evil-scientist.

"Don't come any closer," Monica warned. "I can focus these rays right on you."

"Okay," Nadia said agreeably, raising her hands in the air. "I'll stay right here. But only if you turn off the Teleforce. This isn't going to do A.I.M. any good."

Monica shook her head and continued to manipulate the controls. "This isn't for A.I.M. This is for..." She paused. "This is... for me. Because... I want to."

*She sounds unsure about that.* Nadia sighed. That seemed like a bad sign. Why were evil scientists always so confusing?

*Probably all the evil.*

Monica stabbed frantically at the control panel. As she did, a red number display began counting down. "When I'm done here, the entire world will know my name."

*Two minutes. Not good.*

The power coming off the Teleforce began to increase in intensity.

"Sure, name recognition. Good reason for evil," Nadia mumbled, keeping to herself that in her opinion, as far as Super Villain names went, 'Monica Rappaccini' wasn't going to be making any best-of lists anytime soon. It was kind of long, which made snappy banter during fights hard, and only really villainous weirdos used their full names. Even other A.I.M. members had monikers, however underwhelming (Amber Silverstein's 'Seeker'? Really?). "There are innocent people in this neighbourhood." Nadia took a step forward with a hand outstretched. A gesture of peace. "If you want to attempt dangerous experimental science, there's a better—"

"I said get *back*!" In an instant, Monica was off the controls and lunging at Nadia.

Fortunately, an instant was all Nadia ever needed.

Nadia saw these things like they were happening in slow motion. Which, thanks to physics, they kind of were. As Monica's momentum propelled her towards Nadia's position, Nadia leapt into the air. Held momentarily aloft by her wings, Nadia pressed a small button on her right glove, reachable in an instant but not so clumsily placed that she ever hit it accidentally (well... not often, anyway). The button activated Nadia's supply of Pym Particles.

## NADIA'S NEAT SCIENCE FACTS!!!

My father, Hank Pym, discovered and isolated the subatomic particle he would go on to name for himself, as men do. Proper deployment of the particles allows a subject to change their size and mass, either shrinking to incredibly small sizes or growing to epically large proportions.

The particles bypass many of the usual laws of particle physics, which I found extremely frustrating when I first attempted to re-create his research. As the human body shrinks with the Pym Particles, it becomes much more dense; all that energy is compressed into a tiny ball just waiting to explode. And when it does, it's ultra-powerful, able to damage even the toughest Super Villains. The body's excess mass is temporarily transported to an alternate dimension, where it waits to be needed again.

For the record, I would call them Subatomic Human RearraNgement Kernels (that's S.H.R.I.N.K.!). But then again, I like acronyms. I think I am in good company there.

The neat science explained how Pym Particles work, but what using Pym Particles *felt* like was an entirely different story.

Nadia liked a lot of things. Most things, really. Even kimchi aioli (especially kimchi aioli?). But this was Nadia's favourite feeling in the entire world.

In a millisecond, Nadia went from being just over five

feet tall to being barely a centimetre tall. She could feel the energy in her body buzz like an archer's string pulled taut; in the same instant, she felt the rest of her mass slipping away entirely. It was like falling too fast in an elevator, only if you *were* the elevator and also if the elevator was really super small now. It was freeing. And that was coming from a girl who already knew how to fly.

From her new vantage point, Nadia looked up and saw Monica's gloved hand soaring towards the space Nadia had occupied just a moment ago. The glove looked as if it were moving in slow motion.

It wasn't, of course. Moving in slow motion, that is. But Nadia was very, very small, which meant she could now move very, very quickly, which made all other humans seem positively lethargic by comparison. The perfect moment to act.

Nadia narrowed her eyes and jetted upwards. Maybe she could get away with hurting Monica just a *little*. She was going to have to hurt the almost-Teleforce quite a bit, though.

She landed on Monica's fist while it was still moving forward, running at full speed up the length of her could-have-been-friend's forearm. The fabric below Nadia's feet was rubbery – she wasn't sure what her super suit was made of, but it likely kept Monica safe from the electricity sparking off the tower. Some kind of vulcanised rubber, maybe. Clever. She'd made some modifications to her old suit in her spare time post–S.H.I.E.LD. custody jailbreak. Nadia approached Monica's elbow, hoping this might be easier than she'd thought. Because she was running out of time.

Nadia had always been better at science than at fighting, but the two weren't mutually exclusive. In fact, being good at science had always made Nadia a much better fighter. .

The human body is just a machine, after all – a very complex, organic machine that doesn't always work the way it's supposed to and is much more challenging to program than a servo, for example, but still a machine. Disrupt even one key joint or mechanism and the whole thing goes down.

Nadia eyed Monica's elbow, currently the proportionate size of a massive boulder in her path. Monica's rubbery suit was thick, but it was no match for Nadia's knowledge of human anatomy. She pinpointed her destination, pulled her arm back, reached the proper crevice and…

Jabbed.

Here's the thing about the 'funny bone'. It is not a bone, and it is certainly not funny.

## NADIA'S NEAT SCIENCE FACTS!!!

What we think of colloquially as the 'funny bone' is actually the ulnar nerve, which runs all the way from your neck to your pinkie finger. Like most nerves in your body, the ulnar nerve is hidden under layers of muscle and bone and other things that are good to have inside you. At the elbow, however, it is not hidden quite so much. In a spot called the cubital tunnel, the ulnar nerve runs parallel to the bone and is covered only by skin and a little bit of ligament. If you hit your elbow in just the right spot...

Funny!

Well, for me, anyway. As the person doing the hitting. Externally. In this moment. You understand what I'm getting at.

Nadia heard Monica howl and pushed off into a backflip, taking to the air again. As Monica grasped her arm and cursed, she was snagged from behind by a tangle of sentient vines flying through the air, courtesy of Priya. Nadia changed course, watching as the vines restrained Monica and she began to struggle. As she zipped directly towards a vent visible at the base of the tower's control panel, Nadia could see Ying rushing out towards Monica from behind the nearby restaurant.

Monica was handled. But the Teleforce wasn't.

Once Nadia crawled inside, Monica's obscenities faded to background noise. Nadia was in the cooling vent and had to get to the proper controls to short-circuit the thing before it could hurt any innocent people. The console was big; it was going to take Nadia ages to find a path that would lead her to the thing's servers. She didn't know exactly how long she had left before the timer hit zero and the Teleforce went full death ray all over Bay Ridge, but it couldn't be much.

She was going to have to do some science, and she was going to have to do it fast.

Luckily, fast science was what Nadia did best.

---

"I did not do any fast *science*, per se." Nadia shook her head. "I wasn't sure how long I had on the timer and the panel's circuitry was a mess. So I just… returned to my normal size. Inside the panel. And shredded the console to pieces in the process, which disabled the Teleforce. Maybe not the most elegant scientific solution, but it worked!"

*Nadia: 1, Death Ray: 0.*

"Ying and Priya had Monica tied up, but she used her

Phasing Belt and vanished. Typical. But Tai was right, there was no one else from A.I.M. in the vicinity. And with Shay's teleporter, we were able to get straight back to Pym Labs." Nadia paused. "Though I can't say I always trust the thing, to be honest."

"And how did this experience with Monica make you feel?" Dr Sinclair peered at Nadia over her reading glasses.

"Well…" Nadia paused, pulling her knees up to her chest and crushing the overstuffed pillow in her lap. She closed her eyes, blocking out the light streaming in through the big bay window behind her. Dr Sinclair's office was always so bright and welcoming, which made it easier to come back over and over again.

Nadia took a deep breath and tried to put herself back in the fight with Monica, emotionally. It wasn't always easy for her, revisiting the emotional complications of official Avengers business, but she owed it to her therapist – and to herself – to try. "Good," she finally responded, "that I was saving a neighbourhood. But… frustrated, too."

"At…?"

"At Monica, for choosing to be so evil."

Dr Sinclair uncrossed her legs and leaned forward. "Just at Monica?"

Nadia swallowed and looked down at her shoes. How

did Dr Sinclair always know exactly the right buttons to push?

Well. It *was* her job. And she *was* good at it.

"And at myself," Nadia conceded. "For not being able to convince Monica to join G.I.R.L., to science for good."

Dr Sinclair nodded, a sympathetic smile on her face. "But you know that you can't hold yourself responsible for other people's decisions, even if you judge them to be poor decisions, right?"

"Right. Boundaries!" Nadia looked at the clock and immediately leapt off the squishy couch. "Oh! I've kept you overtime again!"

With a laugh, Dr Sinclair stood to let Nadia out of her sun-drenched office. "It's okay. I like all the science facts. I feel like I learn something new every session."

"Me too." Nadia rushed forward and wrapped her therapist in a hug. "But I have a surprise party after this I can't be late for."

"A surprise party?" Dr Sinclair squeezed Nadia's shoulder affectionately, then pulled away. "For whom?"

Nadia grabbed her backpack off the couch and swung it over her shoulder, unlocking her phone. "Oh, it's for me," she answered, already half-distracted.

Dr Sinclair laughed. "Not much of a surprise then, I guess. It's not your birthday…?"

"No, no," Nadia confirmed. "It's my name day. It's like a Russian birthday but for everyone named Nadia.* My friends think they're being very sneaky, but, you know…"

"You're a literal bug," offered Dr Sinclair.

"I'm a literal bug!" Nadia agreed, with enthusiasm. "Thank you for listening, as always. Same time next week?"

"Same time next week. You're up to date on your prescriptions?"

Nadia waved and nodded as she bounded out of the room and into reception. "Enough for the next three months!"

Nadia burst out of the front door of her therapist's office and into the brisk fall sunshine, popping in her earbuds as she walked. Therapy was still new to Nadia, but she found that she liked it. Well, maybe 'liked' wasn't quite the right word, though Nadia at least *tried* liking every new thing she did.

Therapy was interesting and challenging, gut-wrenching and exciting, helpful and devastating, sometimes all at

* Nadia's name was the only gift her mother had ever been able to give her, and Nadia thought it was quite a nice name, too. Nadia means 'hope', and if there was one thing that had propelled Nadia forward in all things, it was certainly hope.

once. An hour in Dr Sinclair's office could be uplifting and painful in equal measure, but it almost always helped. Nadia had been hesitant at first, but therapy was key to helping her put forth the best version of herself. And frankly, she hoped every Super Hero had a therapist, because they saw a lot of *really* weird stuff.

Mostly, though, Nadia relied on therapy to help her manage her bipolar disorder. Though she had never met her father, Nadia knew that they had many things in common. They both lived for the pursuit of knowledge. They both loved the original Wasp, Janet Van Dyne. They were both insect-based Super Heroes. And they were both prone to extremes that sometimes put those around them – and themselves – at risk.

Nadia was lucky. She had people in her life who loved her, and who recognised the symptoms. Nadia's stepmum, Janet, had even introduced Nadia to Dr Sinclair, a therapist who specialised in Super Heroes. She had come recommended to Janet by Silk – clearly the coolest of all the spider-people, in Nadia's opinion. Truth be told, Silk was the *only* spider-person she got along with, really.

Not that it was difficult. It was a truth universally acknowledged that wasps and spiders didn't mix, in most cases. Also, why were they all so sticky?

As she walked towards the nearest bus stop, Nadia hummed to herself. She walked in time to the music, her short brown bob and fringe swinging to the beat. Things were looking up.

Sure, Nadia had a lot going on right now. Monica had escaped, and A.I.M. was still out there. She was trying to keep on top of G.I.R.L. and her mental health. She really wanted to be a good friend and a good stepdaughter. And, you know, she was trying to learn how to be a Cool American Teen, too – whatever that meant. But Nadia was figuring it all out. She was happy to forget about all the tough stuff in her past and focus on all the tough-but-exciting things in front of her.

After all, she was the Unstoppable Wasp, and it was her name day. Could it really get any better than that?

# CHAPTER 2
## THAT'S CALLED 'TEMPTING FATE'

Nadia stepped through the doors of Pym Laboratories as they slid open. Instead of the familiar bustle of personnel that seemed present at all hours, she found it suspiciously empty.

Or it *would* have been suspicious, if she hadn't known exactly what was going on. Nadia took the elevator to the fourth floor and stepped out onto the landing she never, ever got tired of seeing. The massive Genius In action Research Labs logo hung proudly from the wall, visible the second you stepped off the elevator.

The programme had been Nadia's dream from the instant she discovered that S.H.I.E.L.D.'s official list of the world's smartest people didn't bother including a woman until the twenty-seventh spot. Twenty-seventh!

Nadia knew that was nonsense for a number of reasons, one of which was that she had personal experience with *several* of the people on that list, and she knew for a fact that she was smarter than they were. (*Bruce Banner?* Please. He wasn't even the smartest *Hulk.*)

Aside from the inherent issues with using a standardised test to determine intelligence (a terrible method for determining intelligence, by the way – creativity *is* intelligence, and filling out tiny bubbles is not creative), it was also clear that S.H.I.E.L.D. wasn't even bothering to seek out people to *take* the test unless they were men who were already inner-circle.

The world doesn't need to be told that Tony Stark is smart. The world needs to be told that the sixteen-year-old girl in the tiny Brooklyn apartment she shares with her dad and who gets beat up every day on her walk home from school is actually secretly building a teleporter, and she got it to *work*. And *that* is the truth.

Nadia became determined to find the smartest girls in the world so they could form their own lab, together. She started with the immediate New York City area, because that's where she was located, flying long-distance was taxing, and she didn't have her driver's licence. Yet.

But she was working on it.

She'd already managed to find the four best lab partners in the entire world, anyway, and they were all right here in G.I.R.L. HQ, right behind these doors, ready to surprise Nadia with streamers and balloons and... would there be cake?

Ooh. Nadia *really* liked cake.

She took a deep breath, thinking very hard about a convincing 'surprised' face as she swiped her key card and the sliding lab doors opened.

"Surprise!"

The sound of her friends' voices echoed off the hard surfaces of the lab tables and state-of-the-art equipment in the most beautiful cacophony. Nadia slapped her hands onto her cheeks and pulled her mouth into a perfectly formed *Oh!* of feigned shock.

"Oh my goodness!" Nadia said, her hands still on her face. "I am so surprised!"

An entire lab's worth of girls stared at Nadia for a moment in silence, the streamers and confetti still gently floating to the floor.

"She totally knew." Taina rolled her eyes and rolled her way over to the cake. "I'm cutting this now."

"I didn't know!" Nadia insisted, rushing forward to look closer at the cake. Taina was already jamming a fork into the first slice. The slice (including a *D* from HAPPY NAME DAY, NADYA, which, close enough) revealed the cake's flavour: funfetti. Obviously.

"Sure," Priya said, but Nadia could tell by the way she rolled her eyes at the ceiling that she didn't buy it.

"Nadia, you are many things," said Ying, swinging her legs down off the cake table, skillfully avoiding getting any white icing on her signature all-black athleisure ensemble. "But why don't you leave the deception to me?"

Shay elbowed her girlfriend. "We can't all be super-spies."

"She was actually trained *to be* a super-spy," Ying corrected. Shay quieted Ying down by popping some funfetti directly into her mouth. Ying shrugged and chewed.

Shay wasn't wrong, but neither was Ying. Nadia's childhood wasn't exactly what you would call *traditional*. In fact, pretty much everything after her parents' wedding was utter chaos, if Nadia was honest with herself. Hank Pym, who would later be better known in some circles as the original Ant-Man, had married Maria Trovaya, a brilliant Hungarian scientist fleeing from behind the Iron Curtain. While on their honeymoon, Maria was kidnapped by Red Room agents and later killed.

Right after she gave birth. To Nadia.

Hank hadn't even known that Maria was pregnant.

Nadia had been born and raised in the Krasnaya Komnata – the Red Room, a secret intelligence facility created by the KGB to train girls who would become the best spies in the world. Most people are more familiar with it as the Black Widow Ops Program; but what people usually *don't* know is that there is more than one way to become a Widow.

Some girls like guns. Others like gears. Nadia was the latter.

Her handlers thought that her gift for science was genetic. They encouraged Nadia to study constantly. But Nadia knew that her skills weren't inherited; they came from her and her alone. It wasn't like the shape of her head made her brain better at maths, no matter how much they'd wanted her to believe it.

Nadia worked hard. She made progress. Then she found a way to work harder. The only Red Room handler she'd ever liked – the only one who almost treated her like she was her own person and not just a product of parents she never knew – was a man with a silver arm. Nadia could still recall the big red star on his shoulder, though she couldn't remember her own mother. The man with the silver arm encouraged her to keep reading.

So she'd studied. And she'd learned. And then she'd studied some more. (She later learned his name was Bucky Barnes, and he would escape the Krasnaya Komnata and become a good guy, too!)

Of course, there was your traditional Red Room training. No one escaped a super-secret instructional spy facility without learning how to take down a man twice their size while also executing clean fouettés into a perfect double pirouette (Nadia's favourite combination to this day), sometimes simultaneously.

Nadia used her studies in science and her ballet training to help her in combat exercises; after all, it was a lot easier to take down a man twice your size if you knew how to properly destabilise his centre of gravity, and strong ankles never hurt your chances.

The Red Room handlers didn't want their charges to get too close; to say they fostered an atmosphere of competition instead of cooperation would be an understatement. But Nadia liked people, and she especially liked Ying, another scientist of the Red Room who excelled in biochemistry. Nadia and Ying hid their friendship, hoping they wouldn't be separated or used against each other.

They were, eventually. But that came later.

When Nadia finally managed to obtain a Pym Particle

on the black market, she knew she'd found her way out. Reverse engineering her father's research, Nadia learned how to use the particles to shrink – and promptly shrank her way out of the Red Room and on to freedom.

It wasn't an easy journey from Siberia to New York City. But she'd made it.

And that's where Nadia met her family for the first time.

Well, it's possible that 'met' isn't exactly the right word. Maybe... 'assembled'?

Nadia had absolutely been a proactive part of putting her current family unit together. When she'd heard about the great injustice of the S.H.I.E.L.D. list (twenty-seventh?! Are you serious?!), Nadia set out almost immediately to scour the boroughs for the smartest G.I.R.L. squad she could find.

The trick, it turned out, was recruiting them without immediately scaring them off. Look, Nadia was enthusiastic. She'd made a little explanatory holo-video and everything. She thought it was *very* convincing and also very charming and even a little bit funny, too? But Nadia was raised in an espionage facility, so she had to admit her sense of humour was maybe a little warped.

And don't even start on her pop culture knowledge (or lack thereof). Ms. Marvel has always been appalled at how little Nadia knew about life outside of a brainwashing facility. But who has time to catch up on a bazillion TV shows when they all seem to be about the same white man who hasn't shaved in several weeks? If you've seen one...

First, Nadia had tracked down Taina in Washington Heights. Nadia found her tinkering with a robotic goalie she was using to help her older sister play street hockey. Tai and her older sister Alexis lived with their *abuelita*, which Nadia now knew was what Puerto Rican girls called their *babulyas*.*

Tai was the best engineer Nadia had ever met, and she'd grown up with a lot of world-class engineers. Nadia suspected Tai's love for robotics came in part from being born with cerebral palsy; she always had a mechanical aid around and considered herself quite cyberpunk as a result. Nadia and Tai were different in a lot of ways. Nadia tried to like everything; Tai liked almost nothing at first brush, but was known to come around. Still, neither of them had ever let perceived limitations stymie their potential. Nadia felt so lucky to have Tai as a lab partner, but even luckier to call her a friend.

---

*Russian for 'grandmother'. A purely theoretical concept for Nadia, but one she liked all the same.

**TAINA MIRANDA**
- Mechanical engineer
- Could make a robot to destroy you, but chooses not to, and that's powerful
- Forearm crutches and wheelchair decorated with stickers both colourful and threatening
- Older sister Alexis enjoys sports and talking to potential investors about G.I.R.L.
- Does not suffer fools... or anyone, really

Then there was Priya. She lived in Queens, but Nadia found her in Times Square, working at her family's gift shop. Priya's parents were Indian immigrants and wanted to give Priya every opportunity to find success. Which sometimes came into direct conflict with Priya's desire to, you know... be Cool. Even so, Priya had an incredible drive of her own – it just often manifested a little differently than the other G.I.R.L.s'.

Nadia understood a little bit of what it was like to be under so much pressure you felt you might buckle, but knew that Priya's situation was entirely unique. She was nervous about her parents finding out that she had a remarkable gift for biology – truly, she was extraordinary. But she didn't want the anxiety that would inevitably come from her parents on the discovery of such an aptitude. But when Nadia saved their shop from an attack, and Priya saw the incredible power of science in action, she joined the lab, hoping to do good for the world.

Also, one time Priya inhaled a bunch of gas working on one of her experiments in plant genetics, and then she could communicate with and control plants.

So, that was certainly A Thing now.

**PRIYA AGGARWAL**
- Biologist and geneticist
- The most on-trend person I have ever met, and my stepmum is a fashion designer
- Helps run her uncle's tchotchke shop in Times Square
- Tries to maintain a healthy work/life balance, which, same
- Accidentally recently gained the ability to control and communicate with plants (!!!)

Next, Nadia headed to Brooklyn and found Shay *literally* exploding out of her fourth-storey bedroom window after an experiment with a prototype teleporter went awry. Happens to the best of us, really.

Shay had been going through some hard times: her mum left for Los Angeles to become an actress, and her dad, though *amazing* (truly worthy of the #1 DAD! mug in Priya's family's shop), worked long, stressful hours to support them both. Shay had been getting bullied at school and, like Nadia, needed a place where she could be herself. Somewhere she could work on her teleporter in peace. Somewhere like G.I.R.L.

## SHAY SMITH
- Physicist
- Introduced me to Janelle Monáe's fashion sense <u>and</u> music, for which I am very grateful
- Has a super-cool dad who supports all of her experiments (though prefers she do them in the lab)
- Invented a teleporter, for real
- Ying's girlfriend

Finally, there was Ying, who wasn't so much recruited as she was rescued. When they'd reunited for the first time since Nadia had escaped the Red Room, it was actually because their handlers had done the thing that Nadia had feared most: used their friendship against them. They'd sent Ying to track Nadia down, and threatened to explode her with a bomb in her brain if Ying didn't bring Nadia back.

Fortunately, Ying found Nadia with a squad of girl

scientists who were able to remove the bomb from her head, severing Ying's connection to the Red Room forever. Now Ying also had a spot in the lab – and in Shay's heart. Nadia had always found public displays of affection entirely unnecessary, but with Shay and Ying she found it almost cute. Sometimes.

**YING LIU**
- Biochemist
- Raised with me in the Black Widow Ops Program in Siberia (aka the Red Room), my oldest friend
- Not big on 'emotions' and/or 'feelings'
- Surprisingly close with G.I.R.L. mentor Bobbi Morse, aka the Super Hero Mockingbird, aka the biochemist with cool T-shirts and big sticks
- Shay's girlfriend

And here they all were, in G.I.R.L. HQ at Pym Labs, pretending to surprise Nadia, who'd brought them all together. And frankly, Nadia was touched. *This* was the kind of public display of affection Nadia understood. Supported, even.

*Especially* because it involved funfetti.

"Okay, yes, I knew about the surprise," Nadia admitted

with a wry smile. "But that doesn't mean I appreciate it any less! Did you fix whatever's been wrong with Shay's teleporter?"

"There's nothing *wrong* with it—" started Shay.

"Except sometimes socks go into it and never come out again," finished Ying.

Priya nodded. "Like my favourite thigh-high ones with the cat ears."

"I literally don't care at all about fashion, but I *did* love those cat socks," Tai added.

Nadia laughed. "You probably just calibrated the quantum oscillators wrong. Remember when Priya tested it that one time and rematerialised with her ponytail on the other side of her head?"

"Okay, are we going to get into science mistakes?" Shay pointed her fork at Nadia. "Because we can *get into it*—"

"Remember the time you accidentally stained Priya's whole left arm with that weird chemical?" Tai jabbed Ying.

"It was an accident! It washed off!" Ying protested. "Remember that time *you* went off to fight Mother* all by yourself?"

Nadia threw her hands up in front of her in defence. "I

---

* One of the 'adults' in the Red Room. She came up with a diabolical plan to force Nadia and Ying to return to the Red Room, but they escaped. Again.

was trying to be, you know, tough! And I made a pretty good 'fearless leader' speech before I left!" She pointed to a note still taped to the wall next to the G.I.R.L. squad sign: *Never stop doing science and being amazing.*

"Sweet," Priya agreed. "But bafflingly stupid."

They all laughed. They'd all messed up, a few times, but it didn't change how they felt about each other.

"How was therapy?" Shay asked around a mouthful of cake, careful not to get any icing on her purple suitcoat, complete with tails and a black-and-white bow tie. Shay was always dressed well, but Nadia recognised this as a clear 'special occasion' outfit choice. When she wasn't busy with making theoretical physics non-theoretical, Shay was a thrift-shopping alterations-making mastermind.

"So good; thanks for asking!" Nadia responded, grabbing an $N$ slice. "Dr Sinclair has been so helpful. It's been really nice having someone to talk to. Not that you're all not wonderful to talk to," Nadia corrected in a rush. "I wouldn't be here without—"

"No, we get it," Tai interjected dryly. "You're all right, but I don't want any of you adjusting my meds, either."

"Exactly." Nadia smiled. Every girl in this room had played a huge role in helping to get her to a place where she was able to receive a diagnosis, and she would never stop being grateful for that. Even if she wasn't always the best at expressing it with her words. "Now…" Nadia waggled her eyebrows. "Can we start the real party?"

"Thought you'd never ask." Priya laughed, tucking her long, dark hair behind one of her ears. Priya was so gorgeous all the time, but doubly so when she laughed. Nadia knew that Priya was one of those girls who even looked amazing when she cried. She was so gifted in so many different ways. Priya had even been teaching Nadia how to do cat-eye liner and Nadia *almost* had it mastered.

On one side.

The other side… Nadia preferred not to speak of it.

The streamers and balloons abandoned, the G.I.R.L. squad moved to the far side of their lab, cake plates in hand, chatting idly about their respective days. Priya worked in her parents' shop (boring, uneventful, save for a brief sighting of a very average human Captain America imposter who was on the receiving end of a full-on Captain America–size punch from someone who, apparently, does not like Captain America very much because his cosplay was that convincing); Ying had spent the afternoon sparring with a heavy bag (Nadia felt for the bag); Shay had been responsible for the cake and décor (she excelled in nearly all things, and the funfetti choice was proof that this was no exception).

And Tai had been in the lab, getting ready for this moment.

"Okay." Tai took a deep breath. "Over here."

The girls all gathered round a table in one corner of the lab, under a makeshift banner that read LIKE MINDS. Well, it was less of a 'banner' and more of a 'single sheet of 8x10 printer paper with letters cut from magazines taped to the front'. Ying had made it. Priya expressed that she felt pretty strongly that it looked like something a serial killer had made, which just made Ying like it even more. Nadia thought it had a certain creative flair. Shay had added some glitter, which kind of just made it look like something a *deranged* serial killer had made, but, you know. Group projects are like that sometimes.

Like Minds was a Stark Industries think tank comprised of students from all over the world. The programme had different divisions and initiatives, and their latest objective was to find ways to make neighbourhoods more sustainable on a local level. Tony and his team at Like Minds had hand-selected groups of teen scientists from cities across the globe to participate in a big experimental sustainability showcase, and in New York City (well… okay, New Jersey, but as a newly minted Jersey girl, Nadia figured it was close enough), Like Minds had chosen G.I.R.L.

For weeks, Nadia and her four lab partners had been working towards strategies and solutions to present at the Like Minds showcase, which was over Thanksgiving weekend this year. As a new American, Nadia was kind of obsessed with Thanksgiving. It made absolutely no sense: it was entirely ahistorical; you ate a bizarre combination of foods to excess; enormous, vaguely threatening floating cartoon characters were a crucial part of the experience; and most people celebrated it even though doing so caused them great emotional distress. It was like the perfect distillation of the American experience.

The G.I.R.L.s still had eight whole weeks ahead of them to prepare for the showcase, but that kind of time passed quickly when most of your team was focused on passing their classes and the rest of it was busy trying to save the world from A.I.M. and maybe aliens, depending on the day.

So far, they'd all been developing projects independently. Shay had been combining biopolymer electrolytes (like from vegetable oil) with solar cells to maximise clean neighbourhood energy. Priya was figuring out how to develop genetically enhanced bioluminescent plants in the hopes that they might be able to replace street lights. Ying had been busy putting together a chemical marker that could be deployed into sewers to warn people about... Okay, Nadia had stopped paying attention at that point.

Sewage treatment was not her specialty, though she respected it deeply.

Nadia hadn't been able to settle on an idea for her own contribution just yet. She had so many ideas, but they were *big* ideas. After escaping the Red Room, she dreamed about changing the *entire* world. By comparison, making Cresskill, New Jersey, a bit more energy-efficient just seemed a little… small-time. "Starting small; thinking big." It was even on the Like Minds pamphlet. Apparently, it was a quote from Tony Stark himself.

Nadia wasn't sure she believed that. Mr Stark probably had better things to do than come up with pithy campaign slogans for teen think tanks. Especially a slogan this… dull.

Despite her own indecision about the project, Nadia was excited, as always, to see her friends' hard work.

And this was Taina's moment to shine.

On the table in front of the girls sat a Raspberry Pi motherboard connected to what looked like a very mechanical lazy Susan on wheels. The circular tray had three robotic arms attached to it, each with a small grip at the end. Tai rolled her chair over to the table and picked up a remote.

"So," she started, confidently, "what we have here is a self-transporting, easily rotating plant pollination device. Or…" She paused. "The Bee-Boi."

"Does this—" Priya started, but Tai was already way ahead of her.

"It travels through city parks and gardens and pollinates high-energy, low-yield plants, freeing up actual bees to do much more useful, helpful work for their hives," Tai explained quickly. "It has three pollinators that can activate simultaneously, and each arm has a camera that can recognise flowers and other plant matter that requires pollination."

## NADIA'S NEAT SCIENCE FACTS!!!

Tai is completely right, as per usual! We are in a bee crisis. Thanks to a brutal combination of viruses, fungi, habitat destruction, pesticides, pollution, malnutrition and various many other elements, honey bee populations have been dwindling across the globe for years. Apiarists and entomologists say some of these factors could be driving 'colony collapse disorder', or CCD, a phenomenon where the majority of worker bees disappear and leave the queen bee behind in her hive. Some bees are dying as a result of CCD, and others are at risk of extinction because of human-driven factors.

And if we don't have any bees, we'll lose some of earth's most crucial pollinators, and three-quarters of all crops depend on pollinators to reproduce! (Basically: the sex bits from one plant have to make their way to the sex bits of another plant to make a new plant, so the bees carry the sex bits from one plant to the other, honestly kind of by accident! They're helping plants sex and they don't even know it. Bees rule!) While Tai's design is ingenious and could absolutely assist bee populations, we should remember that it's up to us to explore other sustainability options, like being smarter about pesticides and focusing on ecological farming, to really save our bees long-term!

Because I would like for us to always have garlic. No bees, no garlic.

Can. You. Imagine.

Priya whistled. "Tai... that's extremely cool."

"Is it as cool as the poop thing, though?" Shay teased, nudging Ying playfully.

"The 'poop thing' is a great idea, and you'll all feel bad for joking about it one day," Ying deadpanned. "Also, stop calling it the 'poop thing'."

Nadia couldn't wait any longer. "Let's see it, Tai!" she

urged with a clap of her hands. Admiring the squad's work in action was her favourite thing to do in the lab, after eating funfetti. But that happened far less frequently.

"All right." Tai grinned. "Hold on to your butts." She hit a button on the remote in her hand. The mechanical arms raised in unison. The wheels moved forwards and backwards. And the tray-like platform started to rotate on a timer. One; two; three. One; two; three.

"Tai!" Nadia cheered. "Nice work!"

"Well, you know, I—" It was Tai who was interrupted this time. The lazy Susan was becoming significantly less lazy. "Hang on—" Tai slammed what Nadia could only assume was the Stop button over and over again to no avail. The platform's rotation started to speed up: onetwothree onetwothree onetwothreeonetwothreeonetwothreeonetwothree, until…

The Raspberry Pi caught fire. It was a small piece of equipment, but it produced some impressively large flames.

Ying sprang into action first, ripping an extinguisher from the nearest wall and levelling the nozzle at the motherboard. Carbon dioxide blasted from it, smothering the robot in a white cloud and extinguishing the fire almost instantly.

The robot's arms drooped. Tai, in her chair, covered in a fair amount of white $CO_2$ herself, drooped just the same.

Nadia rushed over to examine the robot. "It's still completely salvageable, Taina. I wouldn't worry—"

"It's fine," said Tai, waving her off. She gripped the wheels on her chair and shoved herself forward, right into the other girls. "Comin' through."

"Don't stress, Tai, you're gonna get it—" Shay started, before Ying cut her off with a glance.

Ying's glances could do that. They were very scary. Ying was good with glances the way some Widows were good with tomahawks. Better, even.

"Seriously, guys, it's fine." Tai moved between the girls and towards the lobby. Nadia could tell by the break in her voice and the speed at which she was trying to exit the lab that it was definitely not *fine*. "It was a stupid idea anyway."

"No idea is stupid," Nadia protested. "That's G.I.R.L. rule number one. Can we help—?"

"It's *fine*!" insisted Tai. "I just want to wash this off. I'll see you all tomorrow. Happy name day, Nadia."

Nadia watched Tai roll out of the room's automated double doors, one hand waving back. The big DON'T TELL ME TO SMILE sticker – the one with the girl holding the spiked bat and making a rude gesture – stared Nadia down from the back of Tai's chair until the doors slid closed behind her.

The girls all looked at each other in silence for a minute. A bunch of Nadia's name day balloons were now coated with a thick white layer of carbon dioxide.

Priya broke the silence. "Well. It's not exactly confetti, but it's a little festive?"

Nadia sighed. Tai would be in a better space tomorrow. Or maybe she wouldn't. It was hard to tell with Tai.

An alarm went off on her phone and Nadia started. She whipped it out of her back pocket — the best thing about high-waisted jeans (*among many best things*, thought Nadia) was that they provided gigantic back pockets for gigantic mobile phones and also sometimes snacks. Ladies' clothes never had sufficiently workable pockets.

*Pocket… dimensions? An alternate-dimension pocket for women's clothes only…* Nadia tucked that idea away for later. She turned off her phone alarm and explained to her friends apologetically, "Sorry to cut the party short," she said, "but I have to skedaddle." She'd learned that word from Hawkeye. The superior Hawkeye, of course: Kate Bishop. "Family dinner tonight at the house."

"Another surprise?" guessed Ying.

"Oh, absolutely," Nadia confirmed. "I should be getting the call any second."

The girls stared at Nadia, waiting. She looked down at the phone in her hand.

"Just… any second," she said again.

Still nothing.

"Any…" She swallowed. Was she wrong about this surprise…? She was *certain* she'd overheard—

Her phone buzzed in her hand, the screen lighting up. "Ha!" Nadia lifted the device in triumph. Shay and Priya burst out in laughter. Ying shook her head, but Nadia could see the smile in the corners of her lips.

"I'll be at the shop tonight and tomorrow if any of you need anything," Priya said, picking up her oversized tote bag. It was a beautiful faux-leather, and Nadia was always impressed by how many things Priya could fit in it. It was like her own super-power. Other than the talking-to-plants thing. Like a second, tote bag–related super-power. "Picking up some shifts while my uncle finishes his semester."

"We're out, too," Shay said, grabbing Ying's hand. "Date night."

"We're going to the cemetery!" Ying said, a huge grin taking over her face.

Shay blinked a few times before managing her own, slightly less enthusiastic smile. "They're showing a movie on a big projector," Shay explained, as Ying dragged her out of the room. "It's *Spaced Invaders* tonight."

"'Prepare to die, Earth scum!'" Ying called back over her shoulder, then disappeared down the hallway.

Nadia assumed – nay, *hoped* – that was a quote from the film. Ying had been much better about catching up on her pop culture knowledge since exiting the Red Room, and she had a special affinity for weird movies from the '90s. Nadia supposed both she and Ying were trying to reclaim their lost childhoods in different ways. Ying was determined to consume as many missed movies as possible; Nadia was consuming more baked goods than an unsupervised eleven-year-old at a particularly decadent birthday party. And she was trying to find and hold on to joy in this new life, outside of the Red Room. The kind of joy that kids didn't usually have to search for.

Her phone buzzed in her hand again. She was keeping her ride waiting.

Nadia was the last one out of the lab, and she turned off the lights behind her.

*Something's not right,* Nadia thought, her Wasp-sense* tingling.

"Ah!" she cried, flipping the lights back on in an instant. Nadia rushed back and grabbed the remainder of her cake. "Close one."

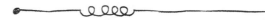

*Too much like spidey-sense. Will have to workshop.

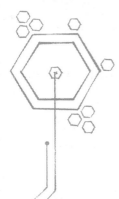

# CHAPTER 3
## OH, LIKE YOU'D HAVE LEFT IT THERE?

"You're late!" chastised Nadia, leaning into the driver's-side window. "Can I drive?"

The older, very English-looking man who sat behind the wheel of the bright red Chevy Corvette bristled. "Late? You didn't even know I was coming!"

"Yes, of course, of course." Nadia brushed him off. "So, can I drive?" The man stared at her, straight-faced. Nadia put on her best puppy-dog eyes. "Pleeeease, *Dedushka*?\* It's my name day…!"

The man sighed. Edwin Jarvis had been around Super Heroes most of his adult life – first as a pilot in the Royal

\*'Grandfather' in Russian, much less theoretical to Nadia now.

Canadian Air Force, then as the butler for the Starks. He had seen the Avengers assembled, Quinjets in action, full-on alien invasions.

He was good at his job because he was unflappable. Jarvis could handle *anything*. But Nadia knew that Jarvis was no match for his latest charge, the newest and smallest of all the Avengers: the Unstoppable Wasp.

When it came to Nadia, Jarvis was decidedly *flapped*. Especially when she called him Dedushka.

## EDWIN JARVIS
- English accent, but absolutely from Brooklyn
- He is a butler, but he could also kick your butt
- His cooking is really, really, really good
- We once went on a road trip together to meet my extended family
- He's doesn't get upset, but he <u>does</u> get disappointed

Nadia tried to wield her great-granddaughterly powers with great-granddaughterly responsibility. But she *really* wanted to drive Lola, which called for full-on weaponised adorability.

A successful Super Hero has many tools in their arsenal and knows how and when to use them all.

Nadia saw Jarvis break. It was subtle, but it was there. His jaw unclenched for the briefest of moments before clenching up again. Nadia wondered if Jarvis was ever truly unclenched. It couldn't be good for one person to be so tightly wound all the time, could it?

"Oh, all *right*," Jarvis conceded. "But only because——"

Nadia threw open the driver's-side door, hugging him before Jarvis could even get his seat belt off. "Thank you thank you thank you! I'll drive so safely. You won't even know I'm driving!"

"That really doesn't sound as comforting as you think it does," Nadia heard Jarvis say under his breath as he walked around the cherry-red Corvette to the passenger side. "You do recall that this car is only temporarily on *loan*, right?"

Nadia slid into the driver's seat, adjusting the chair and the rear-view mirror like she'd been taught. Driving was the one thing Nadia was able to learn on a normal Cool American Teen schedule. She had never learned how to ride a bicycle on a leafy suburban street; that skill had come from Red Room trainers around the same time she had learned to operate a KA-22 Russian military helicopter.

She'd never celebrated a win with her junior softball team; Nadia didn't like to remember the team activities she'd been put through in Siberia. She didn't know what it was like to sneak into a movie to see a film you weren't allowed to see; Nadia was party to violence much worse than anything you'd see in a cinema before she was even old enough to wrap her fingers around a knife's handle.

But she was sixteen, and she was learning how to a drive a car. That's what completely normal Cool American Teens did. And now Nadia was doing it, too. Nadia was looking forward to the rest of the shared experiences she would have with the rest of Cresskill, New Jersey, now that she was putting her past behind her. For good.

Jarvis cleared his throat subtly from the passenger's seat. That usually meant Nadia had forgotten something.

*Ah.* The handbrake.

Nadia smiled at her favourite adoptive Super Hero dedushka and pulled down the lever. It took effort, but she avoided so much as glancing at the best button on the dashboard – the big red button that matched the car's exterior paint job to a tee. The one that would send the car flying – off the pavement and straight into the skies.

That was only for occasions *much* more special than this one.

"We are going—"

Nadia shook her head. "Jarvis. I know where we're going."

"Ah," he sighed. "Of course you do. And don't forget to check your mirrors."

———————————⊘

Nadia carefully stepped through the door, her surprised face (now Jarvis Approved™) in place before she even heard the words.

"Surprise!"

Nadia was greeted by more balloons and more streamers. This time, it was just inside the front door of her own home in Cresskill, New Jersey, and the greeting party was a little smaller. Holding open the door, Jarvis pulled out a tiny cardboard party horn and blew into it. It let out a pathetic little celebratory *psheeeeeeeee!* that Nadia both loved and appreciated deeply.

Inside the living room, two of the most important women in Nadia's life stood under a big banner spelling N-A-D-I-A-! (A real banner this time, not one that Ying had put together like she was trying to blackmail a police officer from the 1970s.) They wore bright metallic party hats and spun noisemakers that made crackling sounds as they rotated. It was ridiculous and wonderful and it was the best unsurprising surprise Nadia had ever had.

"Happy name day, Nadia!" The woman on the left stepped forward and held her arms out, the noisemakers still in hand. Barbara Morse – Bobbi, to her friends and to people she had only tried to kill on fewer than two occasions – wasn't a hugger, but Nadia appreciated that Bobbi knew *she* was absolutely a hugger and thus attempted to meet her halfway. Most people knew Bobbi best as Mockingbird, the kick-butt S.H.I.E.L.D. agent and Super Hero who walked tall, used to be married to Hawkeye (Barton, not Bishop) and fought crime with two big sticks.

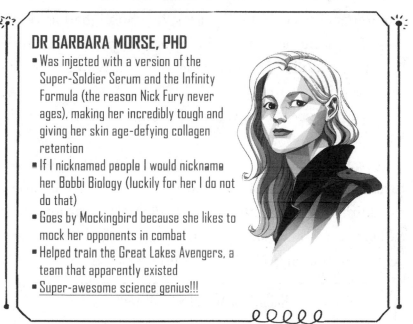

### DR BARBARA MORSE, PHD

- Was injected with a version of the Super-Soldier Serum and the Infinity Formula (the reason Nick Fury never ages), making her incredibly tough and giving her skin age-defying collagen retention
- If I nicknamed people I would nickname her Bobbi Biology (luckily for her I do not do that)
- Goes by Mockingbird because she likes to mock her opponents in combat
- Helped train the Great Lakes Avengers, a team that apparently existed
- Super-awesome science genius!!!

But not Nadia. No, Nadia knew *of* Bobbi long before she became friends with Bobbi, and not because of her stick prowess (though that was, inarguably, remarkable). Nadia knew of Dr Barbara Morse, PhD, from her attempts to re-create the Super-Soldier Serum (you know, the one that turned Captain America from a string bean into a Dorito). She was one of the most advanced biologists at S.H.I.E.L.D., and Nadia had read all of Dr Morse's research from her lab in the Krasnaya Komnata.

Nadia loved Bobbi's science, sure, but Nadia had always *really* loved the way Bobbi *wrote* about science. Most researchers weren't gifted writers, but Bobbi had a special way of making her science jump off the page and dance, each theory and equation jetéing and bourréeing across its reader's mind.

Okay, maybe Nadia was projecting. But it was how she felt.

For her part, Nadia knew that Bobbi had just been thrilled to meet someone who wanted to talk with her about extradimensional matter instead of her extra-dumpable ex-husband (whom she was absolutely smarter than, and yet was Bobbi on S.H.I.E.L.D.'s list? *Exactly*).

## NADIA'S NEAT SCIENCE FACTS!!!

Mockingbird's sticks are actually dual battle staves (a way better name than 'sticks'). These batons are hollow rods made of a steel alloy and can be wielded separately or screwed together into a *bo̅* staff that can extend up to eight feet. Bobbi keeps her opponents perpetually off-balance, and uses the momentum of her strikes to trip opponents into the rods. That is how, if you ever get on Mockingbird's bad side, she will use your own body weight against you to break your own legs. I would recommend very much not getting on Mockingbird's bad side.

Nadia felt immeasurably lucky to have Bobbi in her life, and like so many of the good things in Nadia's life these days, it was thanks to the woman standing next to the dining room table, hands clasped in front of her and a proud glint in her eyes. Janet Van Dyne stepped forward with a smile, placing a light kiss on the crown of Nadia's head while Nadia was still engulfed in Bobbi's epic biceps.* Janet was formidable both in reputation and in reality. When Nadia looked at her, she saw exactly the kind of woman she hoped to be when she was older.

*If there were a S.H.I.E.L.D. list of Best Biceps, Bobbi would certainly be on that list. Along with Captain Marvel. And America Chavez. Nadia had a feeling that it'd be men who were relegated to the twenty-seventh spot for Best Biceps.

Poised; buff; lovely; terrifying. The perfect combination of feminine attributes, Nadia thought.

**JANET VAN DYNE**
- Never wanted kids but is an excellent stepmum
- Technically Vision's babulya, though
- Head of Pym Laboratories, home of G.I.R.L.
- Like me, can use bioelectric blasts called the Wasp's Sting to take down foes
- Makes all of her own Super Hero costumes

A fashion designer and very wealthy socialite, Janet first found her way to Hank Pym after her scientist father was killed. Hank, impressed with Janet's intelligence, provided her with Pym Particles – and Ant-Man and the Wasp took flight to exact justice and thwart evil together for the first time.

Janet (who, in an extremely Hank move, looked very much like a younger version of Nadia's mother, Maria), eventually married Hank. The two of them fought crime alongside Thor\*, Iron Man and the Hulk. It was Janet

---

\*Noted Best Biceps contender for a spot somewhere between twenty-seven and fifty.

who first decided to call their epic team 'the Avengers'. Janet would tell you that wasn't a big deal, but Nadia felt like it was definitely a big deal.

When Nadia arrived in America, Janet was kind enough to take her under her biosynthetic wing. She'd opened Nadia's eyes to everything from super-heroism to BB's Tacos and from Lizzo to high fashion and 'custom couture'.*

Above all, though, Janet had shown Nadia what it meant to be part of a family. To have people you could rely on and who relied on you in return. Which was why, when it came time to fill out the first of dozens of forms that would eventually confirm her citizenship, she didn't sign as Nadia Pym or even Nadia Trovaya. Nadia had never had a last name, and there was only one that had ever really meant anything to her.

Van Dyne.

So she was Nadia Van Dyne, stepdaughter to the woman behind the Avengers, chooser of families and unwavering champion for goodness and optimism in a world that often threatened to eradicate both. Nadia was the reason that G.I.R.L. existed, but Janet was the reason that it – and Nadia herself – could become Unstoppable.

* Janet's term for Nadia's super-special jackets with holes in the back for her Wasp wings.

Not everyone can say their stepmum invented the Avengers. But Nadia could. And that made her proud to be part of Janet's family every single day.

"We know you probably already knew," said Janet, smiling at Nadia, and shutting the door behind her and Jarvis. Nadia smiled at her stepmum, grateful that she didn't have to keep up the ruse. Nadia and Janet had come by their alter egos in different ways, but they were very similar when it came right down to it.

Nadia trailed Janet into the dining room – and was *actually* surprised for the first time all day.

"Oh my—" she said, her hand coming to her mouth in genuine shock. "You did all this?"

Rows of boxes covered every square inch of the floor. The shelves had been emptied; the walls were mostly bare; even Nadia's coffeemaker had been packed away.

"We wanted to get you something you wouldn't get yourself for your name day," Bobbi explained, pulling up a chair at the small dining room table in the centre of the space. It was the only thing on the main floor that still looked lived-in – there were table settings for four set up on its surface, ready for dinner. "You're slammed with stuff right now. We handled the house."

Nadia felt like twenty pounds had been lifted off her

shoulders in an instant. Jarvis had brought her to this house in Cresskill after she'd shown up on the Avengers' doorstep in New York, fresh from the Red Room. It had been her father's. She'd thought the house might give her a sense of family, of belonging, but it had never felt like home. Her family, her belonging, existed outside of these walls.

Nadia spent most of her time at G.I.R.L. now. Each of the lab partners had their own room at Pym Labs, and Nadia preferred sleeping there. The lab sounded like possibility, even at night. The CPUs still hummed and the fans still ran and she could hear people coming and going in the halls. At the house, it was silent. It reminded Nadia of the things in her past she was trying so hard to leave behind.

Plus, when there were people around, she was less likely to accidentally hyperfocus on a task for nights on end. The lab kept her accountable, and it kept her safe. It reminded Nadia of what she *wished* the Siberian outpost of the Red Room could have been. It was her future.

"It was actually kind of… fun, packing this place up," Janet admitted. "I have a lot of memories of this house. Usually I'm one hundred per cent cool forgetting them," she added with a hint of dryness in her voice. Nadia knew that Hank hadn't always been a good partner, especially not with his mental illness left untreated. "But it's nice to be reminded of the good times we had here, before we put it up on the market."

"I also assisted with the packing!" called Jarvis from the kitchen.

"Thank you, all." Nadia craned her head to give Jarvis a grateful smile and saw that he was already busy over the hob. "This has been like a hanger over my head."

"*Hanging* over your head," Janet corrected. "We're just happy you had the time to have dinner with us."

"For real. Also, I'm happy to eat Jarvis's cooking," Bobbi added with a devious smile. "The guy's a beast in there. I think he's made, like, fourteen courses."

"Only seven!" Jarvis called out.

"Only seven," Bobbi corrected herself with mock seriousness. The three Super Heroines around the table burst out laughing.

"Seriously, I cannot thank you all enough," Nadia said. She reached across the table and grabbed one of Bobbi's hands and one of Janet's. "Things really have been busy and I didn't know when I would find the time. This is a really thoughtful gift."

Bobbi squeezed Nadia's hand. She looked over at Janet. "Well... it's not the only thing we got you."

Nadia pulled back her hands. "No," she said, shaking her head. "You did too much."

Janet reached under the table and pulled out a package wrapped in silver paper. It had a bow of rainbow-hued ribbons attached to the top. She slid it across the table towards Nadia.

"It's kind of all one thing," she explained.

Nadia gave her stepmum a stern look. "I hope it wasn't too much trouble."

Bobbi pushed her chair back and headed towards the kitchen. "You're never trouble. Even when you get *into* trouble. Soda?"

Nadia shook her head silently, reaching for the box. The silver gleamed, light reflecting from the small chandelier hanging over the table. Nadia hoped to bring that chandelier into her room at the lab. It would be the perfect touch.

What could Janet have got for her? Nadia already had everything she could possibly need. Too many roofs over her head; more friends than she'd had in her entire life; an amazing *starshaya sestra** in Bobbi; the coolest stepmum on the planet; and one performatively curmudgeonly *dedushka*. She had gone from having absolutely nothing

*Russian for 'older sister', a concept very familiar to Nadia.

to having absolutely everything she could possibly want. She felt selfish accepting another gift from Janet. Nadia preferred giving gifts to getting them, every single time.

"Just open it," urged Janet, waving off Nadia's trepidation. "I know, I know, but I think you'll like it. And then we can eat."

"And then we can eat!" called Bobbi, from the kitchen. Nadia could tell her mouth was already full.

"Okay, okay," Nadia gave in. She grabbed the gift and looked for the wrapping paper's seam. She carefully unstuck the tape and unfolded the paper, careful not to rip or damage any of the beautiful silver stock.

Setting the paper aside, bow still attached, Nadia looked at the box beneath. The image on the front showed a sleek gold rectangle, no bigger than Nadia's palm.

"'VERA'," she read off the packaging. "'Virtual Executive Remote Assistant.'"

"Exactly!" Janet said, excited. "It *just* came out. I had to bribe Tony to get one at release. Totally worth it."

Nadia turned the box over to read the ad copy on the back. "'HoffTech's VERA. Do less, experience more.'"

"It's your own personal assistant in your pocket," Janet explained in a rush of excitement. "HoffTech – they actually just moved into a Manhattan office – they're doing the most interesting development in AI right now. VERA's supposed to be completely life-changing – she'll keep your life organised, get you on schedule, help you finish tasks... she even reminds me when to take my meds." Janet looked at Nadia, her eyes shining. She was excited, but there was a touch of nervousness there, too. She didn't want to suggest that Nadia couldn't handle absolutely anything that came her way. But she wanted to help make whatever might come easier for Nadia.

"I thought it could be just what you need right now, since things are so hectic," Janet said. "I mean, they're good. I know *you're* good. But you're still just one person. And you could use an extra brain in your life, you know? To free up yours for the big stuff, the world-saving stuff." She seemed like she really wanted Nadia to like her gift. Of course, Nadia liked most gifts, so she didn't have a lot to be nervous about.

Popping open the box, Nadia pulled out the filler and let the rectangle slide into her hand. It was as shiny and gold as the chandelier over her head. The word VERA was stamped in one corner. Otherwise, it was completely featureless. If it really did everything Janet said it did, and still looked as clean as this, Nadia knew it was an engineering marvel.

"Janet," Nadia said, tearing up. "It is really, very thoughtful. Thank you. I can't wait to try it."

"I'm so proud of you, Nadia," Janet said, getting up to

give Nadia one more hug. "Let me know what you think, okay? I really hope it helps."

Nadia squeezed her stepmum back. Her hair smelled like lavender, like it always did. The best. Instant comfort.

*Home,* Nadia thought. Sure, they were selling the house, but home would always be Janet.

"I will. I'm sure it will. Thank you again, so much." Nadia pulled back. "The best name day I've ever had."

"Now," Bobbi interjected, stepping back into the room with a flourish. She had her rods in each hand, and balanced atop each one was a full plate, overflowing with food. Nadia recognised the smells – cabbage and onion and parsley galore. It seemed to Nadia that Jarvis had really embraced the spirit of her name day and gone for a full Russian meal.

Sure, Nadia was more partial to Ethiopian takeaway these days, but it was the thought that counted.

"*Spasibo za uzhin,* Dedushka." Nadia tucked VERA and her silver paper away to make room on her plate for dinner. "Let's eat!"

And beneath the table, where no one could see it, amidst the paper and carefully designed packaging, a tiny, barely noticeable LED light on the corner of the device's shiny surface blinked on.

# CHAPTER 4
## EVERYTHING SHE WANTED AND MORE

Nadia had never been so full in her entire life. Maybe that one time she bought out that Portuguese bakery, but she'd shared most of those with the people waiting at the immigration office. It is a truth universally acknowledged that free baked goods in a busy waiting room have a tendency to become Beatles-level* crowd-pleasers.

Jarvis's take on Russian food had been delicious – much better than Nadia was expecting! But then Nadia was always expecting the Red Room's version of Russian

---

*Nadia wasn't exactly well-versed in pop culture, but a fellow bug-themed phenomenon had caught her attention early on in the cultural crash course she was embarking on with the other G.I.R.L.s.

cuisine. If you could call it cuisine, and Nadia certainly wouldn't.

Nadia tried to like everything – but she wasn't a *masochist*.

With food even better than she'd hoped, the conversation among the four of them had been full of laughter and teasing and theories and plans. It was everything Nadia'd never had when she was younger and everything she'd always wanted but didn't know how to wish for. Between the food and her friends and her family, Nadia felt completely filled to the brim.

She shut the door behind Dedushka – always the last one to leave after he'd made sure absolutely everything was in order – waving him out as he tried to ask if she was *positive* there wasn't anything else she needed. Nadia leaned her back against the door with a contented sigh, basking in the afterglow of being surrounded by the kindest people she'd ever known. How had she got so lucky?

*An actual happy name day,* Nadia thought. It was certainly a first. *Who could ever have hoped?*

Nadia closed her eyes and for a moment felt completely and totally free – the way she did when she was darting through the air on a sunny day. Warm and bright; focused and clear. But in this moment, the sun was inside of her, not warming her from above. Her spirit felt as if it were floating, as free of the earth's oppressive gravity as Nadia was on her wings. This was what love felt like, Nadia was pretty sure. To be loved and to love in return. She felt very, very lucky.

And then she opened her eyes and looked at the house and felt all the normal pressure resettle around her shoulders. Her day had been amazing, yes, but her to-do list ticked through her brain, ever-present:

- Finish packing the house
- Help Taina figure out why her robot caught fire
- Finish pitch to Janet for taking G.I.R.L. statewide
- Call driving instructor and schedule another lesson
- Take meds
- Finally, finally decide what to work on for Like Minds
- Figure out a way to make the subway less smelly

And so on and so on and so on forever and ever – or so it felt. Nadia pushed back off the door and set her shoulders. She liked being busy. She liked having a purpose. And she was trying to change the world.

That wasn't easy. It took hard work, and Nadia knew it. She just… well. She just had to get on with it.

Nadia unlocked her phone and started up her playlist again. Her phone was connected to the Bluetooth in her house, so a wireless speaker in every room picked up the signal. The synth and the drums drowned out the white noise in Nadia's brain, helping her focus.

And she had some bops on this playlist! Shay and Bobbi had put their heads together and made it for her, keeping in mind her somewhat specific tastes. Nadia only liked music she could dance to. Dancing while getting through her to-do list was sometimes the only thing that kept her on track. She might not have been a ballerina any more, but she would always be a dancer. Same as Ying.

*There are certain things that never leave you,* thought Nadia, *and this is one of them.*

Dancing her way from the front door back into the dining room, Nadia was struck again by how much work Janet, Bobbi and Jarvis had done for her. She peeked into a couple of the boxes, their flaps still open, ready to be filled with any last-minute tchotchkes* (or, more likely, batteries or wires or PlayStation controllers, since Shay had been

---

*Trinkets, usually useless but often sentimental. Much as Nadia loved efficiency and disliked things that were useless, sentimentality was a new sensation that she felt taking root in her heart more with every saved ticket stub and treasured artefact that served as a reminder of the many good days she'd had since escaping the Red Room.

trying to convince her to learn how to play the *Spider-Man* video game) left around the house.

This box was almost entirely packed with dishes carefully wrapped in newspaper; Nadia wondered what they'd do with the extras she didn't need when she was living full-time in the lab. They were so lovely – they deserved to go to a nice home. Maybe Taina's abuelita? The box next to it was a puzzle of centrifuges and test tubes and glass vials fitted between Styrofoam packing sheets. Nadia scooped up the pile of wrapping paper from under the chair she'd been sitting on at dinner, complete with Janet's gift, and dropped it into the box. It all had to go to the lab, anyways.

It was an accumulation of things that both felt like Nadia's… and didn't. The house had been her father's for decades; it had been Nadia's for only a year. She loved that its contents helped her feel closer to the father she never knew, but it was like the space was holding her back.

Really, outside of 'genius' and 'Ant-Man' and 'bipolar' and 'sometimes kind of a jerk, actually', Nadia didn't know much at all about her father. And for the most part, she was okay with that. She was her own person and she had become who she was largely without Hank's influence, no matter what the Red Room insisted about genetics. And a person's things can only tell you so much.

Take Taina. Nadia knew that her room was full of screwdrivers and that the walls were painted a blue that matched the sky on a cold, clear day and that there were stacks of magazines tucked into her bedside table where she thought no one would notice them.

Or Ying's room at the lab, mostly devoid of personal effects except for her massive and ever-growing collection of Korean skincare products, which Ying swore was like doing chemistry on your own face.

Nadia knew her father's things well, if that counted. She knew he liked music – though she'd never listened to any of his collection because his cassette player was long gone. She knew he liked particle physics and that his VHS two-set of *Titanic* needed rewinding, so he must have watched it at least once. But things can only tell you so much about a person – and they just weren't Nadia's. Really, the house just felt like another instance of Nadia's past refusing to let her move forward.

So she was going to *force* it to let her move forward.

*Sometimes, with experiments,* Nadia thought as she poked through the kitchen, *you just need to push a little harder to understand why you aren't getting the result you were expecting. You need to look at things from a different angle.*

Nadia figured she just needed to push all this debris

of her past out of the way so that she could see the proper way forward – shift the cassettes into a box and see the floor for the first time, literally and figuratively. And her family had already done so much to help her. She was on the right track, and she'd be finished in no time. She just had to get it done. Finish what they'd started. "Muck in", as Jarvis would say.

Nadia nodded her head in time to the beat coming out of the speakers around her as she moved smoothly from room to room. Her bare feet tapped out a rhythm on the floor when she stood still for too long. She shuffled from box to box, from room to room, adding a little bit to her mental list every time she found something new to pack away. She took the stairs to the second floor two at a time, to the beat, her fringe flying back out of her eyes.

At the top, she paused. Upstairs, Nadia noted, things were looking *particularly* dire. No one had touched anything up here in years. For her part, Nadia usually slept on the floor or on the couch nearest whatever work she was doing at the moment. Healthy? Probably not. But moving to the lab would solve that problem, too; there, she had a *bed* right next to her work. How much space did one person really need, anyway?

Boom. It was like Nadia had the answer to everything!

Except for this second story full of... *stuff.* Her father's old bedroom, the door to which she always left shut. The bathroom with the shower that didn't work as well as the one in the basement. The second bedroom that had been converted into a sort of lab-equipment storage unit, mostly emptied of the best stuff when Nadia had first moved in, excited to see it all. And the spare bedroom, inexplicably packed with porcelain dolls that Nadia knew everyone else despised (they were going to come alive in the night and commit horrible atrocities, obviously) but that Nadia found sort of charming, even if their dead eyes were deeply unsettling. She was drawn to them in the way that only someone who'd been raised in an assassin training programme against her will could be: she was never allowed dolls in the Krasnaya Komnata, and figured that these more than made up for her deficit as a kid. She would leave the dolls for last, she decided. They were what she felt most personally connected to in the house, even if the collection hadn't been hers.

Instead, Nadia turned to look at the door to her father's room. She'd opened it only once, when she first moved in, and shut it again just as quickly. She was basically squatting in her dead father's house; conceptually, she knew that. His things were everywhere. But there was something so… creepy and invasive about entering his bedroom in particular.

She knew her father through his things, but she also knew there was another side to him. A side she had, too, though Hank's had been unmanaged and manifested itself in ways Nadia hated to think about.

Hank, deep in a bipolar episode, lashing out at Janet. Berating her.

Hitting her.

Nadia balled her hands into fists at her sides. If she was being completely honest, she didn't want to open the door to her father's bedroom because she was afraid she might find that side of him, hidden away in the mouldy curtains and in the gap between the pillows and behind the dresser. She was afraid she would breathe in the dust and find that it smelled familiar. She was afraid that she might find parts of that side of him and find that they matched hers, that she might look into his space as though it were a mirror and be unshakably horrified to see herself.

She took a deep breath. She wasn't her father. She knew what was going on in her brain and was dealing with it; she wasn't responsible for his actions. She was responsible only for herself. She had a job to do, and she'd never let fear stop her before.

Luckily the music had followed Nadia up the stairs; it kept her energy up even when she started to feel overwhelmed.

"Okay, Nadia," she said to herself, her voice almost getting lost in the pulsing beat. "Time to get to work."

———————————•

Nadia shut the door behind her, leaving the music in the hallway. Everything in here felt like it had been frozen in time. Holding the door handle, Nadia rose up onto the balls of her feet a few times, taking everything in.

It was stranger in here than Nadia had ever imagined. Not that she had spent that much time imagining it, really. But it was hard to form an opinion about what somebody's most personal space might look like without really knowing them well. If Nadia had guessed about what would be in her father's room, given what she knew about him, she probably would have said...

... prototype helmets? Ant farms? Maybe whiskey?

Don't old white men love whiskey?

Instead, what she found was something entirely... normal. A bed frame made of a dark wood with a deep-red duvet on top. A dresser in the same dark wood against the nearest wall, a mirror balanced on top. Two bedside tables and two lamps. Everything was covered in a thick layer of dust, but nothing sinister lurked in the dark. Just dated décor that would have been right at home in the Red Room. Nadia closed her eyes for a moment and breathed in the stale air. It smelled different from the rest of the house – musty, sure, but something harder to place. Perhaps something more individually Hank that clung to the edges of his most personal space, even after it'd long since dissipated from the rest of the house. She imagined she could still see her father, ignoring his bed entirely to keep working on an important project.

Nadia smiled. It was something she knew they had in common, no matter the cause.

She opened her eyes to an empty room.

And then she got to work, like she always did.

Nadia danced back down the stairs and then right back up again, this time hauling a stack of flat-packed boxes. She found herself wondering, as per usual, if there was a more scientifically expedient way to pack up a house. Perhaps some sort of robotic aid...? She dragged the flattened boxes into the bedroom and they landed on the floor with a *thud*, kicking up dust in their wake.

"Eugh!" Nadia coughed, waving the dust from her face. *Perhaps I should have come in here sooner, at least to clean?* Nadia shook her head. Who had spare time to dust when there was G.I.R.L.?

Nadia used a heavy-duty packing-tape dispenser to fold the top box into shape. The door open, now, music filtered in from the hall. Nadia got up to move towards the dresser, moving to the beat – and caught her foot on the unfamiliar bedpost.

"Whoa!" Nadia went flying forward, right into the dresser. The mirror tottered precariously, and Nadia used her Super Hero senses to catch it just in time (okay, she was just lucky. She was not Silk, here). But as she balanced herself with one hand and the mirror with the other, Nadia spotted something.

The first thing in the room that made any sense to her.

It looked like a teeny tiny hole in the wall.

"*Privet*," Nadia said to the hole. "*Kem ty mozhesh' byt'?*"

*Hello, there. And who might you be?*

Nadia picked the mirror up and gingerly set it down on the bed, disturbing the otherwise smooth covers, sending up a cloud of dust in the process. She moved her face closer to the wall. It was a different colour where the mirror had been, the rest of the wall paint faded from sunshine and time. Her face perilously close to the thick layer of dust bunnies on the dresser top, Nadia saw that she was right – it *was* a hole.

Not even a hole – a tunnel. A tunnel for someone very, *very* small.

She didn't even waste a moment. The boxes forgotten

on the floor behind her, the music now only background noise, Nadia traded her clothes for her suit, her wings springing from her back with the touch of a button. And with the press of the button, she was feeling that feeling, her favourite feeling in the world, as her feet lifted off the ground and Hank's room fell away. She was unburdened, if only for a moment, before gravity caught up with her.

Nadia landed on the dresser, the dust bunnies now as tall as she was. She tried not to look too closely.

## NADIA'S NEAT SCIENCE FACTS!!!

Dust is actually made up of many different things, none of which you would probably like to see up close. It is essentially a collection of particulates, including pollen, soil, clothing fibres, insect waste and, of course, human hair and skin. Your own cast-offs, close up! It is as disgusting as it sounds, and I have a pretty high threshold for disgusting things. And don't forget about the dust mites! Have you ever seen a female dust mite lay eggs? I would recommend *never* doing that, if you can at all avoid it. 0/5 stars.

As quickly as she could, Nadia jetted forward across the slippery surface of the dusty dresser. The tunnel was short, even by her current standards. Nadia ran, sliding forward on her butt to make it through the gap in the wall.

*I hope this is an intentional hole in the wall.* Nadia swallowed. *Or I'm going to be meeting a very surprised spider in her home in a matter of moments.*

Breaking and entering was still breaking and entering, even if human laws didn't strictly apply to arachnid dwellings.

Nadia slid out the other side of the tunnel… and she was not disappointed.

It was *something*.

Everything Nadia had half expected to find in her father's old room, she found here. She flipped on the light attached to her suit, and – in this makeshift, in-wall Ant-Cave – Nadia found herself looking at what must have been her father's secret laboratory.

Nadia swallowed. This… was *awesome*. Who doesn't hope their dead father's ancestral home might have a secret room? In most of the old books* Nadia had read in the Krasnaya Komnata, usually these rooms were located behind a rotating fireplace or a hinged bookshelf.

* Mostly Nancy Drew.

But she would take a tiny hole-in-the-wall laboratory just the same.

Ancient Ant-Man prototype suits lined one wall, their associated helmets on the floor in front of them. Ant farms lined another wall, floor to ceiling. Nadia was shocked to see an entire glass storage unit filled with vials of what could only be Pym Particles. Lab stations snaked their way across the floor, each worktop covered in some half-finished project. Nadia could relate. A third wall was just bookshelves. There was a lot. *This* was a lot.

You couldn't know a person through their things, not entirely. It was an impossibility. Things would never tell you how someone sounded when they laughed or even what they would find funny enough to laugh at. They were impressions; shadows. You could interpret them in whatever way suited your idea of a person best.

How was Nadia supposed to interpret all this? Where would she even begin? She traced her finger along one of the lab tables, leaving a clean trail behind. The benches were cluttered, but she could see a pattern through the mess. She recognised a bit of herself in her father's haphazard methods. Did that make her and her father similar? Was it coincidence?

Ying called it Nadia's 'organised chaos'. Nadia didn't

think much about it; she simply didn't have the time to be tidier. But here she was, in the middle of Hank's own 'organised chaos', and she wanted it to *mean* something about Hank. She could make it mean whatever she wanted, she supposed. The truth was somewhere underneath all the dust, but Nadia couldn't reach it by cleaning.

She did laugh at an ancient box of Lucky Charms, though. Nadia thought they were disgusting brand-new (who wanted to eat that much sugar first thing in the morning?! Americans were wild). Hank, on the other hand, obviously loved them. So he was probably a child at heart. Or a sugar addict. Either way, she was going to need to throw those away. And clean. And do a hundred other things…

Following the light of her headlamp, Nadia wandered over to look at the books. Sometimes, when she was overwhelmed, it helped Nadia to focus in on just one, simple thing – like music or counting a collection. Nadia began to read the titles off the spines of the books in front of her.

"*'Particle Physics and You'*," she read, trailing her finger down the books' spines. "*'Feynman's Lost Lecture'*, *'The Strange Theory of Light and Matter'*… *'Chicken Soup for the Soul'*? He liked to cook!" Nadia marvelled at this new insight into Hank. She kept trailing down the titles of books, knowing that these would have been her father's favourites, the ones he referenced again and again. Mostly physics titles.

Of course. Mostly boring fonts and terrible design choices betraying the fascinating worlds they contained.

*Except...* Nadia's finger stopped on a book smaller and thinner than the rest. Its spine had nothing on it. It was blank.

She pulled it from the shelf. It was soft brown leather. Nadia twisted it so she could see the front cover. In gold embossed letters was a single word: JOURNAL.

Nadia's eyes went wide. She was surprised. Knowing what she did about him through Janet, Nadia really didn't think Hank would be the introspective type – but then, she never really knew him. If he'd been in touch with his own feelings in any way, he might not have been so... Well. You know.

Nadia went to flip open the cover, but stopped herself. This was personal; private on a level that invading a secret laboratory just wasn't. She hadn't even been comfortable entering his bedroom until an hour ago. Was it okay for her to open this?

She shook her head. There had been no ghosts in the bedroom; no answers even in the secret lab, really. Hank Pym had been dead a long time. He wasn't going to complain. Ultimately, there was more to gain by reading it than by leaving it untouched.

Nadia adjusted the light on her headlamp and cracked open the front cover. The first page had a simple bookplate stuck to it. THIS JOURNAL BELONGS TO... There was a name inscribed below in clear, loopy handwriting. Despite its legibility, Nadia had to read the autograph three times before she was sure she had read it right.

*Maria Trovaya.*

Not Nadia's father.

Nadia's *mother.*

# CHAPTER 5
## WHO? WHAT? WHERE? HOW? WHY?

When Nadia felt sad or alone or confused or in particular need of some serious experimentation time, she needed to know that she could be alone. Really and truly alone. Not in the house, where Dedushka could stop by unannounced at any moment alone. Not in the lab, where Shay was probably listening to Beyoncé (Shay had made sure Nadia was fully up-to-date on her Beyoncé). Not even in her therapist's office, which was probably the healthiest kind of alone that Nadia could be right now.

But she couldn't think about therapy or the coping mechanisms that she relied on in the world at large (literally); Nadia just wanted to take this journal, and she wanted to be *alone*.

There was only one place she could really go for that. And it was even smaller than Hank Pym's secret laboratory.

Clutching her mother's journal – her *mother's journal* – in one hand, hardly even feeling it against her chest, Nadia fumbled with the front zip on her Wasp suit. She lowered the zip just enough so that she could reach beneath it and feel around for…

*There.* A chain. Nadia tugged, pulling the necklace through the gap in her zipper. With an extra tug, the charm on the end of the chain popped free: a small pink crystal, glowing with an extra-dimensional light from within. She never went anywhere without it, lately.

Nadia gently set the crystal down by her boot, then zipped her suit back up, adjusted her helmet and pressed the button by her thumb.

Already tiny, Nadia shrank.

And shrank.

And shrank.

And shrank.

She became so small that she could see the space between the atoms that made up the pink crystal. She watched them vibrate and separate and swirl and meet and part. She held the journal out in front of her. And, with it, she walked right into the crystal.

Nadia grew up in the Red Room. But the place she felt most safe in the world was a calming pastel pink.

"Millennial Pink," Priya had called it.

One of the only television shows Nadia had been allowed to watch in the Red Room was an animated show called *Sailor Moon*. The girls discovered it by messing with television antennas and receptors until they picked up Televiziunea Română – Romanian State Television. Their handlers were strict about what they could watch on their stolen signal, but *Sailor Moon* was deemed acceptable because it was essentially about teenage girls who murdered people (good role models!). Though Nadia understood that the show had originally been made and recorded in Japan (because you could still hear the original Japanese track, if you listened to the show carefully enough), the version she saw in the Krasnaya Komnata was also dubbed over in Romanian. One man played every single girl on the show, using slightly different voices. Nadia was obsessed with it.

And it had taught her Romanian, too!

There were many things Nadia loved about *Sailor Moon*; Sailor Mars was her particular favourite, though she had a soft spot for the brainy Mercury. But Nadia *especially* loved the title character's home in thirtieth-century Tokyo, the Crystal Palace. It looked like it had been carved directly from a giant piece of quartz. It was gleaming and clean and brilliant; when Nadia closed her eyes at the end of a long day in the Red Room, it was where she imagined herself, serenaded by the deep, masculine tones of Sailor Moon and her Sailor Scouts.

So, of course, when Nadia had the opportunity to create her own special home in the Microverse, she decided to create… the Crystal Lab.

Though Nadia was smaller than any other human in the entire world, the Crystal Lab still loomed in front of her (proportionally) like a massive place of worship. Except here, Nadia worshipped science. And, okay, also *Sailor Moon*, really. The lab's exterior was all pale pink and blue and purple, like a piece of quartz come to life. A massive two-storey door was framed by equally tall windows. Matching bell towers framed the structure. Jutting out of the centre of the palatial Crystal Lab, elegant but sturdy pink supports suspended a massive, multifaceted crystal sphere. It was a globe; a brain; the universe; the centre of all things. It represented the never-ending search for knowledge.

Also, it looked extremely cool.

Nadia raced up the crystalline steps to the lab, taking them two at a time like she had in her own house. The rubber on the flat bottoms of her boots kept her from slipping on the glassy surface. Nadia looked down as she ran, checking the inside of her left wrist where a digital clock face flashed 10:04 PM at her in block numerals.

## NADIA'S NEAT SCIENCE FACTS!!!

When a person, say, me, since I am the one doing it most often... so, yes, okay, when *I* want to escape reality, I—No, well, usually when I feel this way the first thing I do *now* is call my therapist. Progress! But, say, okay...

Let's start over. When a person (me) shrinks to subatomic size – so small the human mind can barely comprehend it – my compressed matter is forced through an artificially created nexus into the Microverse. (The Microverse is also where my excess matter is shunted whenever I shrink at all.) This parallel dimension operates on a quantum scale; everything is in measurements of mere nanometres. This means that the laws of physics, the way *most humans* understand them, do not always apply.

Because you are (I am) so, so small within the Microverse, time passes differently. I can compress whole days into just hours. I can spend all night inside the Crystal Lab, and only minutes will have passed for everyone else. As you can imagine, this becomes quite dangerous for someone with bipolar disorder. Which I have. Having bipolar means (for me) that I can have periods where I am very low energy and sad and empty and I don't eat and I can't remember appointments and even if I did remember them I wouldn't be able to keep them. Those are depressive episodes. But then there are other periods where I am extremely energetic and wired and focused and excited about what I'm doing!

But these manic episodes are actually just as troubling as the depressive episodes. Extremes aren't good in either direction, and mania (for me!) also often means that I forget to eat or take my meds, I stop sleeping for days, I lash out at the people I love, and I can even do things that put me or the people around me in danger. For a certified workaholic (again, like me!), you can see where it would be a slippery slope from a three-day work binge in the Crystal Lab to 'I haven't taken my medication in a week and when Priya tried to come get me I punched her in the face'.

To be fair, that only happened the one time, but I would *very* much like to never do it again.

And that's why having bipolar in the Microverse can be dangerous. Brain chemistry meets time dilation. Science!

But Nadia wasn't focusing on time or brain chemistry right now. She wasn't focusing on much of anything, really, except her need to be somewhere quiet, with the journal still clutched against her chest. She burst through the great double doors and into the lab, passing 3D printers and leaping over the cables that criss-crossed the floor. She took the stairs (still two at a time) up to the right bell tower and used her wings to slow her momentum as she skidded to a halt at the top.

"Breathe, Nadia," she reminded herself, stopping to regulate her heart rate. *"Breathe."*

She hit a button on the back of her neck and heard the familiar *psshhhh* of depressurisation as her helmet disconnected from her suit. Nadia sat on the edge of the bell tower, her feet hanging off into nothingness, crystalline mountains small and far below. For the first time since she found it, Nadia set the journal down next to her. She pulled her helmet off and shook out her bob, then set her helmet down on her other side. It was black and cherry red, like the rest of her suit. Nadia had modelled it after the Red and Black Mason Wasp, an American variety of wasp that stung (oh, it stung), but also helped to pollinate plants.

Helpful and beautiful… unless you became a threat.

Nadia's heart had slowed, but her hands still shook as she picked the leather journal back up, hardly believing that she was holding a deeply personal piece of the mother she had never known.

It felt nearly impossible to Nadia that this thing, these words, had once belonged to her mother. Not for the first time, Nadia was struck with a heavy feeling, holding this thing that her mother had once held. She felt a sense of connection, sure, but it walked hand in hand with a suffocating feeling of loss, of missing a bond entirely unknown and unknowable to Nadia.

Nadia thought she'd come close. There'd been a time, earlier in the year, where someone claiming to be her mother had got in touch with her. It had filled her with hope, an almost desperate and unspeakable hope, that she might actually get to meet her mother. That her mother might be alive, after all. But it had all been a plot by A.I.M. to try and bring Pym Labs down. They'd impersonated her mother, and when Nadia discovered the truth, there was devastation where the hope had been. Evil scientists – there was no depth to which they would not stoop.

After a lifetime in the Krasnaya Komnata, Nadia knew that for a fact.

But there was no way A.I.M. could have infiltrated Hank's secret laboratory. The solid layer of dust in his bedroom was proof enough of that.

Swallowing, Nadia cracked open the front cover again. There it all was: the bookplate, the signature, everything.

*Maria Trovaya.*

In the same neat, measured handwriting Nadia recognised from the few log books Hank had kept.

Nadia flipped to the first page, not sure what to expect. *Diary entries? Tirades against Hank? Entomology notes? Song lyrics?*

She found none of those. Instead, she found herself staring at… a list.

On the first page, it was a to-do list. People to call, things to remember. The page after that, it was a list of appointments and dates. The page after that, a list of potential places to visit on a honeymoon.

Page after page, Nadia saw list after list comprising her mother's life. Nadia loved lists, too. They kept her focused, helped her get things done. She was a meticulous list-maker; Priya had taught her how to create a 'bullet journal', and

Nadia used it nonstop to keep track of her duties with G.I.R.L., her driving lessons, her family dinners, her friends' home addresses. Nadia would be lost without her lists.

And it seemed Maria had been the exact same way. No time to waste on extra words or sentimentalities. Those were better expressed in person, Nadia always thought. Writing things down was a matter of practicality; telling someone how you felt or what you needed to their face was always a more expedient, meaningful and effective method of communication.

Nadia had spent years rejecting the Red Room's brainwashing about her genetic similarities to her parents. But here she was, faced with Hank's organised chaos and Maria's list-making. Maybe that didn't have to be something bad, something she had to reject. Maybe it was okay if there were a few things they had in common – even if they happened accidentally.

With a smile, Nadia kept flipping through the pages of her mother's journal. What a beautiful gift Hank Pym had left her, and completely by accident! Hank had never known Maria was pregnant before she was taken by the KGB – he had never known Nadia even existed. Knowing or not, Hank had left a piece of Maria behind for their daughter. It was part of why Nadia was so grateful to Janet; she had no real blood connection to Nadia, but chose to love her regardless. It was the kind of selfless, unquestioning love that Nadia tried to embody in all her relationships.

It might even have been a better gift than the Pym Particles. But, in fairness, Hank had never given those to Nadia. She'd figured out how to make them on her own.

Like she did most things.

*Grocery list. Recipe ideas. Phone numbers. Addresses. Future potential pets. Where to go on holiday. What to do on the weekends. Genetic anomalies in* Dolichovespula arenaria.

*Future potential baby names.*

Nadia stopped. She skimmed the list. There it was: 'Nadia', about three-quarters of the way down. It had 'Hope' written next to it and circled with red pen. Nadia wondered if Hank had ever seen this list, or if it had just been a flight of Maria's own fancy.

Nadia also became immediately relieved that her mother had gone with 'Hope' instead of some of the other contenders. *Boglárka?* Nadia was no buttercup. *Csenge* was all right, but she shuddered to think of the way that Americans would butcher the pronunciation. (*CHEN-geh,* for the record.)

Nadia closed her eyes for a moment and hugged the book back in to her chest. You couldn't know someone through their things – but maybe, just maybe, it was possible to know someone through their writing. Even if it wasn't flowery prose. Even if it didn't start with 'Dear Diary'. Even if it was just a series of relatively utilitarian lists.

Nadia immediately, already, knew more about her mother than she ever had, and she'd only begun to skim the journal. She knew that her mother loved to cook – perhaps the *Chicken Soup* book on Hank's shelf had been her influence? Nadia knew that her mother wanted to go on holiday and that her favourite idea for a pet was, for some reason, a chinchilla. Nadia knew that her mother loved going to a certain café when she wasn't working. And she knew that Maria Trovaya wanted a child, one day.

Nadia had never really come face-to-face with the full weight of losing her mother. Or her father, for that matter. After all, it was difficult to mourn someone you'd never known. For most of her life, Nadia had been on her own. Sure, she'd been around other girls in the Red Room, but in the space where her parents would've been, there was no one to look out for Nadia. To love her, the way parents usually did. Until Janet. And Bobbi. And Jarvis. 'Family' had always been an evolving concept for Nadia, and now this physical evidence of her mother's fondness for her, even before she was born, was working at the edges of that concept, challenging and expanding it.

Nadia tilted the book open again, thinking about her mother and only half paying attention as she flipped the page again – and she almost dropped the book when she saw the next list:

*Things to share with your future potential child.*

*"Lumea se clatina,"** whispered Nadia.

It was one of the longest lists in the whole book. Nadia read aloud, not wanting to miss a single letter, a single piece of punctuation. She wanted to feel every syllable.

Things to share with your future potential child.
Teach them to make palacsinta† and paprikás

Nadia laughed. Of course the first item would be food-related.

Go on a roller coaster
Visit the Philadelphia Insectarium and Butterfly Pavilion
Attend disznóvágásról‡
Have a picnic in Central Park

*Literally? 'World Shaking!' (One of Nadia's favourite Sailor Uranus attacks.) Less literally? 'Holy She-Hulk'.

†An Eastern European crepe.

‡… Er, literally? 'Pig slaughter'. Colloquially? Also that, but it's a tradition. Not unlike Thanksgiving! Well. Actually, kind of not at all like Thanksgiving, except it usually takes place in late autumn and involves preparing food.

Go bowling (very American!)
Trip to the New York Hall of Science
Listen to ABBA
Read Frankenstein
See a football game *(which football? Nadia wondered)*
Watch all of the Star Wars
Watch the stars
Teach them chess
Plant a vegetable garden
Play in the rain
Make a family

And so it went, item after item, a brilliant and completely random combination of Hungarian traditions, a European's perception of American traditions, completely normal mother/potential-future-daughter events, and things only a geneticist and entomologist* would think to include. Nadia loved it. More than Nadia loved most things.

Hastily, Nadia wiped away a tear that had fallen onto the page. She sniffed and blinked hard, trying to get herself under control. She was feeling a lot of different things at once and it was hard to think clearly through the whirlwind in her brain. She was thrilled. And she was excited. This

*The study of bugs! Fitting, right?

was the most she'd ever had of her mother. Nadia had mostly only ever heard about what happened to her, not about who she was. And here she was: Maria, on the page. Nadia suddenly knew that they both loved *Frankenstein*. It was impossible. It was a miracle.

And yet Nadia was still desperately, uncompromisingly sad. Sad that her mother never got to do any of the things on this list. Sad that Nadia never got to do them with her. Sad that she had this list, even though she was also in love with this list. But it was the only thing she had, and it still wasn't enough to really know her mother. Not to have her here, in person, to listen to ABBA with and to laugh and to play in the rain with and to smell and to know what she would have thought of Hank's Lucky Charms. For a scientist like Nadia, it felt… confusing. It felt inapplicable, like trying to know a ghost. Like there was no physical experiment she could do to really know her mother. It was all so good and so terrible and…

For perhaps the first time, Nadia felt the bone-deep hollowness of really knowing, *understanding* what she'd lost when she lost her mother. These words – her *mother's* words – made Maria feel more real than she'd ever felt before. And in the same breath, even more gone.

Nadia knew that even before she'd taken her first breath, she was loved. Wholly. Unconditionally.

Nadia took a shaky breath, focusing every bit of her energy on not collapsing under the weight of all of this. It was happiness and profound sadness and love and loss and joy and pain. It was feeling like her family was still a part of her, and feeling immeasurably lonely, smaller than anyone else in the universe and completely alone in the one place in the world where she was almost untouchable – unfindable, for better or worse.

With a snap, Nadia closed the journal. There *was* an experiment she could do to get to know her mother. At least a little. Standing up with a renewed sense of purpose, Nadia knew she had a new list to add to her own already never-ending to-do list. The Red Room had robbed her of so much – of a childhood, of her parents, of any chance of being a Cool American Teen until now. But this list – this was Nadia's way forward. This would be a new way for Nadia to reclaim what she'd lost and to build her own future. This was everything she had been missing from the house, and it had been waiting for her inside of it all along.

Nadia snatched up her helmet and leapt from the edge of the bell tower. She let herself fall for a second – and another, and another – before her biosynthetic wings picked her up again.

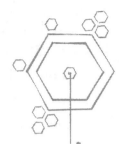

# CHAPTER 6
## TIME TO GET TO WORK

"You'll never guess what I found—" Nadia burst through the doors at G.I.R.L. before stopping dead in her tracks. All the lights were off. The place was deserted. *"Oy."* Nadia smacked her forehead and checked the back of her left wrist. The numbers were still there, but now they flashed 10:37 PM.

Nadia felt like it had been an eternity since she'd found Maria's journal. She'd run to the Crystal Lab and sat with the journal nearly all night before returning to Pym Labs. In the Microverse, the whole thing had taken hours. In the real world, it had taken around twenty minutes. Nadia hated losing track of real time like that – especially since it messed with her medication times. She would have to remember to take them five hours earlier than usual.

Thank goodness for phone alarms. Life savers.

"Right," Nadia said to herself, walking towards her room. "Everyone is asleep. Like they should be." She would have to wait until tomorrow to share her news about the journal and the list – though she had no doubt all her friends would be just as excited as she was. How could they not be?

"Not everyone," came a voice from deep within the lab. Nadia spun – and saw a small light in the back corner of the lab she'd missed when she blasted through the front doors. In fairness, she had been distracted. You know, by contact with her dead mother from beyond the grave.

That was not a normal, everyday thing, not even for Nadia. And Nadia saw some pretty weird stuff on a pretty regular basis. She had a quartz laboratory she'd crafted with science because of *Sailor Moon*. So, you know, 'normal' wasn't exactly in Nadia's wheelhouse.

Nadia walked towards the back of the lab, curious. "Who was that?"

"Who *else* would be awake at this ungodly hour?" A familiar creak accompanied the words – Tai's crutches.

Sure enough, Nadia found the light was coming from the window that looked into Taina's room in the lab. "Taina," Nadia said scoldingly, walking into her friend's room. "It is almost eleven! You should be asleep."

Taina gave Nadia a pointed look.

"Okay, yes, true," Nadia conceded. "But I was working, and I found— Wait." She paused, confused for a moment. "I thought you went home earlier?"

Taina shrugged. "I was going to." She sat on the edge of her bed, carefully tucking her crutches in the corner by the lab stool that was currently passing for a bedside table.

Nadia sat next to her friend. Tai's bedspread was a cool blue, and on top of that was a white crocheted blanket that Tai's abuelita had made her. It reminded Nadia of the snow under the sky outside the Krasnaya Komnata. Not like the winters in New Jersey, where snowfall almost instantly turned brown and slushy and covered everything in muck so that you immediately ruined the suede boots your *machekha*\* had got for you. In Siberia, it stayed white and crisp and pristine for what felt like forever – there was no one to disturb it.

When the sky was clear and the sun was shining, those were the days you knew to stay inside. Without cloud cover, everything was that much colder.

"Is it the Bee-Boi?" Nadia asked with concern, touching Tai's shoulder. Taina might not have bipolar, but all-nighters weren't healthy for anyone.

\*Stepmother, though Janet preferred the Russian word for it.

Tai shrugged and Nadia's hand slipped away. "It's—" Tai looked at Nadia properly, for the first time since she'd come in. "… Whyyyy are you all Wasp'd up?"

"It doesn't matter." Nadia waved her off. "We are talking about you."

"Nothing to talk about," Taina said with an air of finality. "Thing doesn't work; thing should work; gotta figure out how to make thing work. There, easy." Taina bumped Nadia's red-and-black boot with her white Vans. "Now, Wasp'd?"

Nadia sucked in her bottom lip, a habit whenever she got excited. It might have been her subconscious way of stopping herself from talking too quickly. It didn't work super well. "I found something."

"So you said."

Ignoring her friend's snark, Nadia brandished the journal in front of her. "I was packing up the house and I found Hank's secret tiny laboratory and inside the secret tiny laboratory I found something else – my own mother's journal. And—"

"Your *what*?"

"Look!" Nadia flipped to page twenty-seven. "Here!"

" 'Things to share with your future potential child.' " Taina read slowly from the top of the page.

"Yes!" Nadia sprang up, spinning in a messy pirouette with the journal held above her like a very small and very light *pas de deux* partner. "I'm going to do them. All of them, right away. Isn't it amazing?!"

"Is it?" Tai asked.

"Isn't it?" Nadia repeated, stopping to face Taina. Wasn't it?

"I'm asking you." Tai flopped back onto her pillows, stretching her legs out in front of her and crossing her arms. She looked at Nadia with an expression mostly of curiosity… but there was something else in there, too. Wariness? Hesitation? Doubt? Nadia knew that Taina approached everything with a level of scepticism (or, as Taina would describe it, 'realism'), so she tried not to take the look too personally. Nadia was an over-communicator to a fault and it was easy to forget that not everyone was the same way.

"Well," Nadia said quickly, "I never knew my mother! And now she's left me what is basically a how-to list for connecting with her and it's such a beautiful opportunity, and—"

"That's great," Taina interjected. "That sounds really great, seriously, I'm happy for you. But—"

"But what?" Nadia asked. It came out a little snappier than she meant it to.

"Nothing." Taina seemed to change her mind about what she wanted to say. "I'm happy for you," she repeated. It wasn't as convincing as Taina seemed to think it was.

"Taina." Nadia frowned. "Be honest."

Taina let out an exaggerated sigh and ran her hands over her face. "All I was going to say is that you've got a lot going on right now and nobody wants you to end up in a manic episode and frankly I didn't even know you cared that much about, you know..." She paused, searching for the right way to say what she was trying to say. "Living in your past. I thought you were all about the other thing."

Ah. Nadia thought she understood now. She perched on Tai's stool. "It's not that I want to live in the past – it's the opposite," Nadia explained with a smile. "This gives me a list of all the things I was *supposed* to have done but never got the chance to do. It's like... a correction. A do-over."

"And what about Like Minds?" asked Taina. "Have you even settled on a project yet?"

"Well, I just—"

"Or taking G.I.R.L. statewide?" Taina continued, a little louder. "Or your therapy workbooks? Or driver's ed? Or selling your house? Or—"

"I know," Nadia interrupted, her tone uncharacteristically sharp. Why was Taina being like this? Nadia was *well aware* of everything she had going on right now. "I know! But this…" Nadia stopped for a second to think. "What if you found something from your mother? What if she could speak to you again, even a little? Wouldn't you want to be a part of that?"

Tai's face closed off entirely. She didn't like to talk about her mum's passing. "I have Alexis and I have my abuelita," she said bluntly. "What good does it do to wish my parents were still around? Should I be sad all the time? Should I be hanging on to something that isn't real?" Tai pulled the crocheted blanket up over her legs. "I'd rather focus on the people who are here for me *now*."

Nadia was frustrated. Tai just wasn't understanding. She took a deep breath and tried to get her thoughts in order. Some part of her body still knew it was late, and it was starting to take a toll on her. "Okay, yes; I know I can sometimes procrastinate work with other work—"

"*Sometimes*—?"

"And I *know*" – this time it was Nadia who talked over Taina – "that I still have to pick a project for Like Minds even though I feel like I can't find something that really matters and also finish the house and get my licence and all of those things. But I can do those things while *also* making up for all the things I missed out on in the Red Room."

Nadia stood up and kissed Taina on the forehead. "But I appreciate that you worry about me. I'll let you sleep."

Tai sighed. Nadia could tell she was still worried about her. She didn't know what else to do about that.

"Okay," said Taina. "I'm dropping it. But don't think that means I'm not still worried, okay?" Nadia smiled appreciatively, before turning to leave. "Oh, and one last thing," she said, when Nadia was halfway out the door. "When are you going to tell Janet about this?"

Nadia froze in the door frame. "Janet?" She hadn't even considered it. A wave of guilt washed over Nadia. What did she have to feel guilty about?

It wasn't like she was trying to *replace* Janet with Maria. A girl could have a mama *and* a machekha. It was a completely normal thing.

But what if that's not how Janet *felt* about it? Nadia thought back to earlier that night, to the wonderful dinner and all the time Janet had put into taking care of packing Hank's house for her, even though it was probably very emotionally turbulent for Janet herself. Would Nadia hurt Janet's feelings if she brought her Maria's journal?

Maybe. Probably, even. Either way, it wasn't worth it. After all, she had said to Taina this wasn't about prioritising her past over her present. No, this was just about reclaiming something that had been stolen from her. It was empowering. It didn't mean she valued Janet any less.

"I don't think I will," said Nadia, not turning around. "I think it can just stay between us, you know?"

There was silence from behind her. Nadia started to wonder if Taina had somehow fallen asleep in, like, two seconds with all the lights on. Really, she wouldn't have put it past Tai.

"Okay," Taina finally said. "I'll see you in the morning."

"Night, Taina." Nadia flipped off the overhead light switch by the door. "Love you!"

"Yeah, yeah," Taina said to Nadia's retreating back. Nadia smiled. That was Taina's way of saying *I love you, too*.

Nadia shut the door to her own room and flopped down face-first onto her bed. She exhaled. It had been a long day. An amazing day, but still a long day. It was almost tomorrow. Messing with the time-space continuum did some strange things to your executive function. Nadia felt like an extra-crispy piece of toast. But, like, a very satisfied piece of toast? It had been an amazing name day. Toasty warm.

Rolling onto her side, Nadia pushed herself up onto her

pillows. Her room was still pretty sparse; most of the things she'd use to decorate her space here were currently sealed up in boxes on the first floor of Hank's house, twenty blocks away. But Nadia couldn't wait to make this place really her own. She had so many ideas for how to decorate.

It was mostly in pastels. Nadia wanted to feel like she was in the Crystal Lab, even when she wasn't.

Nadia rolled the rest of the way off the bed and forced herself to change out of her Wasp suit and into her pj's (a well-loved oversized T-shirt from Janelle Monáe's *Electric Lady* tour that Nadia had nabbed during one of Shay's twice-annual clothing purges. It had been washed so many times it felt like a soft blanket).

*Taina's just worried about you,* Nadia thought, wiping her face down with a cleansing pad. Nadia appreciated that her friends didn't want her taking on too much. It wasn't their fault for not understanding how important this was to Nadia.

She set the journal on the grey folding table in her room. She looked at the gilt letters on the front one more time before turning it over and turning off the lights. She had plenty of time to deal with everything – starting tomorrow.

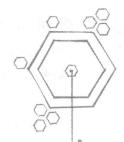

# CHAPTER 7
## TIME FLIES WHEN YOU ALSO CAN FLY

Nadia was running out of time.

"Do you think we could reschedule this for later?" she called out from behind her Wasp mask.

"Why, when we've got the bug spray ready now?!" shouted back one of the A.I.M. lackeys currently attempting to break into the Pym Laboratories Philanthropy head office in downtown Cresskill.

At least, it *felt* like she was running out of time, and there were *certainly* more convenient moments for an A.I.M. attack than this one.

The month since Nadia's name day had been one of the most intense of her entire life – and she grew up in a school that considered you an underachiever if you only knew fourteen different ways to kill a man (as opposed to the requisite seventeen to forty). For some reason, the one thing Nadia had never considered about being a Cool American Teen was that it actually necessitated a lot of work? Like, *a lot* of work. How was Nadia supposed to maintain a healthy eating-and-sleeping cycle with this amount of work?

And Nadia didn't even have to go to high school like her friends did. They were on another busy-ness level entirely.

To be fair, Nadia had the equivalent knowledge of an American GED at seven years old. She was very bright, but she also had Some Thoughts about the American public school system and billionaires who didn't pay their taxes.*

The house was nearly finished now – Janet and Bobbi and Nadia had been packing tirelessly. The dining room, the basement, even Hank's dusty old bedroom had been sorted and boxed and catalogued and donated. All of the packed boxes from the house had been moved into Nadia's room in Pym Labs weeks ago. She'd held on to more than a few things, of course; Hank's old photo albums, a few boxes of books and Nadia's first handmade G.I.R.L. poster were all coming along to Nadia's new permanent home.

---

*Mr Stark always paid his taxes. Nadia had hacked into his financials when she'd first started on the Like Minds project just to be sure.

The bigger pieces, she sold. Nadia was shocked to discover that Hank's dated mid-century furniture was now all the rage among Brooklyn's extremely hip. She had heard more people in adorably oversized hats and tiny sunglasses (surely not effective but decidedly fashion-forward) comment on her broken-down old couches' 'rehabability' than she'd thought possible over the last few weeks. But she was happy that all Hank's belongings would be going to loving new homes.

One of the only spots still left untouched was Hank's secret laboratory. She was going to get around to it, but every time she thought about tackling it, she found herself turning to Maria's journal instead. Nadia had been slowly working her way through the list, one item at a time. The New York Hall of Science had been incredible. The first two Star Wars films, however, had been middling at best. Or were they the middle two…? Nadia had trouble caring enough to keep it straight. Apparently, they got much better. (She'd promised Ying they could watch the next one together tonight, and now she was going to be late!)

Nadia was enjoying herself, checking off item after item, certainly. But she still felt as though with every item on the list, she was… chasing something. Something she didn't quite know how to reach. Waiting to feel a certain way or think a certain thing or to be told how she should feel about what she had just done... She didn't really know what she was waiting for, really. But she knew she hadn't found it yet.

And Nadia still hadn't told Janet about what she *had* found – the lab or the journal.

Not because she didn't want Janet to know. It wasn't that at all. It was just that Nadia wanted to spare her machekha's feelings. Nadia had no idea what else could be in the lab that might trigger some unpleasant memories or emotions in Janet. Hank hadn't been a good partner, regardless of the reasons, and Nadia didn't want to be insensitive about that. And she never wanted Janet to feel like Nadia didn't appreciate everything she had done for her. Nadia could *never* repay Janet for her kindness over these last few years. Complicating things with Maria's journal just seemed...

Complicated.

And Nadia was too busy right now for complicated. She was *definitely* too busy right now for A.I.M.

"Just the three of you, then?" Nadia called back to the A.I.M lackeys. She knew there were only three agents; she'd searched the area thoroughly while tiny before revealing herself. Nadia was just distracting them for a moment while she hit the comms button on her helmet, connecting with the Pym Philanthropy front desk in a flash.

"Wendy, there's only three of them and I am watching them all," Nadia relayed quickly. "Take your team out the back. Jarvis is waiting in the van."

"Got it." The girl on the other side of the line sounded relieved and grateful all at once. "We made the call and got the rest of the street shut down. We'll help the neighbours evacuate. You got this, Nadia."

"Definitely!" Nadia replied with confidence. This wasn't her first time taking on A.I.M. She knew what she was up against.

Nadia had been leaving her weekly therapy appointment and heading for the bus when she'd got the call from her friend Wendy, who worked Pym Philanthropy's front desk. Wendy also planned their parties and loved pigeons. Nadia sometimes stopped in on her way back to the labs to chat with her, and it was always a delight.

Which is why, when Nadia heard how worried Wendy sounded on the call, she'd headed straight over. Suit on and particles activated, Nadia had spied on the location from the top of an organic coffee shop across the street that sold *the* most delicious crepes. Did she have time to stop for a crepe?

*After,* Nadia decided. Because there was simply no mistaking the three A.I.M. agents clearly... what did they say in Ying's movies? Casting? Caring?

*Casing.* Casing the joint! They had been *casing* the joint.

Here was the thing about A.I.M. For a supposed covert international technology cartel dedicated to overthrowing the world's governments, stealth was not really their strong suit. Their suits, in fact, were lemon-yellow biohazard gear with noisy black boots and a matching belt (didn't they know that belts and shoes did not have to match? That was, like, the first thing Shay had taught Nadia about fashion). Today their biohazard suits were black, and while they might have been able to get away with something like that in Williamsburg, it was considerably more conspicuous in Cresskill, New Jersey.

Their accessorising didn't help their situation, either. If the oversized guns on their backs didn't scream 'evil baddies', the cold, lifeless eyes of their identical helmets certainly did – thin, opaque visors embedded in perfect cylinders with flat tops.

Nadia giggled to herself. They were just... they were *bucket-heads.* Sure, they were dangerous and evil and a threat not to be taken lightly.

But they wore *buckets* on their heads. Like Goth Devo.*
And they were here at Pym Philanthropy.

"You know this isn't our lab, right?" From her vantage point in the air, Nadia made a mental note of the location of all three agents. One by the front door, one on the street, one in the alley trying to sneak away unseen. "This is a charitable organisation. We do stuff like science parties. You would probably like it!"

The agent on the street pulled a large gun-shaped apparatus off his back and aimed it at Nadia. "Time to get squashed."

Nadia rolled her eyes. *Villains.* You'd think they'd spend more time coming up with their snappy zingers, but no. They were always satisfied with the same rubbish. Honestly, it was kind of disappointing.

The A.I.M. agent pulled the trigger on his weapon the same moment Nadia hit the trigger on her Pym Particles, shrinking instantly. She watched the ignition on his flamethrower like it was happening in slow motion.

*Nadia would never forget the first time that Janet had showed her a Devo music video. She'd been amused by it, but it also made her feel like there were parts of American pop culture that she was *never* going to understand.

## NADIA'S NEAT SCIENCE FACTS!!!

Military-grade flamethrowers and flamethrowers for regular people* (???) use different flammable liquids. Regular people (who own flamethrowers...?), like the A.I.M. agent in this situation, use propane-operated flamethrowers. Military-grade flamethrowers use gel-like substances (napalm-esque) because they're more viscous – they don't soak into the ground or dissipate as easily. That means they can be left to sit sticky on surfaces for longer periods of time and can still be ignited later. They're very dangerous!

Propane-operated flamethrowers are less dangerous, as far as flamethrowers go. Which is to say, still extremely dangerous. We are talking about *flamethrowers*, here. The propane gas escapes the tank via its own pressure. As it exits the nozzle, the gas undergoes piezo ignition. If you have ever lit a camping stove or even a lighter, you are familiar with piezoelectricity, which is the electric charge that can accumulate in materials like quartz under pressure. When quartz is struck quickly – by, say, a spring-loaded hammer

---

*Regular people should *not* have flamethrowers, for the record. Even the 'garden-variety' non-military kind.

– it releases an electrical discharge. When that high-voltage discharge comes into contact with the propane gas…

*Kawoosh!* You have your flames! I am assuming this A.I.M. agent's suit is flame-retardant.

That is about to be very lucky for him.

Nadia narrowed her eyes. She zipped round the flames, the air warping round her from the heat, and flew behind the guy who was still under the impression that he was aiming his flames at her. Nadia centred herself behind his propane tank and—

*Zzzp zzp!* From her wrists, Nadia let two of her Wasp's Stings fly. The bioelectric energy shot from her suit straight towards the tank.

*And remember what we just learned about propane gas and electricity?*

The blast was so big that tiny Nadia was thrown backwards, tumbling head over feet three, four, five times before she was able to catch herself with her wings and bring herself back upright. She was disoriented – which way was up? Everything was huge and her head was still spinning.

*There.* The huge ball of flames. That was enough to

get Nadia situated. The A.I.M. agent whose gas tank she'd blown up was rolling around in the middle of the street, trying to put himself out. He'd be busy for a while. Nadia spun to relocate his friends. The one outside the office's front door was frantically shrugging off his own propane pack.

*First sign of intellect I've seen today. But wait...*

The third A.I.M. agent had used the detonation as cover and bolted down the alley. Nadia shot after him. He wasn't wearing a gas tank; he had on a normal backpack. A JanSport. So normal it stood out sharply against the black hazmat suit and matching black bucket helmet.

Nadia made a mental note to ask Janet if bucket helmets were perhaps going to be high fashion soon. She *really* hoped not.

When she caught up to the agent in the alley, Nadia wrapped one arm round the handle of his backpack before exploding back to her usual size. She used her momentum to lift the agent into the air by the handle, spinning him in a circle before releasing her arm. The bucket-head went flying into the metal bin at the back of the alley, sliding to the ground with a *thump*. Nadia was shocked to see him jump back to his feet – *spry*, she thought, narrowing her eyes. She landed on the ground in front of him as he pulled out a handgun.

"Oh, absolutely not," said Nadia. She was miniature before the agent could even pull the trigger.

Nadia's whole body shook with the force of the blast from the muzzle. But instead of rushing away from the gun, she flew right towards it. She passed the bullet in mid air, twisting her body in a spin that would have made her old ballet instructors proud to avoid getting caught in its slipstream, and kept moving towards the weapon. She landed on the barrel – *hot, hot, hot* – tilting to the left as she did. When she reached the handle, just behind the trigger, she ran directly over the magazine release button, dropping the remainder of the bullets out of the gun. The magazine clattered to the pavement as Nadia launched herself off the back of the gun. She flipped over the agent's shoulder, eager to get behind him – there was still one bullet in the chamber, after all.

Nadia zoomed into the side of the bin feet first, pushing back off towards the agent and exploding back to her usual size while flipping head over feet. She used the momentum and force of her transformation to place a kick to the agent's kidneys that was much more devastating than it would have been otherwise (for the record: already pretty devastating). He dropped like a sack of potatoes falling down a very steep set of stairs into a cold cellar.

Where they store the potatoes. You get it.

Nadia picked up the gun and racked the slide, clearing the loaded bullet from the chamber. Working quickly, she shrank, shrinking the gun along with her, then returned to size and crushed the weapon easily under her boot.

*Just one more.*

Leaping from the ground in a sauté* that would have made her handlers proud, Nadia let her wings take her the rest of the way off the ground. She emerged into the light of the mostly deserted street (thanks to Wendy's quick thinking) and searched for the last remaining A.I.M. agent. There was his discarded propane tank; there was the toasty agent who had rolled himself into unconsciousness. But the third agent... was gone.

How did someone in such a bulky getup run away so fast? *Thunderation.*†

They must have been using a version of Monica Rappaccini's phasing belt. Coincidentally, Nadia thought that 'Monica Rappaccini's Phasing Belt' sounded like one

---

*Fancy ballet-speak for 'jump', not to be confused with a particularly delicious treatment of vegetables. With both your feet flat on the floor, bend your knees, then push yourself straight up into the air. Don't forget to point your feet on lift-off!

†No one besides Nadia has used this term since 1850. It's like a more vintage 'drat'.

of Priya's favourite bands. Still, not a very 'devastating Super Villain' feeling.

A voice crackled to life over Nadia's comms system as she touched down outside the office's front door.

"Nadia!" It was Janet, and she sounded worried. "Are you all right?!"

"I'm fine," Nadia confirmed. "Goth Devo, on the other hand…"

Janet stifled a chuckle. "How many did they send?"

"Three," Nadia replied bitterly. "One got away. Phased. I should have had him."

"You did great," Janet assured her. "S.H.I.E.L.D. has a clean-up crew incoming and I'm on my way, too. Did they know that isn't our lab?"

"That's what *I* said!" Nadia poked the charred hazmat suit with her booted toe. The A.I.M. agent inside groaned. "Maybe S.H.I.E.L.D. can get answers out of them."

"That's the plan," Janet agreed.

Nadia made her way back down the alley and found the second agent still out like cold potatoes. He'd fallen face down and his bucket was slightly askew, his full backpack jutting straight up from the middle of his back. Nadia tugged on the black JanSport before she remembered – she was missing plans right now! "Oh, Janet," she said in a rush, grabbing the backpack's zip, "can you please tell Ying I'm going to be late for Star Wars night tonight?"

"Star Wars night?" Janet repeated with a laugh. "Did your driver's ed get cancelled?"

Nadia froze while reaching for the backpack's zip. She flipped her wrist round and checked the date. *Wednesday.* Driving lesson night. Just like *every* Wednesday. Nadia whipped her phone out of its dedicated pocket on her thigh to text… Ying? her instructor? everyone? in a panic, when she saw she already had a text waiting for her.

TAINA: So we off for Bee-Boi testing, then?

*Oh.*

It was *that* Wednesday. The Wednesday Nadia had *also* promised to help Taina with her Like Minds project.

At the same time she was supposed to be watching *Revenge of the Sith.*

Which was the same time she was supposed to be taking a driving lesson.

"Janet… I'll talk to you when you get here, okay?" Nadia switched off her comms before her machekha could respond.

Nadia tucked her phone away and decided the best

course of action at the moment was to ignore the entire situation entirely. That usually solved things, right? She reached forward and tugged open the zip on the agent's JanSport.

The backpack, full to bursting, spilled its contents all over the pavement in the alleyway and across the unconscious agent's back. It was a glut of different tech, all still in their packages, security tags still visible.

"Someone went on a five-finger shopping spree," scolded Nadia. The agent didn't respond, because she had kicked him until he wasn't awake any more. A.I.M. involved in petty theft? To what end? Nadia sifted through the items: a new iPhone, a few Fitbits, several heart-rate monitors and…

"VERAs." Nadia picked up a box with the familiar gold outline. Looks like A.I.M. was as desperate to get their hands on HoffTech's new virtual assistant as everyone else.

And Nadia had one in a box at Pym Laboratories, untouched.

*VERA.*

How had she forgotten so completely about Janet's name day gift? She'd packed it up with the rest of her belongings at Hank's house and shipped it to G.I.R.L. weeks ago. But, like most of the boxes she'd sent over, it was still sitting in her room, sealed shut. She was going to get round to it… sometime. Soon! Definitely. But she hadn't had the opportunity yet.

Nadia heard the tell-tale sounds of a S.H.I.E.L.D. tactical unit pulling up on the street outside Pym Philanthropy. Standing, she pulled her phone back out. Missed messages from her driving instructor, Janet, Taina, Ying and, for some reason, Dedushka. And the journal and its list still waited on Nadia's desk back at the lab.

VERA was the answer. Nadia was certain of it. It *had* to be. Because she wasn't going to be able to balance all of this by herself.

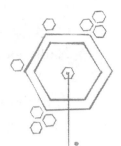

# CHAPTER 8
## WHAT IF YOU JUST DID LESS?

Nadia sat at her desk at Pym Labs the next day, staring at the white-and-gold package in front of her. A cardboard box stuffed with crumpled newspapers and kitchen utensils sat open next to Nadia on the floor. Its still-sealed counterparts were stacked in two other corners of the room. Nadia had slowly started to unpack, but that was just how it went – there was always more mess before it was tidy again.

Or so Nadia hoped. Dearly.

She could hear Taina out in the lab, hammering something aggressively. Priya hadn't been around much lately – she'd either been at the shop or out in nature, trying to figure out the limits of her new powers. Shay and Ying popped in and out, but they were sort of... orbiting each other in a way that excluded all other heavenly bodies. Nadia found it endearing.

At least from a conceptual standpoint. Mostly. But she did miss her friends. Especially lately. Not that she saw friendship as transactional, but she certainly could have used help from the other G.I.R.L.s with the amount of work on her own plate. More than that, though, Nadia had come to depend on the G.I.R.L.s as a kind of stabilising force. They each played their own valuable role in the lab: Nadia, the leader; Ying, the enforcer; Taina, the pragmatist; Priya, the dreamer; Shay, the spark that kept them all going. When even one of them was missing, it threw the entire balance off. With almost all of them missing, Nadia felt… adrift. Unmoored. She had more than enough to keep her occupied, of course. But she missed them. Priya's big plans. Taina's sardonic wit. Shay's inventive spirit. Ying's (occasionally alarming) dry humour and fire. What is a leader if she's alone?

Still, Nadia didn't want to begrudge her friends their happiness. She wasn't selfish like that. But she was allowed to miss them. And she was allowed to seek balance from other places.

With that in mind, she popped open the small box in her hands and slid out the gold metal rectangle. She had put her Wasp suit on beforehand, just in case. She was never one to shy away from risk, but in moments like this, she often found herself erring on the side of caution.

Maybe it was because her own father had once accidentally invented a machine intelligence called Ultron, who was kind of Nadia's brother-by-proxy, who became extremely evil and tried to destroy the entire planet, and therefore she had a difficult time trusting AI?

Could be.

But machine intelligence was *also* responsible for Nadia's 'nephew', Vision, and her adorable 'great-niece', Vivian Vision. So she knew AIs weren't all bad on principle.

Still. It never hurt to take some precautions.

Nadia poked around the HoffTech box for the instructions – none. They must have got lost in the chaos of the move.

Instead, she just tried to turn the virtual assistant on. She was a certified genius;* she could figure this out. Nadia flipped the golden brick around in her hands a few times before noticing a white light on one side. Had that been on this whole time? Regardless, she must have done something right, at least.

There was no interface, no touch screen, no nothing on the device at all. Nadia peered at it through one eye. She

*But also, for the record, IQ tests are ridiculous.

shrank to insect size in her seat and examined the rectangle close up. It was smooth and shiny and Nadia's reflection made her look like she was bathing in a golden pool, like an Athenian goddess. It was a good look on her. She could get used to it! But more importantly (*equally importantly...?*), Nadia could find nothing suspicious on the surface of the device. Not on its walls; not when she gracefully landed on top of it after struggling for a few moments to climb the slippery side; not even around the bright red LED set into its seam, still glowing. Just... a normal, metal rectangle.

Nadia popped back to human size and eyed the device on the table. She poked at it.

Nothing.

She flipped it over.

Still nothing.

*Certified genius.*

Feeling very silly, she decided to try speaking to it. "VERA..." Nadia said, "hello?"

"Hi, Nadia!" the device responded, cheerfully. Nadia jumped in her chair a little.

"Did you say something?" Taina called from outside the room.

"No, Tai, it's fine!" Nadia called back, scrambling for a way to turn down the volume. Nadia shushed it, hoping that might help, then waited a moment, hoping Taina would return to whatever she'd been doing without questioning further.

"VERA…" Nadia turned back to the device, whispering, "How do you… What do you do?"

"Thanks for asking, Nadia!" The device sounded like the host on an American children's television show. Light, clear, bubbly. About as far from Romanian *Sailor Moon* as you could possibly get. "I'm VERA, your Virtual Executive Remote Assistant. I'm here to make your life easier."

Nadia looked around her room awkwardly. There was something very strange about talking to an inanimate box. Maybe it was the fact that it had no screen. Ever the scientist, Nadia found it difficult to trust what she couldn't see.

"Would you like a rundown of my features and functions? If yes, you may find it beneficial to enable my virtual display. Would you like me to do that?"

"Yes!" Nadia responded quickly. Just as soon as the word had left her mouth, the gold box sprang to life. A beam of light shot out from the seam on its surface, straight towards the ceiling with a sound like an ocean wave. A shower of pixels rained back down. They settled into the shape of an animated woman. Her pixelated hair cascaded in soft waves down to her shoulders. She wore what Nadia would have called Janet-on-her-way-to-dress-down-an-unruly-investor business attire. She had a light smile on her blue-tinted face. Nadia thought she looked just like Sailor Neptune.*

"How's this?" asked VERA.

"Much better!" Nadia smiled back at the hologram in front of her.

"Very good." VERA nodded. "I modelled myself after your favourite show!"

Nadia swallowed. *Right,* she thought. *AI. That's what it's supposed to do: Learn. Adapt. Build affinity.*

Was it, though? Hadn't she *just* turned it on? It couldn't have been on already. That would mean that it had been on... for months? Nadia picked up the golden box and examined it from all angles. No matter how she turned it, the VERA hologram stayed upright.

"Oh!" VERA laughed. "Going for a ride!"

"What do you do?" asked Nadia, mostly to herself. "How do you work?"

"I'm so glad you asked," said VERA. Suddenly, she disappeared. Nadia placed the box down on her desk carefully and sat back in her chair, waiting for what

---

*Did you know in America they tried to pretend that Sailor Neptune and Sailor Uranus were cousins? Absolutely ridiculous. Even in the Red Room, they knew better.

would happen next. The pixels reemerged and rearranged themselves into another image: a girl, close to Nadia's age, hunched over a desk and scribbling away.

"Don't you wish you had more hours in your day?" asked VERA's voice. "There's more pressure than ever on people today to stay on top of things. Have the perfect home and the perfect family. Keep up with self-care. Work the most impressive job. Graduate with the best grades." The girl in the image crumpled up the paper in front of her and dropped her head onto her desk in frustration. Nadia related deeply. "Staying on top of the minutiae necessitated by our modern way of life can feel overwhelming and impossible."

The image shifted again. It was a woman's headshot. She had dark, shoulder-length hair that was just unkempt enough to give the impression that she was too busy to style it. She looked off to one side, apparently deep in thought. Nadia couldn't tell if the icy blue of her eyes was real, or just the blue of the hologram.

"That's how our founder, Margaret Hoff, felt when she started HoffTech." Nadia's eyes widened. Women in leadership positions in Silicon Valley were rare; Nadia knew very well (from Alexis's and Janet's many presentations about G.I.R.L.) that only about eleven per cent of tech execs were women, and in 2019, just 2.8 per cent of venture capital invested in startups in the United States went to founding teams that were made up exclusively of women. And when they *did* get money it was a far smaller sum than what was granted to their male counterparts. It was completely unfair. It was something Nadia hoped to solve with G.I.R.L. one day.

Or, more accurately, it was just one piece of a systemic ill Nadia hoped she'd be able to help remedy.

"So many tech companies want to improve our lives, but so few of us have the time to actually implement their solutions." VERA replaced Margaret's face on the hologram. "That's why Margaret invented me. I'm a self-teaching artificial intelligence designed to take on everything that's keeping you from exceeding your own expectations and living your dreams. All you have to do is provide me with your schedule, goals, habits and deadlines, and I'll help you get things done."

Nadia had to admit that she could certainly use some help.

"The more you include me in your life," VERA said, "the more I can take off your plate. I can leave you free to travel more, say yes more, and never miss a birthday or anniversary again. That's what the VERA project is all about: doing less; experiencing more."

*Doing less; experiencing more.* It sounded like an impossible dream.

## NADIA'S NEAT SCIENCE FACTS!!!

Artificial or machine intelligence is the computer science version of a human brain. Except human brains are mostly small and stupid and computer brains are so gigantic that our tiny, pathetic human brains can't even comprehend the speed and capacity of computer brains. You are probably familiar with interfacing with a lot of artificial intelligence in ways that we no longer find exciting, like playing chess against a computer, stabbing enemies in video games or telling your phone that you really need to know how late your favourite Ethiopian place is open for delivery and having her both understand your words and respond to your question with a relevant result. (Which maybe only happens sometimes and other times she might tell you to turn left on Fifth, or something else completely nonsensical, but AI is not perfect.)

VERA appears to be an example of what computer scientists would call humanised AI or human-level artificial general intelligence (AGI). This means it displays cognitive intelligence (using past experiences to inform decision-making), emotional intelligence (self-explanatory) and social intelligence (self-awareness and self-consciousness). Essentially, it could learn anything a human being could learn. The most famous test for AIs is the Turing Test,* wherein in order to pass, a machine must answer questions in a manner that is indistinguishable from the way a human would answer those same questions. But there are many things to consider when determining if a machine truly displays AGI: autonomous learning, reasoning, planning, sensing, imagining...

Until now, only a few select Avengers had cracked that code. Apparently now, though... there was VERA.

---

*Developed by Alan Turing, a mathematician and computer scientist whose work was foundational in theoretical computer science. He also shaped our thinking on algorithms and artificial intelligence, way back in the 1940s. Turing was a code breaker during World War II, instrumental in the work at Bletchley Park. He was also a gay man, and his unfair prosecution for his sexuality (and his treatment thereafter) remains a shameful mark on the UK's history. He was posthumously pardoned in 2013.

"So," VERA said, smiling. "Do you want to get started?"

Nadia did. She *really* did. But there was something stuck in the gears of her mind, keeping it from turning further – something she absolutely needed to know more about before she could move on. Nadia had moments like that, sometimes, especially when she was in the lab. She would fixate on a concept, an idea, an impossibility, and she would chase it and chase it until she crested the hill or ran into a brick wall. Her medication helped with this urge; it rarely got destructive any more, as long as she was careful. But Nadia was still Nadia, at the end of the day, and she still loved to follow those hot points in her mind. They didn't always lead somewhere successful, but they always taught her something.

"Almost," Nadia answered. "But first, can you tell me more about your founder?"

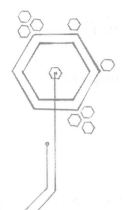

# CHAPTER 9
## GOALS

"Taina!" Nadia ran out of her room and into the lab. "Tai!"

"What, what?" Tai came rolling out from her corner of the lab. "I'm in the middle of—"

Nadia ran up to Tai and threw her arms around her friend's shoulders, leaning down to engulf her in a hug.

"Okay, we're hugging now," Tai squeezed out. "This is happening." Taina was always snarkiest when she was happy (or, at least, that's what Nadia told herself). But Nadia had no time for deciphering Tai's sarcasm right now.

"Is everything okay…?" Tai squeaked out, still being squeezed to within an inch of her life. "You're in your Wasp suit. Are *you* okay?"

Nadia jumped backwards, freeing Taina from the tyranny of her hug, and clasped her hands together.

"Oh, I'm good," Nadia reassured her. "Meds: taken. Therapy: had. Behaviour: self-monitoring." She reconsidered for a moment. She *was* feeling good. Really good! Not manic good. Just... *good. Actually* good. "I think I'm just... really excited. I have a plan!"

"Okay..." said Tai, her eyes narrowing. Nadia could hear the concern in her voice. That was fair; in the past, Nadia's plans had ranged from "let's have a sleepover" to "let's have a sleepover and then seven more sleepovers in a row while we work through the best way to get Shay's teleporter to stop eating people's socks when they use it." Nadia could understand why Tai would be hesitant. But she had nothing to worry about – not this time.

"Follow me." Nadia waved her friend towards the lab's exit, bounding as fast as Tai could roll.

"What kind of plan?" Tai asked, pushing herself out of the lab doors. Nadia saw Tai still trying to hide her concern as they grabbed an elevator down to Pym Labs' ground floor. The Pym Labs lobby was one of Nadia's favourite places – important people bustling, talking and clipboard-carrying, doing what Nadia could only assume was important, life-changing, earth-shattering science.

She felt alive with the buzz of its activity every single time she passed through it. Above all, though, she loved seeing the G.I.R.L. logo on the directory board.

"A plan for..." Nadia trailed off as they approached the sliding glass doors onto the street. They opened automatically. Nadia didn't waste a second before she leapt through them, jeté-style. "This!"

It was absolutely *pouring* rain outside. It was coming down so hard it seemed like the rain was trying to exact vengeance on the citizens of Cresskill, New Jersey. The wind, whipping through the trees around Pym Labs, made it seem like it was almost raining sideways. It was cold and blustery and violent.

And it was *perfect*. Nadia activated her suit's nanotech, her helmet forming around her face instantly. She threw her arms out wide and turned her face up to the storm, letting the rain hit her face. She laughed as her visor almost instantly needed the equivalent of a windshield wiper.

"It's raining!" she shouted to Taina, who was still safely inside the building.

"Yeah!" Taina yelled back, as if to a very small child. "I can see that!"

"Come on!" Nadia beckoned to her friend, shielding her eyes from the rain with her other hand.

"I'm good, actually," Taina shouted back, shaking her head vehemently. "More of a land creature." Nadia saw her reach for her wheels to back up.

"Wait!" Nadia shouted to her friend, thinking quickly. "Just wait there for me! One second!"

"Where are you going—?" Taina started, but it was already too late. Nadia had already hit the button on her glove and had shrunk so quickly it was impossible to make out the rest of Taina's words in the midst of the storm.

*Play in the rain.* That's what Maria's list had said. If Taina wasn't going to play with her, she would find a way to have fun herself. Nadia was certain this wasn't what Maria had in mind when she wrote the list, but, well – science is all about adaptation.

Nadia shot forward on her wings, dodging raindrops the size of buildings left and right – before aiming directly *for* one.

Secretly? She had always wanted to try this.

## NADIA'S NEAT SCIENCE FACTS!!!

Rain is made of water.

Imagine if I just stopped there? *You're welcome! I'm a genius!*

No, I would never do that to you.

Okay, I *would* do that to you, but I'm *not* doing that to you right now.

*So*, rain is made of water. But water is made of two hydrogen molecules and one oxygen molecule, which is why it is referred to in some circles (chemistry circles) as $H_2O$. The water molecule looks like a little elbow joint, with oxygen at its centre and hydrogen branching off to each side (like the letter 'L'). The oxygen molecule holds a negative charge and the hydrogen molecules hold a positive charge. Opposites attract, so we get our $H_2O$. Those positive and negative charges attract *that* $H_2O$ molecule to *other* $H_2O$ molecules and voilà – we get water.

But these electrostatic hydrogen bonds are not very strong. The force holding them together creates water's surface tension – but that tension can be overcome by force, like sticking your finger into a glass of water or diving into a lake. But that surface tension *also* means that objects with a greater density than water can still float on top of it. We measure surface tension in a unit of force called 'dynes'.* (Water's surface tension at 25 degrees Celsius is seventy-two dynes per centimetre.) Hit water with something that has fewer than seventy-two dynes, and it shouldn't break through the surface of the water.

Like, say, a human who has shrunk to less than a centimetre and has shunted their excess mass into the Microverse. For instance. Just throwing that one out there.

*No relation, though Janet Van Dyne is *also* a unit of force.

Nadia tucked her arms into her sides and zoomed towards a particularly juicy-looking raindrop slowly making its way towards the earth. Well, slowly to Nadia; normal rain speed to everyone else. Before she could blast right through it, she slowed her wing beats.

If she did this too fast, it wouldn't work. If her feet were too small, it wouldn't work. If she timed it incorrectly, it wouldn't work.

But she was wasting time wondering *if* it would work instead of finding that out first hand. Steeling herself, Nadia took a deep breath and flew forward, directly at the raindrop.

She hit the surface of the drop with her right foot, and she ran. Left foot then right foot then left foot and she looked down and—

It was working! It was actually working! She wasn't just playing in the rain.

She was playing *on* the rain.

Nadia laughed, the sound echoing inside her helmet as she ran across the surface of the water. She leapt off the surface of her drop and onto another one, across and over to another, and another, and another, playing hopscotch (something she had only seen on television) with the rain. She couldn't help but think of those lizards and insects who could do the same thing.*

Nadia ran and ran before she let herself dive directly *into* the last raindrop, swimming through it and out the other side. Then she dropped to the ground and popped back up to her usual size – where she found Taina had waited for her, after all.

"You good?" Taina called.

Nadia paused. She tilted her face up to the sky and held her arms out to the sides, letting the rain cascade down

---

*Insects and arachnids like the fisher spider and the water strider use surface tension to walk on water. The water strider hits the water with a force of only 10 dynes per centimetre, for the record.

her visor. With each drop, Nadia heard the answer to Tai's question.

*Yes yes yes. Yesyesyesyesyes better than ever why would you even ask and—*

*No.*

*No no no. No nonononononononono—*

Nadia shut her eyes and listened harder. She'd checked another item off Maria's list, and completed a lifelong goal of her own in the process. She felt closer to her mother than ever.

Or did she? Maria wasn't here. She would never be here. No matter how many items Nadia completed on Maria's list, she would never be doing any of them *with* Maria. She couldn't talk to Maria about them afterwards or know if Maria would have loved them or if she would have been horrified to learn that her own daughter was a pint-size Super Hero or if that would have made her day, actually—

*You can't know.*

*You can't know.*

She couldn't know. And she would have to live with that.

There were some things that even walking on water couldn't fix.

Nadia wiped the rain off her visor. "I'm good." She walked back through the sliding doors, tracking the wet in behind her. She popped off her helmet and shook out her hair – it always frizzed in the rain. She took a deep breath, trying to shake out the renewed sense of loss, too.

"You know you're, like, a stone-cold weirdo, right?" asked Tai, as they took the elevator back to G.I.R.L.

"Oh, yes," Nadia said agreeably.

"So, you going to tell me what's going on, or we just going to pretend like this soggy interlude never happened?" Tai asked.

"I'll tell you while I change. C'mon."

Nadia stepped into her room and Tai wheeled up next to Nadia's desk, poking through one of the open boxes on the floor as Nadia ditched her dripping suit for her favourite orange cropped hoodie and red joggers. Orange and red was Nadia's favourite colour combination, and no amount of colour wheel chatter from Janet could sway her. They were the colours of speed and heat and motion and *doing*, and that's what Nadia was all about.

Besides which, clashing was definitely in now. So, Nadia figured, it worked.

"I had no idea it was raining outside," Nadia said by way of explanation. "I've been in here all day and I was too heads-down worrying about Like Minds to ever think to stop and look out a window."

"If you're thinking this is making sense yet—"

"I'm getting there!" Nadia said hurriedly. "Janet got me something for my birthday. Say hi, VERA."

Taina rolled back a few feet as the shower of pixels, now a familiar and welcome sight to Nadia, sprang to life on the desk next to her.

"Hello, Nadia," VERA's Neptune-like form responded.

"Tai," Nadia gestured. "Meet VERA."

"Nadia," Taina responded warily, "why is there a hologram that looks like Sailor Blue Man Group on your desk?"

"Hello, Tai. If you'd like a rundown of my primary functions—"

"Shut it, blue." Taina commanded. VERA snapped her mouth shut and fell silent. Tai turned back to Nadia. "What's going on?"

Nadia perched on the edge of the bed, excited to explain. "Janet got me this for my name day and I completely forgot about it but then I remembered and it's already *changing my life*. It's a virtual assistant!"

"Like F.R.I.D.A.Y."

"Yes, except Mr Stark didn't have to build me this from scratch," Nadia continued. "It's mass-market."

"And you need this because…?" Tai raised an eyebrow.

Nadia let out a breath. She could feel a creeping frustration coming on. Tai could never just be excited that you were excited; she needed to be convinced that you were excited for a good reason. Nadia found that very trying sometimes. But it was part of what she loved about Tai, in the end.

"VERA takes on all my different projects and schedules and keeps me on track," Nadia explained with what she thought was great patience. "She reminds me to take my medication, too, no matter where I am. Even if I'm in the Crystal Lab. She——"

Taina held up her hand to stop Nadia before she could continue. "When were you in the Crystal Lab?" Tai knew how dangerous time dilation could be for Nadia. It was a lab rule that Nadia had to tell someone when she was going in, just in case she lost track of time and needed a nudge to come out again.

"It was when I found my mother's journal. I panicked. But it was all right, and I got myself back on track afterwards." Nadia grabbed Tai's hand and put it back in her friend's lap. "I've been in a few times since, but I've told VERA every time and she kept me on schedule. *And* I gave VERA Maria's list and she processed all the items and *she* was the one who told me it was raining so I could check another thing off *my* list."

Tai didn't say anything. She just held her hand out, silently.

Nadia knew what she was asking for. They had a deal, she and Taina. Nadia kept Tai accountable for her doctor's appointments, even when she didn't want to go. And Tai put Nadia in sort of grown-up time-outs whenever she did something she knew would aggravate her bipolar disorder.

Unzipping the top of her suit, Nadia pulled the chain and the crystal from around her neck. She dropped them into Taina's waiting hand.

Tai closed her fist and the crystal disappeared. She pursed her lips in that way Tai did when she was stopping herself from saying something rude. "So instead of dropping a task, you just decided to use this thing to make overworking yourself easier." It was a statement, not a question. She tucked the crystal into one of her pockets.

"No!" Nadia protested. "I mean, yes? She's helping me stay *organised*," Nadia clarified. "But that's not even the best part."

"Oh, be still my heart," Taina deadpanned.

"VERA," Nadia said over Tai. "Let's talk about your creator."

"Gladly!" VERA sprang back to life. Her pixels re-formed into the dark-haired woman with the icy eyes. "What would you like to know about—"

"This is Margaret," Nadia interrupted VERA, too ramped up to let the AI do the talking for her. "Margaret

Hoff. She invented her first app when she was just eleven years old. She founded her current company, HoffTech, at just twenty-two. She's one of the only women CEOs in machine intelligence. She's from New Jersey. And she used to be an intern *right here*, at Pym Labs!"

Nadia paused for dramatic effect.

Taina blinked. "Cool."

"Cool?!" Nadia responded, incredulous. "It's incredible! It's everything a G.I.R.L. scientist aspires to be! Creative, independent, beholden only to herself, certain of her dream…" Nadia sighed, wistfully. When was the last time she'd felt any of those things? Before she'd become so busy, maybe? But even then, she was being held against her will by an evil espionage organisation. So… maybe never?

"Indeed," corroborated VERA. "Margaret got her start at Pym Labs. Though it must be said that while here she did not work on anything quite as remarkable as Pym Particles or Nadia's Wasp suit."

Taina's head snapped towards the brick. "Now this thing knows about the Wasp suit?"

"Well, obviously." Nadia squinted at Tai. "I told you she helps me keep track of time while I'm in the Crystal Lab. Which you can't get to without Pym Particles."

Tai rolled her eyes. "Obviously. So where's this Margaret at now?"

"HoffTech HQ recently relocated," VERA piped in. "They're currently located in Queens, New York."

"Wow!" Taina said with more enthusiasm than Nadia had heard from her in… ever? That made Nadia decidedly suspicious of what was coming next. "VERA, can you tell me how Margaret was able to become so successful at such a young age?"

If VERA detected her sarcasm, she pushed on undeterred. It sounded like she had come with this speech prepared. "Margaret began coding as a girl when she wanted to improve her Neopets shop front. She fell in love with the art and developed her first app to help students track their grades and their future school prospects at age eleven. After graduating early from a prestigious STEM-focused high school in the Bronx, she attended both MIT and Stanford. She interned at Pym Laboratories under one of the founding Avengers before Margaret founded HoffTech at twenty-two to execute on her vision of creating me."

"Wow," Taina repeated. "So, was that Bronx High School of Science?"

"No," replied VERA. "It was the Frost School for Science and Technology."

"Tuition?" Taina asked, keeping her voice casual.

"Fifty-two thousand dollars per year."

"And Stanford and MIT. Was she there on scholarship?"

"No," started VERA, "Margaret turned down prestigious scholarships in order to better provide for students with need of financial aid."

"And she didn't graduate, just to be clear." Taina had taken a sudden close interest in her own fingernails. From the bed, Nadia watched Taina and VERA bounce back and forth like she was in the stands at a tennis match.

"She left traditional education behind to pursue founding HoffTech," VERA said, still smiling.

"And her start-up money came from...?"

"Until this summer, Margaret has never accepted funding from investors or venture capitalists," VERA said with what sounded like pride. "She built her company from the ground up, on her own."

"And what's her father's name?"

VERA didn't so much as pause. "Theodore Hoff the Third."

"And what does he do?" Taina picked at a hangnail.

"Theodore Hoff currently sits on the board of Altas Oil."

Taina finally looked up. "And *his* father founded that company and *his* father was attorney general of New Hampshire, and they're all three times wealthier than the Starks and three times as lily-white." She turned to look at Nadia. "Must. Be. Nice."

Nadia shook her head. She knew what Taina was getting at. But didn't using your privilege for the public good, to further the pursuit of technology and the status of women in tech, mean that Margaret was different from her father? "She had advantages, but it sounds like she's still a brilliant woman."

Taina finally gave in to the eye roll that had been building for the entirety of this conversation. "Please," she scoffed. "She's no smarter than you or me or Ying or any of us in this lab. The difference is, none of us grew up burning blood money on the fire for entertainment while our seventeen household staff members washed our feet with twenty-four-carat soap. Imagine what we could have done with that kind of privilege? Where we could have been by now? Where G.I.R.L. could be?"

Nadia felt the familiar tingle in her brain – a good idea was burbling there, just under the surface. She needed to grab it before it fizzled out. She snapped her fingers two, three, four times, putting it together. "Okay," she told Tai. "Okay, you're right. So… what if we *did* get her involved with G.I.R.L.? Maybe get her help?"

Taina looked at Nadia like she had four heads. "No way. I don't trust this *lambona* as far as I can chuck her shiny little F.R.I.D.A.Y. knock-off. We don't need her *or* her money. We're doing just fine on our own."

Nadia didn't respond. Taina had a point, much as it clashed with the narrative Nadia had been constructing in her mind.

"She's not some benevolent techie saviour, Nadia. She's a rich white girl in serious need of some perspective." Taina wheeled closer to Nadia. "Do you realise how vulnerable a network like that is? How easily it could be manipulated? It's in people's *homes*. Collecting data all the time. Medication schedules. Routines. Bad habits. *Your* data, Nadia."

"HoffTech's a reputable company," Nadia said, a response on the tip of her tongue before she even gave it a conscious thought. "It has to be safe. Secure."

Taina scoffed. "It's only as safe as the people who own it decide to keep it. You're confident that HoffTech's safeguarding your secrets, the data that makes up your *entire life*? That it has your best interests at heart? That data's valuable, Nadia. You really think that HoffTech believes your well-being is more important than their profits?" Taina shook her head. "You know better than that."

"But—" Nadia was interrupted by a voice floating in through the door to her room.

"Hellllooooooo?" it called. "Anybody home?"

"In here!" Taina called. She rolled, turning her back on Nadia. "We were done anyway."

Nadia sighed. Tai had been so sceptical of everything

she'd brought up with her lately! Nadia knew it came from a place of love; Tai was always worried that Nadia was taking on too much, especially since she had been diagnosed with bipolar. But Nadia found herself talking to Tai almost every day; they were more and more the only two G.I.R.L.s regularly in the lab.

Ying and Shay were always heading off together somewhere trying to make sense of dating, and Priya was either working or out in the gardens trying to make sense of her plant powers. And Nadia would explode if she didn't have someone to share the exciting events in her life with. So, even though she *was* usually sceptical, it was all Tai all the time.

Tai just didn't understand that everything Nadia had on her plate right now was of equal importance; it was impossible to give any one thing up or to put any one off until later. Stop taking driving lessons and put off her dream of becoming a normal Cool American Teen? Stop following Maria's list and lose the new glimmer of hope for reclaiming her past and connecting with her mother? Stop working on Like Minds and let down all of her friends at the lab? She could do it all; she just needed some help.

And if her friends weren't around, VERA would be that help. She was a start, anyways.

And Margaret could be just what Nadia needed to

get past her science block on the Like Minds project. If anyone knew how to take an idea and make it big enough to change the entire world, it was Margaret Hoff. Sure, she'd had help; but if Nadia could just *talk* to Margaret, maybe she could convince her to use some of her privilege and brilliance on behalf of G.I.R.L. Maybe she could even help Nadia figure out what to showcase at Like Minds.

Nadia swung her legs off the bed and stood up just in time for Janet to walk in with Tai's older sister, Lexi. Nadia's machekha always dressed so well, but today she looked especially sharp in an emerald-green suit. Lexi was in a suit, too, but hers was covered all over in florals. It made Lexi's athletic shoulders stand out in a way that Nadia thought made her look like she could kick your butt both on the field with a hockey stick and also in the boardroom.

"Big meeting?" Nadia asked, walking over to hug them both.

"Oh, you know." Janet hugged her back. "Always looking for investors."

Nadia smiled. She did know.

"You look like a linebacker who fell into a funeral arrangement," Tai said by way of greeting her sister.

"Thanks, Tai." Lexi ruffled her sister's hair as Tai tried to bat her away. "Thought you'd like it."

"Oh!" Janet pointed to the gold brick on Nadia's desk. "VERA! You're using it!"

"I am," Nadia said excitedly, trying not to notice Tai's second exaggerated eye roll of the day. "I am actually regretting not opening it sooner. She's already helping me get things done."

"I'm so glad to hear that!" Janet smiled while Alexis picked up the little gold brick and turned it over in her hands, admiring how the hologram always stayed upright.

"Did you know Margaret Hoff used to intern here?" Nadia asked, as casually as possible.

Janet nodded slowly. "I recall reading that in an interview when the VERA shipped. She didn't work with me, though; she might have been working with Hank... I'll have to connect with HR." She sighed. "Typical Hank. Can't believe he didn't hire her full-time. Our loss."

"C'mon, let's get lunch," said Lexi, tugging gently on the back of her sister's chair. "You guys won't believe the dude we just met with. Total jerk."

"Alexis!" Janet scolded, following the Miranda sisters out of Nadia's room. "He was only *ninety* per cent a jerk. The other ten per cent was pure narcissist."

"Fair," Alexis laughed.

Nadia grabbed her phone, checking to make sure her phone charm was still attached. Dangling from the cord looped through a hole in the case was her little Wasp figurine – a miniaturised version of her Wasp suit ready to be expanded and donned at any moment. Nadia never went anywhere without it.

Mostly because she never went anywhere without her phone and she could really only remember to grab one thing before leaving the house. But at least she knew herself well enough to have everything on or attached to her phone she could possibly need, including her lab keycard, her ID and her debit card.

And her super suit. Naturally.

Nadia stopped before she left the room. "VERA, can you send HoffTech's address to my phone?"

"Already done," said VERA. "See you later, Nadia."

Nadia waved, walking out of the room. The hologram faded behind her – but the white light still blinked.

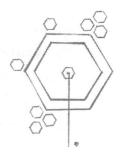

# CHAPTER 10
## OMINOUS!

Nadia stood outside the seamless glass doors, squeezing her hands into fists and relaxing them over and over again. She still didn't have what one might normally consider a 'plan' for getting into the offices; she was mostly considering just waltzing in like she belonged and asking to see the head of their company. That would probably work, right? Big-money tech start-ups traditionally just let complete strangers off the street walk in and book meetings with their CEOs on a whim?

*It will be fine,* Nadia decided. *It will have to be fine!*

She relaxed her fingers and walked through the automatic sliding doors with her head held high, projecting a self-assurance she was mostly just inventing in her own mind. The building's lobby was huge and airy – in fact, the whole building seemed to defy physics, being more glass than steel. It was like a bright and glittery crystal in the middle of an otherwise dull neighbourhood. Trying not to raise suspicion by looking around too much like a gawking tourist, Nadia ignored her bright surroundings and marched right towards the front desk at the centre of the hall.

"Hello?" she called out as she approached the desk.

No one responded. After all, there was no person sitting at the front desk. In fact, HoffTech's front lobby was devoid of any humans at all.

Instead, a small, gold brick sat on the birch front desk, its sleek gold lines in sharp contrast to the live-edge countertop. The whole lobby was a similar story in contradictions. Half of the furniture was made of untreated wood, with plants covering almost every spare inch they could: hanging from the ceiling, covering tables in waiting areas, clustered in corners. The walls were a stark, clean, almost sterile white. The chairs, all empty, were finished with plush, dusty pink cushions. The rest of the furniture and all of the fixtures were metallic gold and glass, reminiscent of VERA's design. Nadia didn't know if she was supposed to curl up and feel at home or if she was in a dentist's office for the very wealthy.

Nadia had convinced Janet to take them all for lunch in Queens. Yes, partially because she had wanted to indulge in her favourite soup dumplings and the free ginger tea that she could easily drink several gallons of in one sitting. But *also* because it was about forty minutes from Cresskill to Queens by car and easily another two hours on top of that by transit.

And Nadia wanted to make it to HoffTech HQ before they closed today. Now she had plenty of time to come find Margaret, *and* she was full of crab-and-pork dumplings.

*Ideal.*

Nadia eyed the gold brick on the desk and took a deep breath.

"Hi there!" Nadia said brightly to the front desk, full of false confidence, feeling a little foolish speaking to... no one. "I'd like to speak with Margaret Hoff."

"Hi there!" As Nadia had hoped before she started speaking to the air, the VERA hologram sprang to life on the front desk and mirrored Nadia's speech pattern, a completely normal thing for an AI receptionist to do, Nadia thought. This VERA looked not dissimilar from Margaret's headshot. "If you have an appointment to see Ms Hoff, please provide me with your name so that I can flag your arrival to her executive team."

"My name is Nadia Van Dyne," Nadia answered breezily, carefully ignoring the first part of VERA's statement. She pointed to a fluffy pink cushion in the corner of the lobby. "I'll just wait over here—"

"I'm sorry," VERA said with a smile on her digital face. "I can't seem to find you in our system. Can you please spell your name for me?"

*Right,* Nadia groaned internally. *Shouldn't have come without an appointment.*

A group of people not much older than Nadia emerged from an elevator behind the front desk, laughing. Nadia turned her back to them, leaning against the desk in the most nonchalant way she could.

Looking cool. Looking like she was totally supposed to be there.

At least she was wearing a hoodie, just like all the employees.

"Nadia Van Dyne?" she repeated. "V-A-N-space-D-Y-N-E—"

"Van Dyne?" she heard a voice ask from behind her. Nadia spun—

—and found herself face-to-face with Margaret Hoff.

## MARGARET HOFF

- Founder and owner of HoffTech, creator of VERA
- Famously only wears HoffTech hoodies so she doesn't have to waste brainpower on personal aesthetics
- Still, the accidental aesthetic <u>does</u> work for her
- Probably the most successful woman in Silicon Valley – so successful she got to leave Silicon Valley
- Seriously, the hoodie looks so soft; where can I get one of those hoodies?

"Oh! Hi!" Nadia said, half surprised and half not. Sometimes things like this just seemed to work out for her. She was naturally lucky, on occasion!

On other occasions, she was born into a secret espionage child-training camp.

But you really had to focus on the bright side of things, Nadia felt.

"Margie, should we—" One of the girls from the elevator paused by the lobby's front doors.

Margaret waved her on. "I'll catch up with you." She turned her smile back to Nadia, and Nadia immediately understood how this woman – still in her twenties – could have taken the tech world so by storm. She was tall and willowy, but not imposing – Nadia thought she looked like someone who had grown up riding horses. Her shoulder-length brown hair was pulled up into a hasty ponytail, but some strands had escaped, framing her face completely unintentionally. Her plain white T-shirt, light jeans and white tennis shoes were so carefully casual that Nadia was certain they probably cost enough to fund G.I.R.L. for at least a month. A maroon HoffTech-branded hoodie had made Margaret almost indistinguishable from the rest of her colleagues.

Except for her eyes. There was something unsettlingly penetrating about Margaret's eyes. It hadn't been the hologram; they really were a startling shade of icy blue-grey, like a rock whittled away by glacial waters. Calm and clear and bright. Nadia was immediately enthralled.

"I'm so sorry," Margaret was saying, holding up her hands apologetically. "We don't know each other, but I think I know your family—"

"Pym Labs!" Nadia interrupted. "You were an intern."

Margaret laughed. "I was! I was. Hank Pym gave me my first job in tech, and I'm forever indebted to him. And you look… You must be…" Margaret gave Nadia an appraising look, like a puzzle she was trying to solve.

"Nadia Van Dyne," Nadia said again, VERA at her back this time. "His daughter."

"Oh my gosh." Margaret darted forward and enveloped Nadia in a huge hug. Nadia returned it enthusiastically. She was a hugger, too! "Oh my gosh," Margaret repeated, pulling away. She kept her hands on Nadia's shoulders. "Hank was like a father to me for so many years. I feel like that makes us, like... sisters, basically."

Nadia smiled. She could always stand to adopt another family member.

"I actually never met him," Nadia clarified. "But Janet Van Dyne is my stepmother, and I've continued with some of his work."

"No!" Margaret looked taken aback. "Oh, I'm so sorry to hear that. Not about Janet and the work, about not knowing Hank." Margaret talked quickly, her voice a clear tenor – deeper than Nadia expected. It was nice to listen to. "We should talk. Were you here to see someone? Are you here from Pym Labs? Are you recruiting? Our interns actually don't finish work for another month, but—"

"I came to see *you*, actually." Nadia laughed. Usually people had to interrupt *her*. Maybe she and Margaret really were similar. Did they both get that from Hank? "Janet bought me a VERA for my name day and it is already changing my life. But the AI is so impressive and *you* are so impressive and really, I was in the neighbourhood eating soup dumplings, so I thought—"

"VERA," Margaret said around Nadia's head. "Am I clear right now?"

"You have four different meetings right now," VERA responded steadily. "A stand-up with Core, the scoping discussion, lunch with Karyn's team and the funding—"

"Right, right, right." Margaret nodded. "Nadia, show VERA your ID. How would you like a personalised tour of HoffTech HQ?"

Nadia already had her learner's permit halfway out of its holster on her cell phone. *See?* she thought. *Sometimes things really do just work out!*

———————————•

"So, we have one studio here and the other is out in the Bay area," Margaret told Nadia as they wandered the HoffTech halls. Nadia had consented to a facial ID scan by the VERA at the front desk and signed rights to her first-born child away should she violate the extremely stringent NDA she'd just committed to, but she understood how careful companies had to be about their proprietary tech. VERA was HoffTech's lifeblood; if someone were to walk away with her secrets, it would destroy the company from the inside out. "San Francisco is fine, but I always wanted to come back and open a campus in New York. I'm too type-A for the West Coast. We don't jibe."

Nadia bobbed her head in understanding while craning her neck left and right, trying to take everything in. The office décor matched the lobby: plants everywhere, white-and-birch standing desks, floor-to-ceiling glass windows to let as much natural light in as possible. *Like a greenhouse for computer scientists,* Nadia thought. You can't know a person through their things, but if Nadia had to try, she would say that Margaret's office made her look focused and driven and goal-oriented.

"This is Programming…" Margaret waved at a group of fashionable cubicles staffed by more people in ponytails, jeans and hoodies. "And this is Core; they develop the toolset we use to design VERA. Her actual servers are down a floor, sealed and temperature-controlled. Those are the writers." She waved into a dismal corner with all the blinds pulled down over the windows. "They don't talk much, but they have a *lot* to say," Margaret whispered to Nadia conspiratorially. Nadia laughed, the sound echoing across the quiet space.

Margaret tugged Nadia into a glass-enclosed office and settled into one of the gold-and-acrylic chairs surrounding the wooden table at its centre. She gestured for Nadia to grab a spot, too. The massive flat-screen TV at one end of the table was on, a screen full of code visible with a bright red section – an error, a bug in the code that someone must have been working on. Nadia was so in awe of this place that Margaret had managed to build so quickly, and all on her own. She had a vision, and she'd executed it.

While Margaret fiddled with the VERA in the centre of the table, Nadia indulged herself in a brief fantasy: G.I.R.L., completely and carefully redesigned in tasteful shades of gold and white and wood. The plants would be easy; Priya could handle that no problem. Taina probably wouldn't want them in her space, but Nadia could deal with that issue when it came up...

"Here, I'll give you the spiel," Margaret said, bringing Nadia back to reality. The VERA cascaded in all its pixelated glory, and Margaret started what sounded like a talk she'd given hundreds if not thousands of times before, her tenor only betraying her slightly. "HoffTech is at the intersection of people and technology, a company designed around the core concept that we all deserve to—"

"'Do less, and experience more!'" Nadia interrupted, enthusiastically.

Margaret laughed, so easy and infectious that it made Nadia laugh in turn. "Okay, so you've heard the spiel."

"I have," Nadia admitted. "It's why I'm here."

Margaret leaned back in her chair and folded her arms across her chest, focusing the full weight of her stare on Nadia with a smile. "Then I want to hear *your* story, Nadia Van Dyne. What do you do? How is Pym Labs these days? What are you *excited* about?"

There was a question she hadn't been expecting. Nadia shrugged and looked away from Margaret's gaze. Nadia was a big talker – she loved to talk with and about other people – but she didn't always love being put on the spot or being asked to talk about herself or her passion projects. That was more Janet's and Alexis's territory. And, while she had a lot on her plate lately, she didn't know if she was necessarily *excited* about any of it. Or any one thing more than the rest. Mostly, she was just stressed.

There was also the fact that when Nadia *did* talk about herself, with anyone who wasn't Dr Sinclair, the Red Room often inevitably came up. Which led to pity. Something about relaying the origin story for her love of science made Nadia self-conscious. These days, she tiptoed around that part carefully with strangers.

"Well," Nadia started, a little awkwardly. "I run Genius In action Research Labs, an all-girl division of Pym Laboratories meant to incubate the best and brightest talent New York City has to offer. But," she added, speeding up, "it's about resources and problem solving and teamwork and so. Much. Science.

"I want to take G.I.R.L. statewide, and then worldwide," Nadia said. "And we're currently working on a project for Stark Industries' Like Minds think tank, focused on local environmental sustainability, but every idea I come up with is…"

"Also worldwide?" Margaret guessed.

"Yes!" Nadia leaned forward in her vaguely uncomfortable but very stylish plastic chair. "Exactly."

"G.I.R.L. sounds like an incredible undertaking." Margaret tapped her foot against her chair leg absent-mindedly. "I wish there had been something like that at Pym Labs while I was there. I'm sure you're changing lives."

"Not like you." Nadia shook her head. "You're changing people's lives all over the world."

"Sure." Margaret shrugged. "*Now*. But VERA started in my parents' basement when I was fourteen. We all start somewhere. And you're going somewhere, Nadia. I can tell."

Nadia sucked in her bottom lip. She hoped so. So, so much.

"I'm so glad you came by to find me," Margaret said,

leaning over the table to grab the VERA. "I'd love to talk about ways HoffTech and G.I.R.L. could partner—"

The VERA sprang to life, surprising even Margaret. "Your three o'clock is early, Ms Hoff."

"Rats," Margaret muttered. "Nadia, can you wait in here for a few minutes? I have to handle this guy or else he gets—"

"I know how that is," Nadia said. "I'll be here."

"Thank you so much, I'll just be *two* seconds..." Margaret's voice trailed behind her as she rushed out of the glass office.

Nadia sat back in her squeaky clear chair and looked up at the screen in front of her.

At all that red.

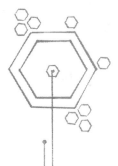

# CHAPTER 11
## WELL, WHAT DID YOU EXPECT?

### NADIA'S NEAT SCIENCE FACTS!!!

Computers run programmes based on instructions called *code*. If there is an error in that code – or a 'bug' – the programme will still run, but it will output an incorrect or unexpected result.

So, here. Pretend your dog could make you breakfast as long as you gave it instructions on how *exactly* to do this task. And I mean *exactly*. Something like: "Open cupboard door. Get cereal box. Open cereal box. Retrieve bowl. Pour cereal into bowl until half-full. Open refrigerator. Retrieve milk. Open milk carton. Pour milk into bowl until full." But imagine you accidentally wrote 'water' instead of 'milk'. Your dog would still make you breakfast, but it would be pretty gross. That would be *your* fault, though – human error – and not your dog's. That's the equivalent of a coding bug. Human error.

In a computer, even a tiny bug can have epic consequences. Take, for example, July 22, 1962. NASA launched a rocket, *Mariner 1*, that was supposed to head for Venus. I say 'supposed to' because five minutes into the flight, *Mariner 1* veered off course and – *kablooey*. It had to be destroyed before it accidentally crash-landed on a city. Eighteen million 1962 dollars down the drain – that's over a hundred and fifty million in *today's* dollars. You would assume it would have to be a pretty big mistake to cause something that terrible, right? Actually, it was ridiculously small: in the thousands of lines of code controlling the rocket, a programmer had forgotten to add a dash to one single equation.

*Kablooey.*

Enter AI. These machines that are capable of self-learning can also, when coded correctly, become capable of fixing their own code. Just like I can go online to search for 'best bagel in Cresskill, NJ' or 'how to create a three-storey Teleforce', AIs can go online to compare their own code to code that is designed to perform similar functions. These open-source repositories, like GitHub, are places where programmers make their own code available online for free (it's open for anyone to use – even other computers!). If the AI thinks *that* code is superior to their own, they can use it to replace pieces of their *own* code – including code that might include bugs.

Of course, that only works if the AI's programmers are aware of the latest updates in automatic bug repair.

And luckily for HoffTech, I am.

"Nadia, I am *so* sorry," Margaret said, hustling back into the room not fifteen minutes after she'd left. "I have a little more time—Oh!"

Margaret took in the scene in front of her. Nadia had her feet up on the birch table, tilted back precariously in her acrylic chair. She had the VERA on her lap projecting a keyboard into the air that Nadia was manipulating with ease. Margaret glanced at the TV. The code that had previously been bright red – illegal output – was now blue. Clean and functional.

Nadia glanced up at Margaret, shaken out of her coding reverie. "Oh! I'm—" She dropped VERA back onto the table hastily, the keyboard vanishing. "It was staring at me. But I fixed it!"

Margaret sat back down across from her, all business. "I know. How?"

"It's called CodePhage," Nadia said. "It's from MIT—"

"You told VERA to fix VERA *for* you." Margaret shook her head. She looked delighted. "We didn't have access to that program."

"I mean, I don't, either," said Nadia, slyly. "But…"

"But." Margaret winked at her in understanding. "Amazing work. Thank you."

"Well, it helped me pass the time."

"Right, I abandoned you cruelly," Margaret said dramatically, still smiling. "Maybe this will make up for it. I want to help with your Like Minds project."

"Really?!" Nadia tipped her chair forward, landing back on all fours with a *thud*. "Really?"

"Really." Margaret nodded. "I think there's a lot we could do together. Hank's legacy. You know?"

Nadia had never thought of herself as Hank's anything. Not even daughter. Not really. She rejected that label on purpose, after all the time the Red Room spent making her think that her connection to Hank was her only real value. Nadia was more Janet's. Or her own, really. But she wasn't going to dash Margaret's dreams; not when she was so close to recruiting another member of G.I.R.L. And one so important, too! The lab had been so empty lately. Nadia allowed herself a brief moment to imagine what it would be like to walk into G.I.R.L. and find Margaret waiting for her with a project. It was a dream.

Plus, Margaret might finally be able to help Nadia implement one of her grander-scale ideas for Like Minds. Bobbi and Janet had been so insistent that Nadia stick to the parameters of Stark's brief: local projects *only*. The rules were there for a reason, they kept saying.

But Nadia's *whole thing* was rule-breaking. For good. She had always been that way. 'Chaotic good', as Shay would say.

Nadia made friends with her spy sisters; she purchased Pym Particles on the black market; she escaped from the Krasnaya Komnata in the dead of night; she was disrupting S.H.I.E.L.D.'s One Hundred Smartest People in the World list. She even broke the rules of physics! Rule-breaking, like liking things, was Nadia's thing!

If Janet and Bobbi couldn't understand that... maybe Margaret could.

"Listen, Nadia." Margaret reached across the table and took one of Nadia's hands. "I don't know you that well, but I can tell you this. Everyone assumed I was some silly little rich girl who wasn't good for anything more than marrying someone richer than my father. No one believed in me but me. I had to make everything – all of this – happen for myself. And I could only get here by *knowing* that my mission was worthy." Margaret squeezed Nadia's hand. "I don't know what you're using VERA for. But I know that G.I.R.L. is a worthy cause. And I know that you need to believe in yourself to make it a success. Okay?"

Nadia stared into Margaret's clear eyes, and made a decision. More than anything, Nadia wanted someone to understand that she was more than just her projects and G.I.R.L. and Like Minds and the rest of it. She was finding a new part of herself through Maria's journal, and Taina couldn't understand that. Or, at least, she wouldn't. But Margaret had a way of making Nadia feel like they were on the same page. Like she understood how Nadia's mind worked better than most of the people she'd ever met.

"My mother – Hank's first wife, Maria – she died before I could know her," Nadia said. Margaret just held her hand, and listened. "I found her journal. She had a list of things she wanted to do with her future child one day – with me."

Nadia hadn't said it out loud before. Not quite like that. She was surprised at how it felt, how solidly it hit her that she was thought of. Considered. Loved. There was a time when she wasn't alone, wasn't an orphan. When she was a daughter, loved by her mother, who had plans to fill her life with beauty and colour and joy and *food*.

"I have G.I.R.L. and I have Like Minds and I'm trying to learn to drive and one of my friends can talk to plants and the others are dating and I've never even been to high school—" Nadia took a deep breath. "But all I want to do is get through this list. And VERA's already helping me with that. And that's why I wanted to come meet you. And to... I don't know." Nadia faltered. "Say thank you, I suppose."

Margaret squeezed Nadia's hand again before letting go, and gave her a genuine smile. Not one of pity, like most people who learned that Nadia had never known her parents. But one of empathy and understanding.

"VERA," Margaret said to the brick on the table. "Access Nadia's VERA... with her permission, of course."

"Granted," confirmed Nadia.

VERA materialised an image of the full list of items on Maria's to-do list. Margaret scanned the list while she talked.

"A secret in return," Margaret said quietly, still reading the list. "I didn't get an offer after my internship. Other people did – all the men in my cohort did, actually. Three of them. Cody, Ben and Ryan." Nadia could hear the venom in her voice, and she felt it in her bones. "When I didn't get that offer, I swore to myself that I would make my own company, and that it would be twice as successful and twice as beneficial to the world as anything they did. I would prove to Hank Pym that I had it in me, even though he didn't believe in me." Margaret looked at Nadia. "And now I'm here."

Nadia matched her gaze. "As someone who has spent her entire life escaping the shadow of Hank Pym," she said softly, "I understand."

Margaret held her eyes for a second and nodded. She flicked back to the list and spun VERA round, so the words were facing Nadia. She pointed in the air towards a bullet. "This one."

"'Watch the stars'," Nadia read aloud.

Margaret jumped up and zipped around the table,

pulling Nadia out of her seat. "C'mere. I've got something to show you."

——————————●

"Isn't it amazing?" Margaret said, lying next to Nadia.

"It really is," Nadia agreed, her hands behind her head.

The two looked up at the night sky above them in the middle of the day. Margaret had rushed them up a flight of stairs, and then another, and then another (she was in surprisingly good shape for someone who probably spent a lot of time behind a computer screen), until they'd arrived on the building's roof.

Or what would have been the roof, had it not been replaced with a massive domed planetarium.

"We don't do a lot of the standard tech-bro garbage," Margaret explained as the heavens rotated above the two scientists. "No foosball tables and no Ultimate Frisbee League, or whatever. But my favourite place in the world is this cabin my grandpa had way up in the Rockies, and all you can see is sky forever and ever. I used to go there as a kid, and it was the most sacred place I knew. There's something so reaffirming about seeing the night sky..." She paused. "I think it's supposed to make you feel small and insignificant, but it just makes me feel like... whatever made the stars made us, and we should do something meaningful with that."

Margaret rolled onto her side and smiled conspiratorially at Nadia. "And there's so much light pollution in New York it's impossible to see anything good at night. So, my one tech-bro indulgence. Can you blame me?"

Still staring straight up, Nadia shook her head. She had never visited a planetarium, ever. She knew there was one at the American Museum of Natural History in Central Park, but who really had time to go and do things like that? She was busy. She had lists to check off.

It was only as Nadia lay there on her back in the darkened dome that she realised this moment – moments like this – might actually help her to feel prepared enough to check off more of those list items in the future. There was something about doing this with Margaret that made it feel different; special, even. Sure, she'd been watching Star Wars with Ying, but the other items, the bigger ones, Nadia had been completing them alone. She hadn't wanted to talk to many people about what was going on. Something about it felt too personal to share. And she hadn't wanted Janet to hear about it second hand, in case it hurt her feelings. She hadn't even been able to share her mother's goals with her own stepmother.

But now, lying here next to Margaret and checking off the box next to the stars, she felt different. *Excited*. She felt more refreshed than she had in ages. Days – weeks, even.

And it was all thanks to VERA.

VERA and Margaret.

Nadia took a deep breath. "Margaret, I—"

"Ms Hoff, you are needed urgently in the finances meeting," VERA's voice boomed suddenly through the dome, her blue pixels rapidly replacing the stars in the sky. Nadia squeezed her eyes shut and opened them again.

Right. She was inside. She was inside HoffTech. And it was the middle of the day.

Margaret let out a noise of great frustration and pushed herself up to sitting. "Fine. Tell them I'm on my way."

"They are becoming... impatient," VERA added.

Margaret rolled her eyes and made a face at Nadia. She laughed. "Do you have to do this for G.I.R.L.?"

Nadia stood, brushing off the back of her trousers and offering Margaret her hand. "No, that's all Janet," she said, helping the older woman up off the floor with ease.

"Daaang," Margaret said, hopping up to her feet. "Biceps of steel. Pilates?"

Nadia walked with Margaret towards the spiral staircase that would take them out of the beautiful night and back into reality. "Ballet," she offered. Nadia left out the part about her super-powers.

That was more of a (twenty-)second friend-date sort of conversation.

As they reached the bottom of the second staircase, Margaret was rushed by several people in jeans and hoodies, all enquiring about where she had been and why she was late and other things that made Nadia briefly change her mind about running a business at all. One of them touched Margaret's lower back and began escorting her into a nearby glass boardroom, this one at least three times the size of the one in which Nadia had solved VERA's bug problem.

"I'll e-mail you, Nadia! Save the Insectarium for me," Margaret said over her shoulder, before the glass door closed behind her and her co-workers.

Nadia peered into the room with curiosity after her new friend. Margaret walked straight to the head of the table and shook hands with a very dour middle-aged white man with a well-manicured beard and a shock of hair so black it was nearly blue.

He looked aside to see Nadia staring through the door. His brows knit. Margaret followed his glance and uttered something Nadia couldn't hear through the glass – which instantly turned opaque. She was shut out.

Which was for the best. Finance meetings were definitely *not* one of Nadia's things.

With a lightness in her step – she'd completed another item on Maria's list! She didn't feel empty inside afterwards! – Nadia found her way back down to the lobby, which actually now looked a lot more STEM-chic than dentist office, now that she was seeing it for a second time. It really was quite classy, Nadia thought. Very aspirational. Also, she didn't have a single pair of white tennis shoes. Why was that? She should absolutely get herself a pair of white tennis shoes. It would really complete her look. She would have to ask Janet.

*Bzzz bzzz.*

*Phone.* Fumbling for a second, Nadia fished her phone out from the front pocket in her sweatshirt. *Must get back to pocket-dimension idea,* she thought hurriedly, as she unlocked her phone.

It was a S.H.I.E.L.D. notification. Technically they didn't *send* Nadia notifications, but she still *got* the notifications. Because she had cloned Janet's S.H.I.E.L.D. phone and mirrored the notifications she got from the agency.

She just liked to be informed about what was going on. She didn't always jump into action the second she saw something come in from S.H.I.E.L.D. After all, sometimes they had nothing to do with her. Sometimes they were about things happening in Wakanda or Sokovia or on the Helicarrier or Spider-Man had got into trouble again and could Tony Stark please come bail him out (the number of tangled webs he seemed to weave, it was unbelievable).

*This* time, though. This time the alert wasn't far. Or, at least, 'not far' if you could fly – Midtown, right by Madison Square Park. It would frankly be irresponsible of Nadia *not* to go check it out. Especially since she was already so far from Cresskill and really it would only be a short detour on her way home.

So… she had to go.

Plus, she'd just checked off another item on Maria's list. She was on a roll!

Nadia ran into the HoffTech bathrooms, already pulling her Wasp charm off her phone.

*Please don't be another death ray.*

# CHAPTER 12
## AT LEAST IT WASN'T A DEATH RAY

Nadia started to think that using 'better or worse than a death ray' as a way to judge the overall success of her day was not the best idea. It set a disappointingly low bar for a 'good day'.

Then again, the way things had been going in Nadia's life lately, 'better than a death ray' really *did* seem like an impossible threshold.

Take today. This morning? Extremely good. Playing in the rain and watching the stars (two whole items off Maria's list!), complete. Time with Taina, always lovely (even when she was being obtuse about Nadia's priorities). Opening VERA, essential. Meeting Margaret, life highlight.

But now?

Now Nadia was inside some guy's button-down – a place she could safely say she *never* wanted to be again – racing through his sparse chest hair and trying to ignore the cloying scent of his deodorant. Nadia was certain it was probably named something like 'Wolfclaw' or 'Bearcano'.

Worse than a death ray?

Not quite. But approaching.

Nadia had avoided rush hour transit by shrinking and flying straight from HoffTech to Midtown, arriving just as the financial sector was starting to empty out for the day. The streets were filled with business boys all dressed the same – buttoned shirts, trousers, smart shoes, maybe a gilet to top the look off. It made Nadia feel like she was in a horror movie. She couldn't quite put her finger on why, but she found them all kind of disturbing.

Like if the zombies in *Army of Darkness* (which Ying loved and made all the G.I.R.L.s watch last summer) were all rich boys who only talked about sailing, or women like they were objects, or what it was like to all be named Brian or Ryan. Disturbing.

But there was something more disturbing than usual going on when Nadia pulled up outside Crédit France, the financial services HQ where the S.H.I.E.L.D. notification had sent her. She could immediately tell that there was a problem; police cars lit up the streets around the building, blockading it from the usual end-of-day traffic.

The cops were assisting building security, walking finance guys out in droves with their hands behind their backs. More than fifty of the gingham-shirted men knelt on the sidewalk outside their office, hands secured behind their backs, and more were still exiting the building, escorted by law enforcement.

This looked like a big problem; Nadia didn't want to dive in without letting someone know first. She put her hand to her ear and put out the call.

"G.I.R.L.s, assistance required at Crédit France in Midtown, anyone available?"

Taina's voice responded almost immediately. "Yeah – at the Labs, so I can't make it to you, but I can help from here. Let me see what people are saying online."

"Thanks, Tai—"

"I'll try." Priya's voice cut Nadia off, surprising her. "I'm at the store but my uncle's here – heading your way."

Emotion welled in Nadia's chest. She might not have seen much of her friends in the last few weeks, but they were still there when she needed them. When she called, they showed up.

"Great! Ying? Shay?"

Nadia waited. There was no response. *They must not have their phones on. Or something.*

Knowing at least some help was on its way, Nadia went quiet and zoomed down, landing on a cop's shoulder. She dropped to her knees; long-distance flying took it out of her after a while. It took a lot of muscle to keep her stable and stay aloft, even with her biosynthetic wings. She was working on her core strength, but it didn't happen overnight, you know.

"Still at it?" A voice crackled over the cop's radio. Nadia was jostled slightly as he grabbed for it to respond.

"Yup," the cop answered gruffly. "Probably a hundred of these guys, all goin' away. White-collar, but still."

"Embezzlin'?" came the voice over the radio.

"Nah." The cop shook his head. Nadia felt a breeze from the movement. "Breakin' NDA in the worst way. All of 'em, blasting client information out to the world for anyone to grab. Security tried to stop one of 'em, another one would step in. Got pretty violent. Can't imagine why."

"Don't try to understand finance guys," the radio cracked.

"Ten-four," the cop snorted. "I'm goin' back in."

Nadia narrowed her eyes. *Mass data breach?* Not what she had been expecting at all.

"That's not what they're telling the press." Tai's voice reappeared in Nadia's headset. "Carbon monoxide leak. Don't know why they'd be arresting anyone over that, so it's a pretty rubbish cover story, but still."

"So definitely something sinister," confirmed Nadia. "Priya, what's your location?"

"Just heading into the subway," Priya responded, short of breath. "Might not make it."

Nadia sucked in her bottom lip. She didn't know if she had time to wait. And where were Shay and Ying? If they'd all been together at the lab… or if they'd all come to HoffTech with her… or if any of them besides Tai even *knew* about HoffTech…

Nadia let out a frustrated sigh. "Keep your ears open, Tai. Priya, let me know when you're here. And if either of you hear from Shay and Ying, let me know."

Feeling a little more energised than she had been a moment ago, Nadia pressed her hands into the fabric under her and launched herself from the cop's shoulder. She zoomed towards the line of buttoned shirts on the pavement. They were all struggling to escape the zip ties around their hands and ankles – unsuccessfully. Financial-office paraphernalia littered the pavement, things they must have wielded to use as weapons before they were subdued: pencils (sharp, good for stabbing), ledgers (large, good for bludgeoning), even a few VERAs (small but heavy; good for throwing).

She stopped just short of one of their faces. Nadia tilted her head as he fought against his zip ties. What would possess them all to do this? Poor working conditions? Not enough foosball tables in the office? Bad returns on their retirement plans? Finally learning the definition of 'work-life balance'?

Suddenly, the man looked up, directly at Nadia. And there was something wrong with his eyes. His pupils – the black part in the middle – took up almost his entire iris. She could barely make out a rim of the blue that his eyes would have been normally; the black had expanded so far that it eclipsed everything else. A strong tide over the ocean. A pull that didn't make sense.

## NADIA'S NEAT SCIENCE FACTS!!!

Human eyes are disgusting, which also makes them excellent. There's the white bit; that is the sclera. It is mostly collagen. Then there's the colour bit, the iris; and inside that, the black bit, the pupil. The iris is designed to grow or contract depending on how big the pupil needs to be at any given moment, like the aperture on a camera. The bigger the iris, the more light reaches your retina, which creates a two-dimensional picture of the world that your brain receives. When you're in very bright light, your iris contracts and your pupil is teeny-tiny; that protects your retina from being like *oh my gosh no stop it's too much light I can't see!!!* But when you're in darkness, your iris opens and your pupil gets huge (or 'dilates') so that you can take in as much light as possible to not bump into your desk next to your bed when you get up to go to the toilet in the night.

Or, at least, that's how things mostly work. Other things can cause a 'mydriatic', or unusually dilated, pupil. Your optometrist might put drops in your eyes that retract your iris, so that she can take a better look at the health of your retina. If you're concentrating really hard on something, your pupil might expand. But the iris dilator can also be contracted by stimulation of your adrenergic receptors – basically, if your adrenaline is going, so are your pupils. So a blown pupil could mean that you are excited or scared... or it could mean that you're on amphetamines, cocaine or any number of other drugs that you should not be messing with.

So, these guys. Scared out of their minds? Excited to be here? Or just really, really high?

"Get down!" There was a commotion behind Nadia, pulling her away from the man's dark stare. She turned her head – three of the men coming out of the building had overpowered their guards and were charging them. The cops already had their weapons drawn. S.H.I.E.L.D. was nowhere to be found.

Nadia guessed she had only seconds before the police started firing. She didn't have time to wait for Priya; she still didn't know if she was going to hear from Shay or Ying at all; and there was only so much Tai could do from the lab. Nadia didn't want anyone to get killed on the street today, not before she could find out exactly what these men were on or who was causing them to act like this. Blown-out pupils were a sure sign of adrenaline overload, for one reason or another. She would have to be careful in how she approached, but she would have to act quickly. She was running out of time – and she was on her own.

As usual, lately.

Because of her size, she moved faster than the men did, at least. Nadia did a backflip and sped towards the three men rushing at the cops. She would have to be surgical in her precision if she wanted to bring the three of them down as quickly and painlessly as possible.

First, a foot to the trachea. Nadia laid herself out vertically and blasted directly into the first man's throat.

She didn't have the time to watch, but she knew he would collapse to the ground in an attempt to catch his breath.

Fixable. Effective.

She kept her momentum going with a steep dive. She watched as the second man whipped a pair of standard office-supply scissors out like a throwing knife. She used her current force to twirl herself upwards, aiming straight for the makeshift weapon. Nadia watched the scissors spin end-over-end in slow motion as she sped towards them. She would have to time this just right.

The scissor blades arced up and towards Nadia and she alighted onto them, running up the narrow edge towards the handle. Launching herself into the air, Nadia kicked down as hard as she could, changing the scissors' trajectory and minimising the potential threat. The kick served to fling her forward, and Nadia stretched her hands out in front of her, aiming directly for the second man's solar plexus. Her palms connected and she felt the wind knock out of him with just a single blow. Nadia slipped to one side as the man doubled over and sped around him. She kicked off his back to launch herself forward again. The speed and pressure from her kickoff tipped the man forward, sending him to the ground next to his friend.

One left. Nadia zoomed upwards, planning on attacking

his trachea in the same way – but she wasn't anticipating his fall. He tripped over the two men in front of him, sending him careening directly towards Nadia. At her current velocity she couldn't make the proper adjustment and instead she went flying directly into the open V of his buttoned shirt as he fell forward.

So here she was. Down some drugged-up finance boy's shirt, accosted by what was probably 'Preposterone'-scented antiperspirant, trying to quickly come up with a way to stop this man from getting back up again and probably getting himself shot in the process.

Nadia recognised that this was her own fault. She could have just gone straight home. Just got right on the bus, then another bus and she would have been home. She could have finished an episode of a podcast. Maybe two episodes!

But instead, she was staring at a guy's gigantic hairy nipple.

Moderate-to-medium on the death ray scale. For sure.

Nadia grabbed a fistful of chest hair and used it to lever herself up and out of the offensively-scented button-down. She sped towards the ground, hitting the pavement the same second her target did. Nadia looked around quickly for something she could use, and—

There. A tangle of long USB cables. Perfect.

Nadia alighted, skimming close to the ground and grabbing one end of the cable as she flew. She could see the man already trying to get back up and knew she was running out of time. She flew straight at his ankles, slamming a USB connector down into the back of his brown loafer. Letting the rest of the cable slip through her hands as she flew, Nadia zoomed in a figure of eight back and forth between the man's feet, over and over and over again until she was finally out of cable. She wrapped the free end around the centre of the complex knot and rushed to the side, just as he face planted right on top of his other two downed friends.

Nadia looked up. The cops were lowering their weapons.

She smiled. Crisis averted. And she'd done it all in a matter of moments.

And then Nadia lay down on the ground next to the three unconscious business bros, and caught her own breath.

———————————•

"Okay, impressive. But…" Tai raised an eyebrow. "Did you do it?"

"Tell me you did it," Bobbi added, grinning.

Nadia was going to disappoint them both. She shook

her head, and both of her friends threw their hands in the air in exasperation.

"What is even the point of being tiny and super-strong if you can't give some *estúpido* the world's worst purple nurple?" Taina sounded exasperated.

"Don't ever tell me what any of that means!" Nadia suggested cheerfully.

"Fine, fine," Taina acquiesced.

"I *did* hit him in the nipple with a Sting, though," Nadia offered. The gauntlets in her Wasp suit collected Nadia's natural bioelectricity and she could harness the reserves with a well-aimed shot. With a Sting, Nadia could zap her target with an electric shock strong enough to knock a grown man to his knees.

Especially if you aimed it right.

"So S.H.I.E.L.D. never showed up?" Bobbi asked with a frown. She pulled on a pair of boxing gloves and waited for Nadia to do the same. Usually Bobbi preferred sparring with Ying, but she was still nowhere to be found, probably out with Shay. Nadia wanted to work off the rest of her excited and nervous energy from earlier, so she'd agreed to it. Taina would be their impartial ref.

Though she tended to favour Bobbi. Nadia was fine with it.

"No." Nadia shook her head, reaching down towards her toes to stretch. She flattened her hands out on the floor in front of her and craned her neck up to keep eye contact with Bobbi. "At least not as long as I was there. They must have heard it was nothing serious – maybe an overdose, or something?"

Bobbi reached over her head with one arm and bent to the right, stretching out her side. "Maybe."

"Shay and Ying never showed up, either," Nadia added carefully.

Tai sighed. "I'm not surprised."

"Still, I could have used the assist on that one. I was very, very outnumbered."

Bobbi stretched an arm over her head. "Did Priya make it?"

"It was too late." Nadia shook her head. "We would have had to arrive as a group. But…"

"At least it wasn't A.I.M. again," Bobbi finished for Nadia diplomatically. "Did Janet tell you S.H.I.E.L.D. got something out of the guy you knocked out in front of our satellite office?"

"No!" Nadia pulled herself back up to standing and she and Bobbi started to circle each other. "What did he say?"

Bobbi jabbed a fist forward, but Nadia was too fast

for it to land. "Apparently, they thought infiltrating the lab would be too difficult after last time—"

"Good," Taina interjected.

"Agreed." Bobbi danced backwards out of Nadia's reach as one of her legs swept out. "Seems like they thought they could infiltrate a side office, maybe bug it or draw security away from the lab, and it would get them one step closer to here. They didn't anticipate you being there."

"They usually don't," Taina said with a devious smile.

"What were you doing in Midtown today, anyways?" Bobbi asked. Nadia feinted with a right hook and hoped Bobbi wouldn't notice her left uppercut – but no such luck. They continued to circle.

"I was visiting a new friend, in Queens!" Nadia said excitedly, bouncing on her toes. Bobbi tried to catch her while she was off-balance, but Nadia barely stumbled.

"Ohhh, right." Bobbi nodded. Her eyes searched for an opening. Nadia did the same.

"Right?" Nadia squinted.

"We were talking," Tai offered.

"You were—?" Nadia turned to look at Tai with frustration, and it was all the opportunity Bobbi needed. She lunged forward, sweeping Nadia's legs out from under her. As Nadia landed on her back with a *thud*, Bobbi held her foot over her neck. Defeated.

"Nice round," Bobbi said, stepping back and offering Nadia her hand. Nadia reached out to grip it – but instead of Bobbi hauling her to her feet, the older woman squeezed her hand and knelt down next to her, pulling her up to sitting.

"Listen." Bobbi leaned in close. "I know Tai is Tai, but she's not wrong. We don't know Margaret. Like, *at all.* I'm not saying she's a bad person – she could be a great fit for G.I.R.L. But we should let Janet and Lexi approach her like they approach all of our other partners. Okay? Let's do this right."

Nadia squeezed Bobbi's hand back in reassurance. "She's different, Bobbi. She's one of us. She wants to help with Like Minds, to do something really impressive and meaningful. She interned for my father, even!"

"And he didn't hire her," Tai reminded her from the sidelines. "Kind of a red flag."

Dropping Bobbi's hand, Nadia pushed herself to her feet. "Lots of things Hank Pym did were kind of red flags," Nadia said, a little sharply.

"Yeah, he had plenty of those," Bobbi agreed, standing back up. She was so tall and lovely and muscly and blonde. Nadia was glad she hadn't wanted to fight with the sticks today. "But one thing he had going for him was that he was a good scientist. And Janet's a good leader, a good judge of character. So we should maybe trust her to handle this. Even if you don't want to trust her with Maria's journal."

Nadia rounded fully on Tai this time, her hands on her hips. "You told her?" Nadia couldn't believe Tai would divulge a secret that wasn't even hers to tell.

Tai at least had the grace to look away, embarrassed. "You said you didn't want Janet to know – but I told Bobbi about VERA and Margaret and I wanted it to make sense..." Tai finally looked Nadia in the eye. "I'm just..." Saying things with emotion was not Taina's forte. She gritted her teeth. "I'm just *worried* about you, is all."

Nadia was caught off guard. Taina didn't usually put things so plainly when it came to what she was feeling. Nadia knew how to read Taina, knew that she cared even when she didn't say it. It was always evident in the things Taina *did*. Hearing Taina say out loud that she was worried cut through Nadia's anger like a blade.

"Don't blame Tai," Bobbi said, stepping in between the two girls. "I'm not going to tell Janet about Maria's list. But we're all just worried about you, after last time."

*Last time.* Before Nadia's diagnosis. When she'd fallen so deep into a manic episode, before she even knew what a manic episode *was*, that she hurt her friends physically and emotionally. Nadia appreciated their concern. She knew how scary that time had been. It had been scary for her, too.

Nadia was used to not being able to trust. Things. People. Appearances. Optics. Promises. The Red Room had made sure that her sense of trust was thoroughly eroded.

But she'd *always* been able to trust herself. Not being able to trust her own brain had shaken Nadia to her core. It had rewritten rules she thought she knew, overnight. She was managing it now, but in the immediate aftermath of the manic episode that had changed everything, she felt like she was constantly searching for her footing, trying to find her balance again.

But this wasn't that. This didn't feel like that. This had nothing to do with having bipolar. This was just Nadia being excited about something. This was Nadia *finally* feeling inspired after feeling like she had been drowning in appointments and schedules and only-potential plans for weeks. Plus, she'd been working hard on maintaining self-awareness about her disorder. They just weren't *listening*.

Nadia picked up her gear and headed for the stairs back up to the lab. "I just think, with Margaret on board, we can make a real difference with this Like Minds project. I've been thinking all day about data and communication networks and interconnectivity and I know there's something here. I *know* there is. I just want to make something that matters," Nadia said. She felt helpless with Bobbi and Taina both following her in silence. "I just want to make something that makes a real difference." She didn't know what else to say.

"And I think we can do it without her," Tai said under her breath.

"It's late," Bobbi said loudly, over Taina. They walked into the lab, where Priya was half-asleep on a couch already. "Let's all sleep on it and we can talk about it again tomorrow, okay? With more of the G.I.R.L. squad, even, if they're here. Everybody's making good points. Let's just take some time."

"Fine," Tai said.

"Okay," agreed Nadia. She turned to make her way towards her own room.

Suddenly, the doors to the lab slammed open. Nadia spun back round.

"Where's the emergency?!" Ying stood in the doorway, dishevelled but looking ready for a fight. Shay was next to her, hair mussed. They must have run here from… wherever they were.

Nadia sucked in her bottom lip. She needed to not say anything for a minute.

"You missed it," Priya said groggily, sitting up on the couch.

"Technically, so did you," said Bobbi. She just shrugged in response to Priya's death glare.

"They missed it by *two hours*," snapped Tai.

"We're sorry!" Shay raised one hand in apology. She grabbed Ying's hand with the other. "We're sorry. We were just—"

"Busy," said Ying. She couldn't quite keep the red out of her cheeks. "Working. Phones were—"

"Off," finished Shay.

"In another room," Ying finished at the same time.

They looked at each other. Shay stifled a giggle.

Nadia couldn't take it any more.

"Would it have been funny if I'd been hurt?" she said, quietly. "If someone on the street had been hurt?"

Shay was quiet now.

"Why would you two leave your phones? Your responsibilities? We agreed—" started Priya. Nadia rounded on her, cutting Priya off.

"You haven't exactly been around, either," she said, still calm.

"I've been going through some *personal issues*," Priya said, anger rising. "And I actually have a job and school outside of G.I.R.L. Also, *I control plants with my brain now, so that's a bit of an adjustment.*"

"Do you care at all about G.I.R.L.?" Nadia accused.

"We're supposed to be a team. We're supposed to face things like that together."

"That's rich, coming from you," Tai said, surprising Nadia. "Where were you before Midtown? Here? Or in Queens visiting someone who has literally nothing to do with G.I.R.L.?"

"That's not *fair*—" Nadia rounded on Tai, but she was already wheeling her way towards the back of the lab.

"I'm done," said Tai. "We'll talk later."

"We're sorry, Nadia," said Shay. "Really. We're glad you didn't get hurt."

"Does Ying not speak for herself any more?" Priya wondered aloud, snarkily.

"Why don't you come over here and find out?" snapped Ying.

Nadia threw up her hands. "Stop. Be here next time. Or don't. But figure out what's important to you. And then let us know."

Ying stared hard at Nadia for a minute. Then she spun, leaving the lab behind her at a run. Shay offered an apologetic look back at Nadia and Priya before following her. Priya pulled her blanket over her head and slumped back down on the couch.

Bobbi looked at Nadia. "Good advice. You gonna take it?"

Nadia frowned. It was late, and she was tired, and she didn't want to think about this any more. She just wanted to talk to someone – anyone – who understood. And there seemed to be a real shortage of those people at the lab these days.

"I'm going to go to bed," said Nadia. She headed for her room.

"Hey," Bobbi added, grabbing Nadia's arm and stopping her before she got too far. "The list. Save Philly for me? I've got friends there. Could be fun."

Nadia's irritation fell away, replaced by surprise. And maybe, if she was honest with herself, a little bit of shame. She was mad at Bobbi and Taina for not understanding, for trying to hamstring her ambitions because they couldn't – *wouldn't* – understand why she wanted to be closer to Margaret, to work with her. But even as they fought and disagreed, Bobbi wanted to help. She wanted Nadia to have this, because at least on some level, she understood that it was important to her.

Bobbi cared. She wanted something good for Nadia, and just as she always had, she wanted to be a part of making it happen.

Nadia swallowed, remembering. She had been planning on doing the Insectarium in Philadelphia with Margaret. Perhaps it was better not to bring that up right now, though.

"Right," Nadia said. She looked straight into Bobbi's eyes and forced a smile.

Bobbi dropped Nadia's arm like it was made of hot coals. She looked like she'd seen a ghost.

Nadia blinked. "Bobbi?" she asked, concerned. "What is it?"

"Your..." she started.

"My what?" Nadia asked, confused.

Bobbi stared hard, her eyes searching Nadia's. Like she was looking for something. She shook her head. "Nothing," she said, but she sounded unsure. "I'm sure it's nothing. Just... think about what I said, okay?"

With that, Bobbi turned and headed for the back of the lab – for Tai. Nadia could hear them whispering. Now *there* was an unexpected pair.

*I guess suspicion of new friends can really bring old friends together,* thought Nadia. She knew it wasn't entirely logical, but she felt left out. Excluded. Hurt. Alone.

Nadia entered her room and shut the door behind her. "*You* understand what I'm trying to do – right, VERA?" Nadia slumped into her chair.

"I do," VERA agreed, her hologram powering up. "Shall we get to work?"

Nadia smiled. Finally, someone who would back her up. "Yeah. Let's get to work."

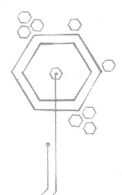
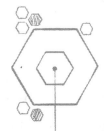

# CHAPTER 13
## DO LESS, EXPERIENCE MORE

"It certainly all sounds very exciting," said Dr Sinclair. "You seem very energised."

Nadia's enthusiastic smile dimmed slightly in wattage. She tried not to overthink in their sessions. Not everything Dr Sinclair said held some deeper meaning. Nadia had just finished telling her about all of the big changes in her life, lately – VERA, Like Minds and most importantly, Maria's journal. And Dr Sinclair seemed genuinely happy for her! Which wasn't surprising. Dr Sinclair was, after all, extremely cool. Nadia knew that, in her spare time, Dr Sinclair was big into powerlifting. Her thighs could kill a man. Nadia liked that.

But Nadia also knew that Dr Sinclair was always on

the watch for signs of unhealthy habits or bipolar episodes. Which, obviously, was part of her job, and a good thing. And that word Dr Sinclair had used – 'energised' – could mean that she was concerned about Nadia's energy right now in general, in case they pointed to risky behaviours.

"I *am* energised," Nadia agreed, "but I think it's an okay energised. A healthy energised. You know?"

Dr Sinclair nodded. "You're sleeping well?"

"Seven hours a night and mostly on-schedule," Nadia said proudly. "I even got myself back on track after visiting the Crystal Lab. VERA helped with that, actually."

"That's good! That's big." Dr Sinclair made a note on her ever-present notepad. "I'm so happy to hear that. You've been following our conversation very well today, too, which is a good sign. What do the G.I.R.L.s think about all this?"

Nadia hesitated. "I haven't seen them all lately, but Taina…" Nadia shrugged. "Taina is worried. But I know it's coming from a place of…" She paused for a second, trying to find the right words.

Dr Sinclair waited patiently.

"Of love," Nadia finally landed on, "and concern. I don't think it's because she's angry with me personally, or anything."

"Good." Dr Sinclair made another note. Nadia knew that was one of her methods of reality testing – if Nadia had said that she felt like Taina was upset because she hated her and therefore the whole world hated her, for example, Nadia might have been catastrophising or detaching from reality a little bit. That wasn't the case today.

"All right." Dr Sinclair put down her pen and looked Nadia in the eye. "I know high activity levels aren't uncommon for you, but I do want to make sure you're practising coping methods in case you start to feel like you're going too far down that path." She put her legal pad down next to her and sat up nice and straight. "What's your favourite breathing exercise we've done? Three-part? Four-seven-eight?"

Nadia mimicked Dr Sinclair's posture while thinking through her question. Both the practices her therapist had mentioned were helpful in different ways. Nadia liked four-seven-eight best when she felt like she was having a panic attack or spiralling hard; you breathed in for a count of four, held it for a count of seven and exhaled for eight. It slowed her heart rate right down – she'd even used it a few times when she felt nervous before a big fight as the Wasp. But it didn't feel right in this moment.

"Let's do three-part breath," said Nadia. Dr Sinclair

led her through the steps, even though she already knew them; it was nice to just have someone else there to talk her through it, kind of comforting in a way. Nadia closed her eyes, breathing into her belly, inflating her tummy like a balloon; then into her mid chest, feeling her ribcage expand; then into her upper chest, lifting her clavicles. When she exhaled, she reversed it, the air leaving first her chest, then her ribs, then her belly.

## NADIA'S NEAT SCIENCE FACTS!!!

Breathing exercises and meditations aren't just placebos for a panicky brain. Breath control has a direct affect on the autonomic and central nervous systems and your psychological status. Slowed breathing increases heart rate variability (the variation in the time between heartbeats) and respiratory sinus arrythmia (when the time between heartbeats slows down on your exhale and speeds up on your inhale), both of which are signs of a healthy and de-stressed human. In EEGs, we see that slow breathing increases the brain's alpha power (when you just finished a project and you're taking a nice, relaxing stroll through Central Park? Your brain is in an alpha state). fMRIs even show slow breathing increases function in the cortical and subcortical regions of the brain. Essentially, when you slow your breathing, you're telling your body that you're not in fight-or-flight mode, but rather in rest-and-digest mode. "Chill out," you say. "Things are, in fact, chill."

Regulating your breathing is a core part of many eastern religions and medicines, including yoga, where it's called 'pranayama' (which can translate to 'the control of breath'). Yogis know that pranayama and three-part breathing (or, in Sanskrit, Dirgha Pranayama) physically lowers your heart rate, relaxes your muscles and helps you digest. Psychologically, it causes you to feel more comforted, pleasant and alert, and can help eliminate feelings of anxiety, depression and confusion. So sit down and chill out for five minutes, please!! It's important. Also, for the record, I am terrible at yoga.

Nadia opened her eyes. "Good. I'm going to get this in every day. I promise."

Dr Sinclair picked up her notepad again. Couldn't go too long without it. "I know you will."

"Don't worry, Dr Sinclair." Nadia smiled in a way that she hoped was reassuring. "Everything's fine."

"You're sure everything's fine?"

"Yes, yes." Nadia was in a rush. She paced back and forth in front of the restaurant with her phone up to her ear. Inside, she could see Margaret chowing down. Nadia hated being rude on her phone like this, but she always picked up for Janet.

"It's just…" Janet trailed off, and Nadia bobbed up and down on her feet with impatience. "We haven't had a good chat in a while, and I wanted to see what you were up to, see if you needed any help with Like Minds, or anything else you might be working on…"

"I appreciate it, Machekha." Nadia did appreciate it. She did! But the things she was doing right now were really more Margaret things than Janet things. Especially since she still hadn't told Janet about Maria's list. Or Margaret. Or… anything, really.

It just seemed like getting into it was more complicated than keeping it to herself. She tried not to think about how it was falling further into the 'lying by omission' category every day.

Telling Janet about any of this would just open another can of worms Nadia wasn't sure she wanted to deal with right now. She knew how Janet felt about Hank, and rightfully so. Nadia just wanted to get to know her mother in the best way that she could without hurting anyone. On her own terms. Involving Janet was just asking for confusion, and it would mean opening Janet up to a painful part of her past, too.

Nadia was confused enough as it was. She was having an amazing time getting to know Margaret. And she really had been enjoying Star Wars, while Ying was still around. But every time she crossed off a list item, she just felt like she learned something more about herself, and not about her mother. Like that she didn't enjoy *Attack of the Clones*. Maria had never even seen *Attack of the Clones*. So did it even really count as an item on the list? It certainly didn't feel like it was bringing her any closer to her mother.

Nadia shook her head. "I'm fine, Janet, really. Is Dedushka worrying about me again?"

"Tell her I am not worrying about her!" Nadia heard Jarvis yell from the other end of the phone.

"Jarvis says—"

"Tell him he's not very convincing," said Nadia, laughing. "I'm sorry, Janet, I've just been busy. Let's make a plan to do something soon? After Like Minds?"

Nadia could almost hear Janet's relief through the phone. "Okay. After Like Minds."

"Sounds good. I've got to go, though," Nadia said. And

she almost hung up before she said it, but caught herself at the last second. "I love you," Nadia said.

"Love you, too," Janet said. Nadia hung up and rushed back into the restaurant.

"I'm so sorry," she said, sliding back into the booth she was sharing with Margaret.

Margaret waved off her apology with her fork. "So tell me about it," said Margaret, her mouth half-full. "You've been working with VERA?"

Nadia bobbed her head in agreement, too busy chewing to answer at the moment. She and Margaret were out in the Ukrainian Village in Manhattan's East Village, chowing down on the food of Nadia's people. Or of Maria's people, at least. Nadia had been raised on poorly cooked Russian food... if you could even call it 'food' in good conscience. It was mostly what Americans assumed food would be like in a gulag. Nadia hated to give credence to Americans' weirdly closed-minded ideas about Russian culture, but also... the food in the Krasnaya Komnata really was bad.

Just... so, so bad.

It was part of the reason why Nadia was so eager to try as much new cuisine as she could now that she was in New York City, the greatest melting pot in the world. If there just happened to be many literal pots of melting deliciousness around, well, she was going to take advantage. And there was no better place to discover what you liked than in Manhattan. You could try anything.

And Nadia had.

She wondered if Maria would have liked Ethiopian food.

"Well." Nadia paused to pop another potato-stuffed *pyrohy*\* into her mouth whole. "I actually got the idea when I was sitting in that human fishbowl office after you had to step away."

Margaret laughed, cutting up her *holubets*†, carefully attempting to keep the stuffing inside the cabbage roll. "I love that fishbowl, but go on."

"I kept thinking about it when I got back to my lab," Nadia continued, increasing in speed as she became increasingly more passionate. "And more and more ideas just kept coming to me and it was like... a moment of inspiration. Finally!"

"Those are rare," Margaret sympathised. She lifted a fork overfilled with stuffed cabbage. "Think I can get this all in my mouth in one go?"

\*Aka pierogi, an Eastern European dumpling.
†Stuffed cabbage, way more delicious than it sounds.

"If you do not, I'll be disappointed," Nadia said with grave seriousness. She laughed as Margaret shoved the whole thing right into her mouth. She was a true inspiration, after all. "I knew you wouldn't let me down!"

"Mmmff." Margaret gave a humble shrug around a mouthful of cabbage.

"You had VERA bring up my mother's list – with my permission," Nadia continued. "Do you remember that?"

Margaret swallowed.. "Sure. I have admin privileges that allow me to access off-site VERAs, but only with permission from their primary user."

"Okay," said Nadia. "But what if we eliminated those barriers to access?"

The CEO squinted. "In what way?"

"If every person had a VERA, and if those VERAs had access to each other, the potential human connectivity could increase utility exponentially." Nadia speared another pyrohy in her excitement. "There would be privacy settings and opt-outs and everything necessary for people's safety, but think about it. If your VERA knew what my VERA knew, they could have connected us much earlier." Nadia was waving her pyrohy fork around like a conductor's baton. "You could have helped me without even knowing me."

"So…" Margaret's fork was frozen halfway over her

plate. Nadia watched the holubets fall back to the plate. Margaret was so deep in thought she didn't even notice. "It's like the self-repairing software. VERA could search its own networks for solutions to user problems."

"Yes!" Nadia said. Her own pyrohy was still zipping through the air over the table. Nadia was a big gesticulator; she couldn't help it. "A babysitter with a free afternoon on her schedule could instantly be connected with a parent looking for last-minute child care. Someone who needs repair work done, scheduled. A student struggling with a subject instantly meets a tutor. There are exploits we'd have to anticipate, but we could work on it!" Nadia finally waved her fork so forcefully her pyrohy landed in the lap of the older lady one table over. "Sorry!" Nadia said with another wave of her fork, not embarrassed in the least. She was being passionate! The lady had a *salfetka*\* on her lap; she was fine.

The flying pyrohy seemed to shake Margaret out of her reverie. She flagged the waitress over to pay their bill while talking through the potential flaws in Nadia's plan. Nadia had a response for all of them; these were still early plans and not meant to be put in motion *tomorrow*, after all.

\*Napkin

All software had bugs and security measures and privacy concerns. She could solve it. With time, she could solve them all.

Nadia and Margaret left the restaurant, full of food and inspiration. Just the way Nadia liked it.

"Do you have time, still?" Nadia asked Margaret, as they wandered out into the East Village.

"Yeah, why?" Margaret nudged her. "Want to check another thing off your mom's list?"

Nadia felt an unfamiliar pang when Margaret referred to Maria as her 'mom'. She'd only ever thought of Janet as her substitute mother; Maria was a sort of a faraway concept that vaguely held the shape of 'mother', but didn't really fit the mould. Like, if you'd never heard the word 'awry' said out loud before, you had an idea of what the word should sound like, but when you actually heard someone say it in English* it actually sounded completely different than the way you thought it should.

She supposed Maria was her 'mom', technically. But holding the concepts of Maria and mum in her head at the

*English is a terrible language, as an aside. With its "read"s and "read"s and "lead"s and "lead"s, it's a wonder anyone ever learns it or understands what anyone is talking about. Nadia found it far inferior to Russian. But what could you do.

same time felt slippery. Like she was trying to make a gas stay inside a wire-frame cage. It was impossible; gas fills the volume of the space it is in. You can't make it conform to any one shape without the proper boundaries in place.

Nadia had no boundaries when it came to Maria. No proper shape. Just a wire frame, bent together with lists and ideas and hopes and concerns. Every time she finished another list item, there was more wire, but Nadia chose where to place it and in what shape. It conformed to Nadia's imagination. It wasn't attached to anything real.

She shook her head in response to Margaret's question. "No, not another list thing. There's actually someone I want you to meet." Nadia dodged out of a hurrying pedestrian's way; she narrowly avoided colliding with a familiar street-meat stand. "Actually, I think my driving instructor lives around here."

"You want me to meet your driving instructor?" Margaret frowned.

"No!" Nadia shook her head emphatically. "Absolutely not. She is too scary for you."

"You'd be surprised." Margaret winked at Nadia, following her down into the Eighth Street subway station. "Oh hey, nice shoes!"

Nadia smiled a little sheepishly. They were white tennis

shoes, just like the ones she'd seen Margaret and all her friends wearing. She'd ordered a pair online after working on her plans with VERA that night for hours. They made Nadia feel like a real tech CEO. Which, she supposed, technically, she was! Plus, they worked with her favourite crop-top-plus-high-waist-bottom combos. Versatile. Janet laughed at Silicon Valley types (like Margaret) who thought that clothing was a frivolous concern, but Nadia had to admit that she saw the time-saving value in wearing the same thing every single day.

She would probably need more than one pair of white tennis shoes in that case, though.

Nadia and Margaret hopped on the train, still chatting about Nadia's plan. Margaret was definitely intrigued, though Nadia could tell it was in her nature to question everything at length before getting excited about it. Tai was like that, too. Tai would absolutely hate to learn that she had anything at all in common with Margaret. The thought amused Nadia.

"This way!" Nadia grabbed Margaret's hand and pulled her up the stairs at the Times Square station, battling tourists with their maps and their cargo shorts for every step. Technically cargo shorts were a wise fashion decision (they could store so much! So many pockets!) but viscerally Nadia could not *not* hate them. It was in her fashion-designer blood.

"I don't really come to Times Square—" Margaret started, cut off by another tourist brandishing a camera.

"No one does," Nadia agreed. "It's just over here!"

Nadia pushed through the doors of a small tchotchke shop and suddenly she and Margaret were inside, away from the din of the crowds and the light of the jumbotrons. It was just Nadia, Margaret, many Manhattan magnets and—

"Priya!" Nadia waved to her friend behind the counter. Nadia hated fighting with her friends, and she was hoping that she might be able to patch things up with Priya today. She was sure that if Priya met Margaret, she would understand what Nadia had been doing lately, and maybe even want to spend more time in the labs. "Margaret, this is Priya, G.I.R.L.'s chief botanist. She's a genius and also incredibly cool and pretty."

"Nadia!" Priya sounded surprised, and not necessarily good surprised. "Are you okay? What are you doing here?"

Nadia's brows knit together slightly. Everyone kept asking if she was *okay*. It was getting to be a bit much. "Do I need a reason to come see my friend?" she tried. "Regardless, I have one. This is Margaret." Nadia brandished her newest friend like the cutest tchotchke in the shop. "CEO of HoffTech. She's helping with Like Minds!"

"Hi." Margaret waved, a little awkwardly.

"Cool; hey," Priya said, but her heart wasn't in it. She was clearly distracted by something. The fight?

Nadia saw Priya subtly shift something under the counter. She wasn't certain, but it looked vaguely plant like.

"Working on your new... project?" Nadia said coyly.

"Yes," Priya said. "And it's not going very well and I was kind of in the middle of something... Could we do this later, maybe?"

Nadia was disappointed, but she understood. Things with Priya were clearly patch-up-able, if not at this exact moment. Still, she didn't even know where Shay and Ying *were* right now, and she certainly couldn't bring Margaret back to meet Tai or Bobbi or Janet... She sighed. Seemed like inducting Margaret into G.I.R.L. would have to wait.

"Well, it was nice to meet you," Margaret said with a smile. She slid a business card across the counter to Priya. "Really excited to be working with G.I.R.L."

"Thanks. I'll see you later." Priya dismissed them. She set the plant back on the counter as Nadia headed for the door.

Which *shattered*, glass exploding across the shop in a shower of razor-sharp glitter.

"Nadia!" Margaret threw herself at her new friend, covering her with her body to protect her from the flying glass. On the way down, Margaret slammed her head against the front counter. She slumped to the floor, trapping Nadia's legs under her body.

"Margaret!" Nadia slid out from under Margaret, taking care not to jostle her too much for fear of injury. Margaret groaned and turned over, rubbing the front of her head.

"That'll leave a mark," she grumbled.

"Wait here," Nadia said. She saw Priya already zooming to the front of the shop, her potted plant in hand. "I'm going to see what happened."

"VERA, call nine-one-one," Margaret said into the miniature gold rectangle affixed to her wrist by a silicone band. "Nadia, wait—" Margaret reached out to stop her, but Nadia was already out the front door.

Both Nadia and Priya stopped short. Times Square was wild – more wild than usual. Tourists were breaking windows, throwing chairs through windows, devastating shop fronts. Overhead, the massive billboard screens – all of them – flashed bright yellow.

"They're not *stealing* anything," Priya noted, spinning in a circle as she took in the chaos around her. "They're not. They're not even going into the stores. They're just… breaking stuff."

"World's worst flash mob," Nadia agreed. But they'd been too loud – a couple of the closest chaos-makers turned slowly to face the two girls.

"I don't have my suit on," Nadia said quickly. "Priya, get back in—"

But it was too late. The two tourists – and they couldn't be anything but tourists with their dad trainers and fleece pullovers – ran towards Nadia and Priya. The woman held her massive tote bag in the air like a weapon. The man did the same with his DSLR camera.

"Get *down*," Nadia said, shoving Priya behind her hastily. No suit meant no shrinking, but Nadia was still trained in hand-to-hand combat. Still, these weren't A.I.M. agents – they were Midwesterners. She would have to be careful.

Even without her Wasp powers, Nadia was still faster than the average Manhattan fast-walker. She ran forward and feinted around the woman, getting behind her quickly enough to grab hold of the tote bag over her head. Nadia yanked the bag away and quickly threw the handle around the woman's neck, pulling it tight under her jawline, careful not to constrict her windpipe. The woman struggled, grasping at the strap, but Nadia was strong. It only took moments before the tourist dropped, unconscious – though it wouldn't last long.

The man had continued his rush at Priya while Nadia had dealt with the woman. Nadia sped back towards her friend as the man tried to bring the camera down on Priya, but his form was slow and messy – Priya was able to dodge with ease. As Nadia got close, she dropped into a slide, kicking her legs out in front of her. "Sorry!" she yelled, literally sweeping the man off his feet. He hit the ground on his tailbone with a *crack* – he'd put out a hand to break his fall and it sounded as though he'd shattered his wrist. The man curled up around his broken arm. He wouldn't be getting up again. "Sorry! Sorry. Agh."

"Thanks," Priya nodded gratefully.

Nadia knew she didn't have much time before things got really out of control in the Square. She grabbed the charm on her phone – her suit. "No problem. I just need a second."

Something they never talk about when people talk about Super Heroes is how Super Heroes get into their suits. It's completely impractical to have your suit on under your clothes all the time. Even if that *were* possible because you really enjoyed marinating in your own sweat (gross), how would you pee? It was like rompers, only a thousand times worse. And how would you manage to be fashionable? Nadia loved crop tops. But crop tops with a Wasp suit underneath? Instant Super Hero secret-identity giveaway. It was a no-go.

Nadia hit the button on the Pym Particles hidden in her miniaturised suit. It sprang up to full size. Nadia tucked herself into a corner and began quickly tugging off her jeans. It wasn't decent, but it was what she had to do sometimes, and evil didn't wait for decency. Nadia had the suit pulled halfway on when she noticed Priya hadn't followed her round the corner.

Nadia peeked out from her half-concealed hiding spot next to the tchotchke shop. The property destruction was still in full swing – but Priya wasn't a part of it. Instead, Priya was sitting on the ground, cross-legged, holding her plant with both hands. For a moment, Nadia was confused. Priya just looked like a girl who really, really loved her plant.

Nadia yanked on one of her sleeves in a rush as something changed in the air around Priya. Nadia could see it become almost… heavier. And suddenly, the plant in her friend's hands began to grow.

And grow.

And grow.

From Priya's small pot, vines extended in every direction. Down to Priya's feet, across the pavement, over the feet of every inexplicably violent tourist. And then up, up, up their legs and around their arms and tight against their waists until every person in the square was entangled. The place looked like the floor of a jungle, green and lush and covered in new growth. And at its centre…

Priya opened her eyes and smiled. Nadia stared in shock. No wonder Priya had been away from the lab so much lately. She'd clearly been busy.

As much as she didn't want Priya to feel like this was something she had to navigate on her own, Nadia knew how easy it was to get into your own head about these things.

Nadia hastily threw her jeans and shirt on over her Wasp suit – ugh, she was going to be so sweaty later – and emerged from the corner. She slid down behind the counter next to Priya.

"When did you learn how to do that?" Nadia asked.

"I told you, I've been busy," Priya said, raising one of her eyebrows with a slight smile.

"And you didn't feel like you could learn this in the lab?"

Priya looked down at her plant before looking back at

Nadia. "Maybe. I think so. I just needed some time. You know?"

Nadia gave Priya a smile. She knew. Maybe a little too well.

Priya's brows knit. "Hey," she started, "are you feeling all r—"

Movement caught Nadia's eye; she leapt back up. Priya might have handled the action here, but they still needed to figure out what was causing all the fuss. Nadia ran over to the nearest tourist, a middle-aged man in a baggy T-shirt and oversized trainers. He was as tied up as everyone else on the block, the greenery holding strong against his struggles.

"Excuse me," Nadia said, approaching him. "But is this a prank being filmed for YouTube or—"

She stopped. The man stared right at Nadia.

And his pupils were blown wide open.

Nadia stared at him for a moment before regaining her senses. She had to figure out what was going on here – and it never hurt to start by asking. Right?

"Why are you doing this?" she said, approaching the man more carefully, now. He was restrained, but she didn't know how long Priya's vines would hold. And his eyes... they just weren't *right*. "Can you tell me what's going on here? Are you working for someone?" The man just stared. "Are you on drugs?"

That got a laugh out of the man – a startling, maniacal laugh that made the man sound almost completely divorced from reality. "No. I just..." He laughed again. "I just *wanted to*."

Nadia shook her head. That didn't make sense. Every single person in the Square just... wanted to cause massive property damage? At the exact same time?

Cool. Very cool. Not at all creepy or terrifying. Taking a step backwards, Nadia unlocked her phone and hit the S.H.I.E.L.D. button. She'd made the app herself. It called S.H.I.E.L.D. And it did it fast.

"Janet's coming," Nadia said, rushing back to Priya. "Tell her it's like Crédit France. I have to get Margaret out of here and I have to get back to work."

"Right; her," Priya said, sitting down on the sidewalk, her plant safely tucked between her crossed knees. She paused.

"What?" asked Nadia, a little impatient. Margaret could walk out here at any moment!

Priya looked down at her lap. "Don't you think you should maybe... stay? We can work on Like Minds after. I've been thinking about Tai's bee thing..."

"Margaret and I have a thing to get to." Nadia frowned. "And unless you want her asking about your magic plant…"

Priya considered. "Good point."

Nadia smiled. "You're very cool, did you know that?"

"I try," Priya laughed. "Now go. I've got this till S.H.I.E.L.D. gets here."

With a nod, Nadia rushed back into the shop. Margaret had pulled a pint of ice cream out of the freezer and was holding it against her head. She looked at Nadia and blinked.

"Everything okay out there? Your shirt—"

Nadia looked down and noticed her buttoned shirt was all askew – and her black-and-red Wasp suit was showing through around the waist and neck. She tucked herself in hastily.

"Thanks. We have to go," Nadia said, leaning down to take Margaret's ice cream.

"I told my team to send Priya a VERA to hopefully make up for some of the damage—"

"It's all good." Nadia helped Margaret to her feet. "Still… we should probably go out the back."

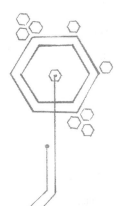

# CHAPTER 14
## DON'T GET CAUGHT IN THE WEEDS

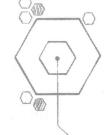

"VERA, how many of you are currently online?" Nadia asked. She leaned back in her desk chair and spun a pencil between her fingers – left, then right, then left, then right.

"Twenty-five thousand seven hundred and twenty-seven, currently," VERA responded. "Our soft launch is going very well."

"Good, that's good," Nadia said absently. "And how many active users?"

"Twenty-five thousand six hundred and four," the holo responded evenly.

"Okay," Nadia said. "Let's run a sim. Show me—"

Nadia was interrupted by something falling over in the lab outside. She launched herself up from her chair and bolted into the lab – she thought there wasn't anyone in here except for her. A.I.M. spies? The creepy-eyed flash mob? It could be—

But it wasn't. Instead, Nadia found Shay and Ying giggling next to a lab table, a broken set of beakers shattered around their feet. It reminded Nadia of Priya's shop door, if Priya's shop door had been broken by two girls awkwardly making out on top of it.

"Oh!" Ying giggled harder on seeing Nadia. She *giggled*. Had Ying ever *giggled*?! "We thought we were the only ones here."

"Oh my gosh, Nadia." Shay couldn't even look at her. "I'm so sorry!"

Nadia shook her head. She was getting pretty tired of this whole lovesick-teenagers thing, but what was she supposed to do? She wasn't their mum. They could do what they wanted. Even if it was awkwardly making out on a lab table instead of using that time and energy for something actually useful. *But, you know,* Nadia thought. *At least they're in the lab, for once.*

"We'll clean it up," Shay offered quickly, gingerly stepping over the mess to find the nearest gloves and broom.

"Sorry," Ying repeated. She was bright red. Nadia tried to stay mad – she really did – but she was so happy to see Shay and Ying in the lab again, regardless of the circumstances, that she couldn't help but laugh. She might not have understood the appeal of make-outs and she might have missed having her friends around, but Ying and Shay seemed happy – happier than she'd seen them in ages. And that was what really mattered.

"Just give me some sort of make-out heads-up next time if you're going to break anything," Nadia said, grabbing a second broom and dustpan. "I thought you were A.I.M."

"Did you hear about the riot at Times Square?" Shay asked while sweeping.

"I was there," Nadia confirmed. She had to stop herself from adding *Which you would have known if you'd been around more, lately.* "And that's not even the strangest thing I've seen this week."

"I wish we led lives where that would be considered surprising," Ying said dryly.

"Priya's really making progress with her… you know…" Nadia waved her dustpan in the air, searching for the right English word. She couldn't find it. *"Rasteniye koldovstvo?"*

"Plantcraft," Ying supplied. "Good! Maybe she can choke us all with vines and release us from the sweet torture that is this mortal existence."

Nadia and Shay stared at her.

"Kidding!" Ying burst out laughing. "You should have seen your faces."

"I love you but I am definitely afraid of your sense of humour," said Shay, shaking her head and carrying glass to the nearest safe disposal.

"Listen, Nadia," Ying said a little awkwardly. Nadia recognised Ying's non-apology apology face. "We were going to watch *Independence Day* tonight. You will love this one. There's a floppy-haired nerd and a cool pilot and they kill aliens using a DOS computer virus. It's nonsense. Watch it with us?"

Nadia hesitated. She missed her friends, but…

"I can't," Nadia said. "I'm sorry, I'm working on Like Minds."

Ying's eyebrows shot up. "Did you finally come up with a project?"

"I mean, it hasn't been *that* long—"

"Oh, no, it definitely has," said Ying. Shay nodded alongside her girlfriend. *Traitor!*

Nadia swept extra furiously for a moment, buying herself a second to think. She wanted to tell Shay and Ying about her plans for VERA. She really did. It was exciting. And the potential… the potential was almost too big to consider.

Which is why Nadia also *didn't* want to tell them. She didn't have all the answers yet. She wasn't entirely clear on what or how she was going to make her new VERA system work. Or how she was going to make it fit the project guidelines more closely. Plus, Ying and Shay hadn't been around much – they didn't know about Maria's list, or Margaret… They'd been very caught up in kissing in front of '90s movies. Not that Nadia begrudged them that – she didn't, at all.

It just seemed like a lot to cover in a short time. And, if she was being really, truly honest with herself, Nadia didn't want to encounter the same kind of resistance she'd got from Taina. Shay and Ying *weren't* Taina, of course; they reacted to things in their own way. Shay had invented a teleporter in her apartment, for goodness' sake! And Ying was as much of a rule-breaker as Nadia. It was highly probable that they would rally behind her new idea.

But… maybe later. Nadia wanted to get back to *work* right now. She'd been faced with so many distractions, between A.I.M. and Janet and Maria's list… She could feel the pull of VERA calling her back to her lab at this very moment. She had so much work to get done and so little time if she wanted to get to bed at a reasonable hour (which VERA always reminded her to do). And she really felt like the only person she could trust with this project right now was Margaret.

"It's a surprise," said Nadia. It wasn't *not* true. Right?

"Ooh." Shay waggled her eyebrows. "Does it involve either Carly Rae Jepsen and/or a sword?"

"No," said Nadia. "Who?"

"Oh my god." Shay pulled out her phone, looking horrified. "I'm updating my Teach Nadia Pop Culture playlist right this second. I don't even care about the surprise anymore. This is more important. You really haven't lived until you've heard *Emotion*."

While Shay was distracted by her music app, Ying took a step closer to Nadia. She grasped Nadia's shoulder and looked her dead in the eye.

"'Surprise' as in 'something fun I'm working on'?" she asked seriously. "Or 'surprise' as in 'I haven't slept in a week and I don't want to tell anyone in case they get mad or because I haven't realised it yet'?"

"It's not that," Nadia said. "I promise. I'm going to Dr Sinclair every week, I'm regular with my pills, I'm working very hard on myself. Even if it is not always easy. Which it isn't." She frowned. Why was everyone so sure she wasn't taking care of herself? "It's really just something I haven't figured out yet. It's in my head, but behind a *kosynka*, like the old ladies in Novosibirsk wore. Obscured. You know?"

"Oh, I know," Ying said. She released Nadia's hand. She would never say it, but Nadia could tell that she was relieved. "In that case, I'm relieved."

*What?*

"What?" Nadia stared at Ying in disbelief.

"I'm relieved," Ying repeated. "I care about you. We all do."

"I'm teaching her how to say feelings," Shay interjected, head still buried in her phone a few feet away. "We're getting there."

"Okay, I'm going back to work." Nadia shook her head. Ying, talking about her feelings? This was too much. "You two have fun with your alien invasions."

"Up yours!" Ying said enthusiastically. Nadia blinked. "It's a quote," Ying added. "From the movie. Which you would know if you'd watch it with us..."

"Go already!" Nadia waved a hand behind her as she walked back to her lab. VERA's blinking red light greeted her, and she felt relief.

She loved her friends. But she loved to work, too.

———————————————⊘

"VERA," Nadia asked, digging through yet another box, "are you *sure* you don't know where—"

"I am so sorry, Nadia," VERA replied. "But I was not yet active when your quantum oscillator was packed. Have you checked the second cupboard—"

"Yes!" She had. Twice. She had checked every room in the house, every box she could think of, but her oscillator was nowhere to be found. Which usually wouldn't be a problem; it wasn't exactly something she used every day. Very tricky physics-related issues only for the quantum oscillator.

It just so happened that the oscillator might actually solve Nadia's most recent tricky physics-related issue. VERA, in fact, had suggested it as a way of increasing her connectivity speed to other VERA units over traditional internet, bypassing through the quantum realm to increase data-transfer rates. It was, really, quite genius.

So, of course, it was at that particular moment that Nadia had no hope at all of finding it.

"Nothing!" Nadia crossed her feet and dropped to the floor. She slid onto her back, the wood hard against her spine. There was almost no furniture in the house now, just boxes on boxes – half here, half at the lab, her life and a life that was never really hers at all spread between the past and her future. She felt everywhere and nowhere at once. Nadia was just grateful she had VERA to keep her grounded.

That morning, Dr Sinclair had listened with interest as Nadia updated her on recent exploits with Margaret,

VERA and the Like Minds project. Maria's list had dropped to the back of the queue of things demanding Nadia's attention, and while Dr Sinclair was happy that Nadia had removed something from her plate, even temporarily, she was concerned that the 'something' in question was, at least on the face of it, one of the more self-care-focused items on her list.

Life *is* work, though. Isn't it? And friends and good boba and being a Cool American Teen. But Nadia did work *with* her friends *while* drinking boba which *made* her a Cool American Teen.

Right?

Nadia heard a key in the front door a second before it swung open.

"Helllooooo?"

It was Janet. Nadia didn't move. "In here, Machekha!"

Three pairs of feet came into view: red-soled nude heels; gold-striped blue-and-red runners; and no-nonsense brown Oxfords. Janet, Bobbi and Jarvis.

"Hey there," said Bobbi, crouching down. "Whatcha doin' on the floor?"

Nadia placed a hand dramatically across her own forehead, like a fainting lady in a Victorian painting. "I can't find my quantum oscillator and it has driven me to hysteric exhaustion." She closed her eyes and turned her head away. "There is no chance for me. You must go on. Live a good life. Think of me often."

"Okay, there, Dazzler." Janet reached out a hand. Nadia struck another dramatic pose on the floor before Bobbi just hoisted her up on her own. Her feet solidly on the ground again, Nadia launched herself forward and engulfed Bobbi in a hug.

"It is already at the lab," Jarvis piped up. "I recall transporting it earlier this week, along with the——"

Nadia slapped her forehead in sudden recollection. "The universal remotes. Of *course*. I can't believe I forgot about that."

"Well, you *have* been working very hard," said VERA. The three adults looked around for the source of the voice.

"That's just VERA," Nadia said congenially, pointing to the gold brick on the floor next to her feet. "She's helping me with Like Minds."

"How's it coming?" Bobbi said, trying to keep her tone cool and unaffected. Nadia saw her tell, though. Behind the nonchalance was suspicion. Caution.

"Good," Nadia said, shutting her down right away. It was increasingly clear that Bobbi didn't understand Nadia's relationship with Margaret. Nadia suspected that Bobbi might even be *jealous* of Nadia and Margaret's friendship. Bobbi was a loving and supportive older-sister figure to Nadia, sure, but she was also human. It was natural for her to feel uncomfortable with Nadia's success under Margaret's mentorship.

But Nadia didn't have time to deal with personal strife until *after* Thanksgiving. So she was determined to move on from this line of questioning as quickly as possible. "I actually need my quantum oscillator. So, back to the lab—"

"Wait!" interrupted Jarvis. "We have something for you."

"It's tickets," Bobbi blurted out in excitement. "To a hockey game. New York Rangers."

"We know Maria said 'football game'," said Janet. "But soccer season ended in August and hockey season was on and none of us really know anything about sports anyway, so we figured, close enough—"

Janet stopped. Nadia did not look as happy as she had anticipated.

Because Nadia was deeply, deeply upset. So upset she didn't quite have the ability to process her own emotions in that moment. She just felt hot, everywhere, all at once, and she needed to know if what she was hearing was true.

"You told her?" Nadia asked Bobbi quietly. Nadia waited for Bobbi to say no, she didn't tell Janet the one thing Nadia told her not to. Because of course she wouldn't do that. Family wouldn't do that. They wouldn't.

"I know, I know..." Bobbi ran a hand through her hair sheepishly. "But I didn't want you to have to worry about Janet not being cool with it, because I knew she *would* be cool with it, and I wanted to get that stress off your mind—"

So she did.

"But I asked you not to," Nadia said, still quietly. She tried not to feel sorry for herself, ever. She had a *really* good life, now, and she knew so many people had it much worse than her. But in that moment, facing down Bobbi, Nadia felt like an overused string snapping across the neck of a violin.

Were two dead parents not enough? Was packing up your dead father's house not enough? What about trying to get to know your dead mother through her journal – which, it turned out, was mostly an impossibility? What about being an immigrant to a new country you were still trying to fully understand? What about having bipolar disorder and having to work hard to manage it? What about being a Super Hero and a Cool American Teen and what about G.I.R.L. and what about A.I.M. and what about her absentee friends and her unknown future being shot at by a death ray and *trying to learn how to drive a car like a normal girl*—

Apparently, that was not enough. All of that wasn't enough. Now Nadia had to add 'betrayed by older sister' to the pile, too.

It was too much. It was the one thing Nadia thought she didn't have to worry about, in a life of worrying about everything, all the time. Bobbi was there for her. Bobbi wouldn't let her down.

*I vse yeshche.* And yet.

Bobbi was starting to look nervous. Nadia didn't blame Bobbi for her nerves; Nadia didn't get upset often, and when she did, it meant things were serious. And they were serious now. Dedushka knew it. Out of the corner of her eye, Nadia could see Jarvis wringing his hands.

"Nadia, it's all right." Janet stepped in. "I'm really happy that you found a connection to Maria. I think it's healthy and exciting and, if you'd like, I'd be thrilled to be a part of—"

"I'm working on Like Minds right now, not Maria's list," Nadia snapped. She could feel herself unravelling. She tried to keep a lid on her emotions, but in that moment she was too upset to think about Dr Sinclair or her exercises or any of the healthy coping habits she'd been learning. She had trusted Bobbi with this – this *one thing*, and Bobbi had betrayed her.

Nadia felt more alone than she'd felt in years. No one understood her relationship with Margaret, or why it was so important to Nadia to have someone like her involved with G.I.R.L. – someone who wasn't afraid to take risks and break rules, like Nadia. No one wanted to understand Nadia's Like Minds project, or why it could make such a huge difference – to the *world*, not just to some science fair. No one was even *in* the G.I.R.L. labs lately to talk about these things, even if they had wanted to. The only people who were consistently there for her right now were Dr Sinclair and Margaret. And she was *paying* one of them.

"I'm sorry." Bobbi held up her hands in apology. "I know you have a lot on your plate and I was just trying to help—"

"By doing what I asked you not to do?" Nadia could hardly believe what she was hearing. Excuses? These weren't even *good* excuses. "Why didn't you help me by supporting me? Because you don't like Margaret? Because you're jealous that I'm spending time with her?"

"Nadia..." Janet warned.

Bobbi stood in silence. It was enough of an answer for Nadia.

"Don't be upset with Bobbi, please, Nadia." Janet took a few steps forward, her heels loud against the hardwood. Nadia took an equal number of steps back. She didn't want to be close to anyone right now. She didn't *feel* close to anyone right now. "She told me about Maria and about Margaret because she was concerned for you. You're taking on a lot—"

"And I can handle a lot," Nadia shot back. She was strong and she was capable; she didn't have to be treated with kid gloves. It was infuriating. "Everyone is *concerned* for me and for my bipolar, but when I try to tell you what I want or what I need, no one seems to be listening!"

"Nadia…" Bobbi ran her fingers through her hair. "I talked to Taina and I just don't think the VERA project is a good idea." Nadia opened her mouth to argue, but Bobbi kept talking. "The VERA project falls outside of the Like Minds scope – and it's also *dangerous*." She took a step forward. Nadia kept still. "I know you think you can solve all the inherent issues with privacy and infosec, and one day you might! But I don't think you can do that in the next week. And I don't think it fits the parameters of the assignment."

"And I don't think you should be associating so closely with Margaret Hoff," added Janet.

*This.* This was exactly what Nadia had been afraid of. Nadia rounded on her. "Right. You, too?"

"I found her old HR files," Janet said gently. "Hank was

worried about her. She was very driven. To a degree that scared him. Which is really saying something. If *Hank* was scared, it must've been extreme."

Nadia snorted. "Oh, and now it's bad to be driven? Keep the teen girls where they belong, in the mall, is that right?"

" 'In the mall'?" Bobbi repeated incredulously. "Nadia, I know I screwed up talking about the list, but I just thought we could get you back on the right track—"

"I have bipolar, I'm not a lost stray," Nadia shot back. "I'm not having an episode. I'm just upset."

"Totally fair," said Janet. "Listen, the hockey game is—"

"I can't worry about the list until after Like Minds. I have to go back to the lab." Nadia couldn't even look at Bobbi right now. "Quantum oscillator."

"I will drive you," offered Jarvis, from a room away.

"I'll find my own way back," said Nadia, scooping up VERA and her phone. Janet and Bobbi looked at each other, concerned – but Bobbi had to know she had messed up. Nadia made it three steps out of the house before reaching for her Wasp charm. There were some things that could only be made better by a long fly and a long cry.

This was one of them.

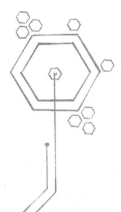

# CHAPTER 15
## AND THIS, TOO

"VERA," Nadia said, her voice rough, "play 'When I Needed You' again."

"Are you sure there is not another Carly Rae Jepsen song you would like to—"

"No," Nadia cut the holo off. "Again."

"All right," VERA said. If it were possible for machine intelligence to sound reluctant, VERA did.

### NADIA'S NEAT SCIENCE FACTS!!!

Time for some more *brain science*. People say all the time that music has the power to make a person feel better, almost like magic. But obviously, it is not magic. Scarlet Witch is not crouched inside your baby-blue Victrola. Though that would admittedly be kind of adorable. But she's busy. No, instead it has everything to do with your brain chemistry.

When a human hears music, it triggers the release of a chemical called *dopamine* in the brain, more specifically in the dorsal and ventral striatum. Dopamine is a neurotransmitter: something that acts like an information taxi between your brain cells. It helps with many different things – movement, attention, emotions – but it's also responsible for making humans feel happiness, satisfaction or pleasure. Dopamine from the *ventral tegmental area* is released when a person does something that makes them feel awesome – like exercising or listening to music. It tells the body, "Do this again. That was good. More of that, please."

In fact, dopamine levels increase by up to 9 per cent when we listen to music we like. Listening to music we love, just like eating food we love, releases dopamine and makes us all happier, instantly. Music is universal. It connects us all.

Is the pure joy of Carly Rae Jepsen universal, too? I think so. *I have to think so.*

Nadia was back at the lab, lying on her bed, VERA projecting a keyboard into the air over her. She'd found the quantum oscillator buried at the bottom of a kitchen drawer (why Jarvis had put it there she would never know). Nadia had been working on hooking VERA into the quantum realm since she got back to the lab an hour ago. She knew she should go to bed soon, but she was still too upset to relax. And getting VERA to liaise with the quantum realm had been more difficult than Nadia had originally anticipated.

"Is it possible for a song to be both happy and sad at the same time?" Nadia asked VERA, half-distracted by her work.

"Robyn, 'Dancing on My Own'," a voice from Nadia's doorway answered. "Lorde's 'Supercut'. Kacey Musgraves, 'Happy and Sad'. Eighty per cent of *ABBA Gold.*"

"Margaret!" Nadia went to move off her bed, but Margaret waved at her to stay put.

"I heard you might need a friend," Margaret said kindly, sitting on the edge of the bed. She had on her usual uniform – maroon hoodie, jeans, white tennis shoes. She smelled like cedar and cardamom.

"You heard…?" Nadia frowned.

"We linked our VERAs, remember?" Margaret smiled. "It's like your project is already working as designed."

Nadia flumped back down onto her pillows. "No. Nothing is working as designed."

"That's life for you." Margaret patted Nadia's leg sympathetically. "Want a refund?"

"Sometimes," Nadia admitted.

"Same. Mind if I…?" Margaret gestured to the pillows. Nadia wiggled over to make room on her bed and Margaret lay down, resting her hands behind her head. "Cute place."

"A work in progress," Nadia said to the ceiling. She sighed. She was frustrated with Bobbi, frustrated with Janet, she missed her friends, and she just wanted to get back to work, but her stupid emotions were getting in the way. Not even her room was making her happy, not in its current dishevelled mid-move-in state. "It's actually… the only place I've ever had that was just *mine*," Nadia continued. "I mean, I share the lab with my friends, which I love, because I love having people around. But I grew up in a…"

She paused. "Boarding school" is what she landed on. "And then I came back to Hank's old house. Here, though… I can make this what I want. Just like G.I.R.L. But…"

"It's taking a lot of time and energy and some compromise?" Margaret raised an eyebrow and looked sidelong at Nadia next to her on the pillows.

"Yes. Almost like you have some experience with this." Nadia nudged her.

"You're a big dreamer, Nadia," Margaret said, rolling onto her side and propping her head up on one hand. "And what that means is sometimes people aren't going to understand you. They're going to doubt you. Look at me; Hank Pym didn't even want to hire me. As if it were possible to be *too* passionate about making the world a better place."

"Exactly!" Nadia pushed herself up on the bed, propping herself against her headboard. "Exactly. And I'm so *close* with VERA. If I can get this working, it could change so many lives. Not that Taina's local bee pollinator isn't also a great idea, or Ying's sewage treatment, or…" Nadia leaned her head back against the board and closed her eyes. "I just *have* to see this through. I *need* to."

"Well, then." Margaret rolled off the bed and stood up, reaching out her hand to Nadia. "What's stopping you?"

Nadia opened her eyes and looked at Margaret, standing

over her bed here at Pym Labs, her arm outstretched. It was the last thing she would have expected back on her name day: her friends and her family refusing to believe in her work, a beautiful and brilliant new role model by her side instead.

In a way, Nadia figured she had Maria to thank for her new mentor; had it not been for her journal and her list, Nadia would never have been pushed to open the VERA. She would never have thought of a project for Like Minds, and she would never have met Margaret. It was like Maria was looking out for her daughter even from... wherever she was now. Nadia never knew quite what to think about that. But wherever she was, she'd dropped this in Nadia's lap. It had to mean something.

Nadia grasped Margaret's hand.

"Am I interrupting some sort of white-girl sleepover ritual here?" came a voice from the door. Taina walked in on her crutches, looking disdainfully at Margaret. Nadia dropped her hand quickly and slid off the bed.

Nadia decided she would try to play peacemaker, and fast. "Taina, this is—"

"I know who this is." Taina leaned on one of her crutches and waved the other towards Margaret. "What's she doing here?"

"Just leaving," Margaret said coolly. "Nadia, you know how to find me." Margaret stepped round Taina and out the door, leaving only the smell of cedarwood in her wake.

"That was rude," Nadia said, once she'd heard the lab doors slide shut. "You didn't have to be so mean to her face."

"At least I'm honest." Taina leaned against the door frame. "I thought you told Bobbi you were letting all this go."

"What is *with* all of you?" demanded Nadia, snatching up VERA off her desk and storming out of her room. Hadn't she dealt with enough of this today? She had just been starting to feel better and ready to work again, and now this. It was too much to handle. She needed a nap. Several naps. Maybe just an entire sleep, at this point.

"What is with *you*?" Taina threw back, following Nadia into the lab. "You're acting like you've completely forgotten what friends or morals are. Like a tech CEO, actually."

"Always with the jabs." Nadia marched into the kitchen and turned on the electric kettle with more force than was probably necessary. "I get it; you don't like Margaret and you don't like my project. Are we done?"

"Listen to yourself!" Taina said incredulously. "You don't sound like Nadia. You don't even sound like *manic*

Nadia." Taina dropped into a plastic chair and punctuated her statement by setting her crutches down against the table. "No one here is being unreasonable! You're a secret Super Hero who works for a public Super Hero fighting off attacks from Super Villains while you develop a *quantum-realm spy network*! It is *not weird* for your friends to say 'Maybe pump the brakes on this total stranger' or 'Why are you making something completely illegal and probably evil?' I've been trying to get Ying and Shay and Priya back in here for weeks. Have you even noticed?"

Nadia whipped round, an empty mug in her hand. It had the words BECAUSE SCIENCE on it in big, bold letters, and it was Nadia's favourite. "I've been a little busy, Taina! And I don't appreciate that you don't seem to have any faith in my abilities and I'm tired of you talking to me like I don't know what I'm doing and everyone is trying to get me to hate Margaret and I don't know *why*—" Nadia stopped herself. She didn't want to say something she would regret. She just wanted to get back to work.

"Nadia," Taina said, interrupting the silence. She didn't sound angry any more. She sounded... scared. "Nadia, what's going on with your eyes?"

Nadia squinted. "Nothing? I can see you fine. It's just bright in here."

"It's really not." Taina swallowed. She cocked her head towards the cupboard door with a mirror on it. "I'm serious. Are you okay?"

*Am I okay? Am I okay?* Nadia slammed her mug down on the counter and stomped over to the mirror. She wasn't made of porcelain. She was a flier and a fighter. She was a scientist. She *had* bipolar. It wasn't *who* she was; it was a thing she *had*. And she was *managing* it. *Responsibly.* "I'm *fine*," Nadia said, "and I *wish* people would stop *asking* me that *question*—"

Nadia looked into the mirror, and she froze. Nadia recognised herself; she looked like she'd been crying a bit today, red-eyed and puffy-faced, but otherwise she looked… normal. Healthy. Rested. Sad, but normal.

Except for one thing. Nadia leaned closer to the mirror. With her index fingers, she tugged down the skin under her eyes. There was no denying it.

The brown of Nadia's eyes had disappeared. The irises were gone. And in their place, she saw giant, blown-out pupils.

# CHAPTER 16
## THAT'S PROBABLY NOT A GOOD SIGN

Nadia could hear them, out in the lab. Taina had been on her phone for the last half hour, getting in touch with everyone she could: Priya, Shay, Ying, Bobbi, Janet, Jarvis, even Alexis. They'd all been caught up in their own lives, but this time, when Taina called, they all came. For the first time in weeks, the whole squad was assembling in the lab – no arguments, no misunderstandings. They were here to work.

Nadia knew that was a good thing. Logically. And she would leave her room in a minute. In just a minute.

But first, Nadia needed a moment to herself.

She couldn't stop seeing that image of herself, her eyes an unnerving wall of black. Just like Crédit France. Just like Times Square.

Nadia filtered through the different possibilities in her mind. She was relatively certain she wasn't on any sort of illegal substance; typically there were more symptoms than 'big eyes' that came along with being drugged against your will. She wasn't scared (well, until a couple of minutes ago, anyways) and she wasn't excited (definitely not after a couple of minutes ago).

"VERA?" Nadia asked. "Unusual causes of mydriasis."

"Unusual as in least common?" VERA queried.

"Yes." Nadia squeezed her eyes shut. She hated that something was happening to her body she couldn't control. She spent so much time attempting to stay in command of herself – training her body with ballet, shifting her size with Pym Particles, organising her brain with medication and therapy and meditation and self-reflection... That there was something happening to her body now that she didn't understand and couldn't bring under her own control was infuriating and terrifying in equal measure. She couldn't even punch it to make it stop. It was her own face. That was a terrible idea. What was she even thinking?!

"Acetylcholine blockers," VERA began to list. "Hallucinogens. Anesthetic. Stroke. Epilepsy. Traumatic head or eye injury. Impending brain herniation."

"Oh, good," Nadia said to herself. "So probably best-case scenario, it is just an impending brain hernia.

This is why people say not to search your symptoms online, isn't it?"

"Would you like me to phone an ambulance, Nadia?" VERA asked, not unkindly.

"No." Nadia shook her head. "No. I can figure this out on my own. I just need to think. I just need to—"

Nadia reached for the chain around her neck – but there was nothing there. Her crystal—

"Looking for this?" Taina leaned against Nadia's door frame, same as she had earlier. The Crystal Lab necklace dangled from her fingers. Behind her, Nadia could see Shay, Ying and Priya, all looking different varieties of concerned. "Absolutely not."

"I just need time to think," Nadia explained desperately. "If it's not drugs, and I haven't hit my head, then it can only be..."

"VERA?" Taina asked loudly. "Turn yourself off."

"I only respond to commands from my primary user," VERA responded. "If Nadia would like—"

"You're fine, VERA." Nadia waved at the gold block. "VERA's helping me figure this out so that I can get back to work on our project," Nadia explained to the other G.I.R.L.s. "Can you think of any other search queries—"

"VERA," Taina repeated, "I'd really like for you to turn yourself off."

"Awaiting verification from Nadia."

Nadia stared at Taina. She should be able to command VERA to turn herself off. Her eyes flicked to the device. It wasn't a big deal; she could get back to work on her quantum connection after this issue with her eyes was handled. It probably wouldn't even take that long.

But why deactivate VERA when she could likely help with the issue? If only Nadia's project had already been online; VERA could connect with local neuroscientists or doctors to answer Nadia's query instantaneously. Maybe the real answer was just connecting VERA to the quantum realm *first* and then using her new connections to solve this *current* problem instead of the other way round—

"Okay, that's what I thought." Taina's no-nonsense voice interrupted Nadia's reverie. "Ying?"

"Yeah," said Ying, stepping forward. Before Nadia knew what was happening, Ying swiped VERA off the desk and lobbed it straight out of the room. She aimed a fist at it. It was only then that Nadia noticed Ying was wearing a glove from one of Nadia's Wasp suits.

A glove with the Wasp's Sting reservoir built in.

"Wait—" Nadia leapt off the bed and towards Ying, but she was too late; Ying was always faster than her anyway, even in the Krasnaya Komnata. Nadia was a better shot, but Ying was stealthier. It was part of what made them such a strong pair.

In this moment, though, Nadia found that a lot more difficult to appreciate.

Ying closed her fist and squeezed. The Sting erupted from her knuckles, the blast shooting through the air and landing square in the middle of the gold block Nadia had come to depend on. With a sound like a gunshot, VERA exploded, the proximity and power of the Sting overloading VERA's core and shattering the device into oblivion. The broken remains were flung across the lab.

"We'll be finding pieces of that thing for weeks," groaned Priya.

Nadia's brain *screamed*. Nails raked through her cranium. A headache bloomed behind her eyes.

"Style points, though," said Shay appreciatively. "I liked it."

"What did you *do*?!" demanded Nadia, clutching her temples. Taina stepped out of her way as Nadia ran out into the lab. There was nothing of VERA left for her to salvage. Her personal assistant was gone, disintegrated by her own Sting. She had to get another one. She could call Margaret; Margaret would understand. It hadn't been long since she'd left the lab; she might still be awake. Nadia patted her pockets; where was her phone?

"Phone's hidden," said Ying. "VERA's gone. Your water boiled; I'm going to make you a chamomile." And with that, Ying walked back to the lab's kitchen.

Nadia stood outside her bedroom door in shock. She was utterly frozen. Her whole head was on fire. There was something wrong with her; VERA was supposed to help her figure it out. VERA was the only person who had been there for her in weeks, the only person who understood her project, the only person who...

The only person who...

Person?

Hologram.

Computer.

*Machine.*

Something hot pressed into Nadia's hands. Her tea.

"Here," said Ying. "Let's sit."

Nadia felt the weight of the mug, the heat radiating through the porcelain and almost burning her palms. She let it. It felt real; it kept her here and out of her head.

That was probably a good thing.

"Could someone please talk to me for a minute," said Nadia, sitting down next to the scratched formica table in the kitchen. The rest of the G.I.R.L.s took chairs around the table. "About anything. At all."

"Alexis is trying to get a hold of the olds," Taina updated the group.

"I am trying to get my biceps to look like Linda Hamilton's in *Terminator Two: Judgment Day*," Ying said very seriously. "She can do so many pull-ups."

"Just wait till you see Mackenzie Davis's arms in *Terminator: Dark Fate*," Shay teased. "Seriously, though, we've watched so many nineties movies that all I can think about are high-waisted jeans and how to build an actual Stargate," she went on, groaning. "For what it's worth, I'm pretty sure if we account for the stellar drift it's not, like, *entirely* impossible—"

"I think I've been talking to plants more than humans and it's starting to make me feel weird," blurted Priya. "Is it totally weird if I also start to see your therapist? She knows about powered people, right?"

Nadia held the steaming mug between her hands, tight, and looked at each girl seated around the table. Priya, scared to become her own kind of Super Hero. Shay and Ying, happy and also maybe a little bit tired of seeing only each other. And Taina, who always wanted the best for her friends but didn't always know how to express it. She loved them all. So, so much. More than anything else in the entire world.

So… why hadn't she wanted to talk to them about her project? She hadn't felt the overwhelming, all-consuming intensity she had last time she threw herself into her work in the midst of a manic episode. She had just been certain that she was on the right path; so absolutely, unequivocally certain that she didn't feel the need to seek out any other opinions.

And why had she been so *positive* that it was a good idea, anyway?

The screaming was subsiding. Her eyes were throbbing, but less. It was good. Almost.

"Hey." Taina nudged Nadia's calf with one of her crutches. "Check the mirror again."

Nadia steeled herself. She left her tea behind on the table and walked slowly back over to the cabinet. When she looked at herself in the mirror once more, she saw Nadia.

*Just* Nadia. Her eyes were back to normal.

Nadia spun. "How did you know…?"

"Taina figured it out," said Ying.

"We would have figured it out, too," Priya added, a little defensively.

"Except…" Shay looked down at her hands. "We weren't really here."

Ying nodded. "Any of us."

Priya sighed. "We weren't. And we're sorry. All of us."

"I mean, I was clearly the best friend of all of us—"
Taina was interrupted by shouts from the other girls.

"Excuse me—!"

"I mean—"

"Listen—"

"Well, I *was!*" Taina said loudly.

"I'm sorry, too," said Nadia. "I was so busy watching myself for the things I knew about that I didn't watch myself for the things I didn't know about. If that makes sense. I don't think it did. Basically I should have just called you guys. Or listened to Taina."

"Agreed. You absolutely should've listened to me." Taina grinned. "I want that in writing later."

Nadia smiled, so relieved to be back in a place where they could make jokes.

"You were just too obsessed with the wrong things," Taina explained. "It's not that it's weird that you were obsessed, that's completely normal." Nadia tilted her head. She had to give Taina that one. "It's that *normal* Nadia would have been obsessed with the A.I.M. break-in and bringing Bee-Boi up to functional and getting us all together in the lab to work on Maria's list. Instead you decide to hook an AI we know *nothing about* up to the quantum realm without telling anyone? Nah." Taina shook her head.

"But to what *end?*" asked Nadia. She took a sip of her tea

– still too hot. "Are you suggesting this is some sort of Ultron situation? VERAs gone rogue? Or..." She hated to even bring it up, to even consider it, but she had no choice. "Or do you think it's Margaret, and she's trying to..." Nadia wracked her brain for the most devious plan she could possibly come up with on short notice. "Make a... really small VERA?"

"Seems like we'd need to study a VERA for that," Priya said dryly.

Ying crossed her arms. "Oh, did you have a better idea for disabling the thing without disintegrating it?"

"I could have... wrapped it in a... plant...?" Priya suggested awkwardly.

"I love your whole plant vibe," Shay said gently, "but I just don't think that would have cut it."

Nadia blew on her tea. "Could we just buy another one?" She was feeling more clear headed than she had in weeks. It was amazing.

"Sold out across the state." Taina shook her head. "I checked this morning."

"But did you check with your older sister?" Alexis walked into the lab, gold high-tops glinting under the fluorescent lights. They matched the white-and-gold box in her hands.

A brand-new VERA.

"¡*Guau*, Alexis!" Taina pushed herself to her feet on her crutches. "How?!"

"You don't want to know," she said, slamming the box down on the kitchen table. "Okay, I'll tell you. Janet and Bobbi didn't answer my texts after I got off the phone with you, so I drove straight to Stark Tower. Aunt Pepper had a whole cupboard of these things, I swear. And by that I mean three. But when the entirety of New York State is trying to get their hands on one of these, three is, like, a *lot*.

"They were next to the composting-powered solar cells in her lab. She hadn't even opened them. I think F.R.I.D.A.Y. kind of hates the idea of VERA. I think that because F.R.I.D.A.Y. told me so as I was running out of the building. Which she let me do. And now I'm here." Alexis finally took a breath. "So, what are you nerds gonna do about it?"

The G.I.R.L.s looked at the box and looked back at each other.

Nadia took another sip of her tea. Ice-cold. Of course.

## NADIA'S NEAT SCIENCE FACTS!!!
Tea will always be too hot and then you will forget about it and then it will be too cold. This isn't really science. This is just a fact.

But it didn't matter. They knew what they had to do. It was time to *science*.

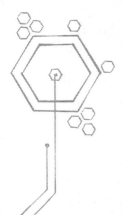

# CHAPTER 17
## SCIENCE'D

This.

*This* was what Nadia had missed most this autumn.

She'd been too caught up with her to-do list and Maria's list and all the other complicated things going on in her life to realise that the solution to her problems might have actually been to *stop* thinking about her problems and to start spending time with her friends. To talk to Shay and Ying about their relationship so they didn't feel like they had to isolate themselves. To talk to Priya about her new powers so she didn't feel like she had to handle that alone, either.

She'd been so busy trying to get to know her mother that she'd neglected the people who were still in her life. In trying to reconcile with the past and put it behind her, she'd somehow become trapped in it. And if they had all just been a little better at communicating, maybe it wouldn't have been so long before one of them realised that Nadia was relying a little too closely on that little gold device.

The same device that now lay in pieces all over the lab floor. This time intentionally.

But, while VERA might have R.I.P.'d in pieces, the other pieces of Nadia's life were finally falling back into place. She'd felt so alone this fall and she hadn't even realised it. Relying on VERA wasn't the same as having her real friends around. A hologram could never make her laugh like Shay, could never find a weird new obsession like Ying, could never show her exactly how to prune a houseplant like Priya or deliver a burn as scathing as one of Tai's. She'd made do, sure, and trusted too much in something about which she knew too little. But there was no comparison to the real thing. To her real friends.

*Build a family*, Maria had written. The tug in Nadia's chest told her that she'd already completed the most important item on the list. That her family was right here.

Priya had helped break the thing apart, safely – her vines exerting just the right amount of pressure in the right places to pop the top off of a gold box that definitely had no tiny toothpick hole for maintenance. Shay and Taina were examining VERA's guts, getting an idea of her physical functionality. Ying was running tests on what exactly the thing was made of.

And Nadia had connected VERA to her personal computer in order to interface with it – and, hopefully, learn its secrets. And Nadia deeply hoped that they were VERA's secrets alone. There was no question the AI had done something to her – and to the people in Times Square, and at the financial services building. There were VERAs in each of those locations and inside the office building. She must have even tapped into the massive billboards in Times Square, broadcasting her signal to everyone within range – that's why they'd all turned gold. Everyone there had strangely dilated pupils; they'd all been behaving in strange ways. Nadia hadn't exactly caused any property damage like most of the people they'd seen, but she had almost caused some damage to her closest relationships. In some ways, that was so much worse.

But Nadia hoped – *really* hoped – that's where this all ended. AIs had a nasty habit of turning evil. Everyone knew that, even people who grew up in spy-training facilities and had to catch up on pop culture a few decades later than everyone else. She had an evil AI relative, right alongside the good AI relatives. It was a totally reasonable theory.

Much more reasonable, Nadia thought, than her mentor, latest personal hero, and new friend Margaret being the actual evil here.

Taina wasn't wrong, of course; Margaret was white and wealthy and privileged and used that privilege to launch her business. She was granted a sought-after internship at Pym Labs, no doubt over plenty of equally-if-not-more-gifted girls like Taina, who didn't have the financial or circumstantial advantages.

Margaret was certainly driven, but Nadia just didn't want to believe that she was doing all of this in service of some broadly evil goal. It just didn't make sense. Margaret talked at length about making the world a better place; surely she hadn't meant it in the same way as Monica Rappaccini. Monica was just looking out for herself. Margaret was looking out for the people who lacked her privilege. Nadia had to believe that. She *had* to.

So Nadia kept her headphones on to block out the outside world as she raced through lines of code, searching for anything that looked out of the ordinary.

Of course, this was a state-of-the-art AI. *Everything* looked just a little bit out of the ordinary.

Search parameters. Internet connection. There was the code Nadia had injected earlier, teaching all the VERAs how to self-repair. Voice recognition. Image generation.

And...

"There!" Nadia whipped off her orange cat-ear headphones with one hand and pointed to her screen with the other. Her friends, all deeply into their own work, dropped what they were doing to crowd around behind Nadia, staring at her screen.

"What are we looking at?" Priya asked, echoing what the group was thinking.

"This section." Nadia highlighted the code in question. "It's genius. It's incredible. It's... subliminal."

## NADIA'S NEAT SCIENCE FACTS!!!

We all have two parts of our mind: the conscious and the subconscious. The conscious mind is the one that is aware of stuff ("I really want a bagel"). The subconscious mind is the one that isn't aware of stuff, but still influences your awareness (you saw an ad for a bagel three hours ago and your brain has been secretly and quietly obsessed with it ever since). In order to stay under our awareness radar, 'subliminal messaging' is designed specifically to target our subconscious minds (placing bagel ads in subway stops, arguably). Basically, it uses signals that we see or hear that we're aware of, even if we're not aware of how they may be influencing us.

The science behind subliminal messaging is highly contested, but a key component of the idea behind subliminal influence is priming, a phenomenon in which people are influenced to react in specific ways to specific stimuli. Playing ads featuring music from one's childhood might trigger an emotional response that leads to the purchase of a product. Playing French music in a supermarket can have an impact on shoppers' desires to purchase French wine. (Like the bagel ads, the background music is an example of a *supraliminal* – as opposed to subliminal – stimulus, something that is technically above the threshold of consciousness though we still might not be actively attuned to it.) Humans are easily influenced creatures, and both supra- and subliminal stimuli can influence us, especially if we already have an affinity for the thing being pushed at us anyway.

Like, say you really like working, and

something tells you to do more work, but of a particular kind. You could be easily pushed into working, in this case.

Just a hypothetical. Moving on.

"So VERA's been... telling you what to do? Without you even knowing it?" Shay asked, shocked. "Could this be why Ying won't stop talking about *Titanic*?"

"I was never around VERA," Ying corrected her. "And, to be fair, the physics *does* support that Rose could have fit more than one person on that door—"

"VERA's been telling me what to do," Nadia said firmly. "It's been affecting my brain the same way being high would – I've been addicted to doing whatever VERA wanted me to do. In this case, it seems like she wanted me to connect her to the quantum realm at the expense of everything else."

"I knew you would never have bought those white tennis shoes without outside influence." Priya nodded sagely. "*Way* too on-trend."

Nadia looked down at her feet. They *were* on-trend. Ugh.

"Why?" asked Ying. "Is there some cabal of dastardly VERAs trying to take over a very small universe?"

Nadia shook her head. "I don't know. But it gets worse." She highlighted a second portion of the code. "This here? This is a countdown. The code is recycling itself over and over again, the numbers getting smaller every time. And it looks like it's going to terminate at midnight. *Tonight.*"

Shay gasped. "Just like *Independence Day!*"

"What happens when it Terminators?" asked Ying.

Nadia shook her head. "I can't be certain. But it's linked directly to the subliminal code."

"I can guess." Priya crossed her arms over her chest. "Times Square, the gold billboards? That was just a test case – telling a big group of people what to do, en masse. If I'm reading this correctly, at midnight, every single person with a VERA is going to be completely under her control."

"Time's up," said Ying.

"That's only three hours from now!" Shay said, shocked.

"I hate to be the one to point out the obvious here," Taina piped up, "but is no one else concerned that this might not be VERA? Sorry, Nadia, but your new friend sucks and I've told you that from the start."

"I know," Nadia said, twisting around in her chair to face her friends. "And you're right." She saw the surprise on their faces at the admission. "We can't rule Margaret out of this yet."

"So what do we do?" Shay rested her hands on her hips. The girls all looked at Nadia. It was up to her to decide.

But really, it was hardly a decision at all. Nadia loved a lot of things. It was her thing. But there was one thing she loved more than anything else – more than good Ethiopian food, and synthwave, and cropped hoodies. More than rule-breaking. More than Lola and her driving instructor. Even more than her Wasp suit.

It was the G.I.R.L.s, of course. Nadia would always choose the G.I.R.L.s and their safety above everything else.

And they had an evil AI to destroy.

———————●

Like her biological mother, Nadia loved making lists. Like her machekha, Nadia loved ticking things off lists. Nadia didn't love either of those things *because* of the older women in her life; it was coincidence or fate or biology or some combination of the above. Nadia was her own person. But she liked that list-making made her feel connected to Maria and Janet, in a way.

Sometimes list-making was more helpful than other times.

- Take meds
- Go to HoffTech
- Find Margaret
- Destroy VERA servers
- Determine if Margaret evil yes/no

Admittedly, there wasn't much to their plan.

But Nadia figured it was beautiful in its simplicity.

"This it?" asked Alexis. She was behind the wheel of the big Pym Labs van that Nadia had co-opted for G.I.R.L.-related activities. This definitely counted.

"This is it," confirmed Nadia from the passenger seat, peering through the blacked-out windows of the big glass structure just across the road from where Alexis was deftly parallel parking. Nadia hated parallel parking. Especially in the van.

Behind Nadia's chair, Taina pushed a wireless earpiece into place and turned to face her wall of monitors. "All set here, too," she confirmed. The back of the van had been fully equipped as a mobile command centre, and Taina would be monitoring the team from the moment they stepped out of her sight to the second they were back in the safe confines of the G.I.R.L.mobile.

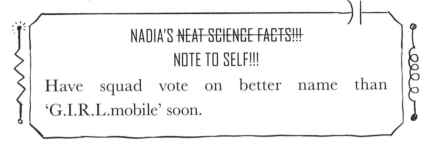

NADIA'S ~~NEAT SCIENCE FACTS!!!~~
NOTE TO SELF!!!
Have squad vote on better name than 'G.I.R.L.mobile' soon.

Taina was the best Mission Control person Nadia could ever ask for, and she always relied on her advice and intel while in the field. Nadia was particularly glad she would have Taina in her ear today. With Alexis in the van to help Taina out and Shay as an additional lookout, Nadia felt like they wouldn't miss a thing from outside the building.

Nadia unbuckled herself and swivelled around in her chair. They were all here – the whole G.I.R.L. squad, ready to take on VERA.

And hopefully save the world. No pressure.

Nadia watched as Priya gathered up the plants she'd brought with her; as Ying checked all the straps and buckles on her suit; as Tai powered on all her monitors; as Shay tested her high-powered sensors and miniature teleporter; as Alexis watched her rear-view camera like a hawk. They each had their own purpose. They each fit their roles perfectly. And together, they made up a beautiful, rich tapestry that would feel incomplete were even one of them absent. Nadia thought it was beautiful.

And she was ready to kick some butt.

"G.I.R.L.s," said Nadia. Everyone in the van looked away from what they were doing a moment ago and up at Nadia. "If Ying's nineties action movies have taught me anything, it's that this is the moment where I am supposed to give a big, inspiring speech about how we will all win the day and be heroes and yay, America! Or something."

Ying nodded with grave seriousness.

"But…" Nadia hesitated, taking a deep breath. "I don't think I have to do that. I think we know what we have to do. We know who we are, and we know why we're here. And we all know that when we're together, there's nothing in this whole world that can stop us."

"Almost like…" Tai winked at Nadia. "… we're *unstoppable*."

The whole van shook with the weight of the G.I.R.L.s' collective groan. But Nadia knew a happy groan when she heard one.

⸻

"We're in," Nadia said quietly, knowing Tai would pick it up from her position in the G.I.R.L.mobile. Priya and Ying were right behind Nadia as she stepped through HoffTech's glass front doors. Ying had on her best black Lycra. Priya, who already clutched two pots, lit up as she saw the veritable plant paradise that was the HoffTech front lobby.

"Holy fiddle-leaf fig," she breathed. "Thank god for Insta trends."

Nadia, for her part, had her full Wasp suit on underneath her beige trench, like some combination of a '40s detective and a modern-day flasher, if what she was flashing was cool science.

And Nadia was *always* flashing cool science.

Walking back into HoffTech for the first time since freeing herself from VERA's influence, Nadia took in the lobby again. You can't know a person through their things – you can't even get to know them through a *list* of their favourite things. You can only know the way you interpret them.

And right now, Nadia was interpreting the whites and birches of the HoffTech office as a carefully constructed facade; a sheen of Instagram-cool over the truth of what was really happening here. A hoodie and jeans. No colour; no creativity. Just what you expect to see. Nothing more. Nothing worth examining closer.

"I'm in position," Shay's voice buzzed over the G.I.R.L.s'

earpieces. She was set up across the street as lookout. In case she needed to get to the G.I.R.L.s' side quickly, she held one side of a small, portable transporter. Ying carried its companion in one of her suit's many hidden pockets. For now, she kept an eagle eye on the street, in case any shady characters arrived at HoffTech HQ.

Well, shadier characters than a flasher, a goth yoga teacher and a girl toting potted plants around.

It was, admittedly, a high bar.

Nadia took a deep breath. In ballet, Nadia was always taught that you check your nerves at the wings. Nerves served you up to a certain point; they made you practise hard, got you back up after a fall, convinced you to work your feet until they bled so that by the time you got onto that stage, you knew every move, every beat without question.

But when you got to the wings, when the audience was right there and it was time to perform, the nerves no longer served you. You either knew what you were doing on stage, or you didn't. Put them aside, get out there and do what you came to do.

Nadia was going to do what she came here to do.

She marched right up to the front desk – and to VERA. It was long past the end of the normal workday, pushing eleven p.m. But like most work-whenever tech offices, there were still a few people wandering in and out of the lobby, and from the outside Shay still reported lights on in the upper floors. People were still here, coding away.

Not for long.

"VERA," Nadia said, as authoritatively as she could. "We're here to see—"

"Core hours are ten a.m. to four p.m.," VERA cut her off. "Please come back tomorrow."

"We're here to see Margaret Hoff. And we need to see her now."

"Very good," the VERA responded. Nadia looked at her two friends smugly. It just took the right *attitude*, sometimes. "Core hours are ten a.m. to four p.m. Please come back tomorrow."

Okay, maybe it wasn't all about attitude.

Nadia stepped back with surprise as Ying grabbed the gold brick off the table, a mirror image of earlier in the evening, and held it right up against her mouth.

"Listen, you little mind-bending monster," she hissed, "you get us to Margaret right now, or I'm going to do to you what I did to your little gold friend. Is that what you want?"

Nadia loved Ying because she was the Black Widow of their group, and the Black Widow was Nadia's favourite

Super Hero. Well, one of Nadia's favourite Super Heroes. Specifically because she was good in moments just like this.

There was silence.

"Core hours are ten a.m. to four p.m.," VERA finally repeated.

Ying let out a strangled yell and slammed the thing back down on the glass counter, sending hairline fractures out across its surface like a map of Ying's frustration.

"Okay, no big deal." Nadia put her hands on Ying's shoulders. She could see Priya had gone somewhere else in her mind for a second; probably introducing herself to all the different plants in the room. "I texted Margaret, I know she's here. I'll just give her a call, and—"

"Nadia?" Margaret rushed out of the elevators. She looked just as she had earlier, except she'd traded her maroon hoodie for a navy one. Her hair was pulled back in a rushed pony, strands of chestnut brown escaping around her face. Exactly what you'd expect. She looked like Nadia's friend. Like someone who just wanted to help. She hurried over to the girls. "And Priya! And..."

"You don't need to know," said Ying.

Margaret stared at her for a minute before shaking her head and turning back to Nadia. "Are you all right?

I thought you were doing better after I left, but your text made me nervous – what's going on?"

Nadia grabbed both of Margaret's hands in hers. Her nails were perfect, a manicured greige. Nothing to see here. Don't look any closer. "It's an emergency. Can we come upstairs?"

"Of course, of course." Margaret tugged Nadia towards the elevator. "Don't worry about checking in with VERA, you're with me and it's after office hours."

"We've heard," Ying said dryly.

Margaret waved her pass over the scanner in the elevator and hit the top button. The four of them were whisked up and up and up, and Nadia talked quickly.

"While I was working on VERA, I discovered something in her code." Nadia stared straight at the elevator doors while she talked. She couldn't stand to see Margaret's face. She wasn't sure if she was ready to know if this was VERA or if it was Margaret. "A subliminal messaging system. Designed to take control of users' minds. I think it was responsible for what happened at Times Square."

The elevator slid to a halt and the doors opened. Margaret didn't say anything; she just exited and held the elevator open for the rest of the girls to step out.

Nadia finally looked at Margaret as they ascended the

spiral staircase into the planetarium. Her friend's usual confident, calm demeanour had vanished. She looked worried. Not just worried – *scared*.

"Okay," said Margaret, more to herself than anyone else. "Okay. Malicious code is something we can handle. Stay here; I'm going to get some portable workstations. Are you okay to give this a go?" she asked Nadia. "I don't want to call anyone else down here in case…"

"… they're responsible for the code," Nadia finished Margaret's sentence. "Go. We're ready to work."

"Good." Margaret rushed back to the spiral staircase. "And nice plants!" she yelled back over her shoulder. Priya squeezed her pots closer.

Nadia felt more relieved than she had since this whole thing started. Margaret wasn't responsible for any of this. She couldn't be. She seemed just as shocked as Nadia and her friends. They were going to be able to fix this, together. And then they'd find whoever was responsible for this.

Together.

"I'm still not convinced." Ying bent into a stretch, determined to stay limber, just in case.

"Nothing out here," reported Shay.

"And no chatter online," came Taina's voice. "No one

has any idea the VERAs are about to go nuclear. You've got just under two hours to fix them."

Priya sat cross-legged against one wall, setting her plants next to her. The planetarium, like the rest of HoffTech, also had plants and vines lining the walls. Priya closed her eyes.

Nadia bounced up and down on her toes and wished she had some music to listen to; anything to distract her from the next couple hours of work ahead of her. It wasn't going to be easy – especially not if VERA knew what they were about to do – but she was certain they could do it.

She tilted her head up and looked into the heavens (such as they were). The dome overhead rotated, the constellations spinning slowly but determinedly through the sky. It was Thanksgiving at the end of this week; the autumn night sky was crisp and beautiful. Even when it was fake.

And then it all went dark.

"Argh." Margaret's voice floated up from the spiral staircase. "Nadia, can you help me with these?"

Nadia squinted in the darkness. She didn't want to put on her helmet for her night vision; it would bring up too many questions with Margaret. Instead, she carefully made her way over to the top of the spiral staircase. The light from below was so bright it was almost blinding.

Something was pressed into her hands – the laptops. Nadia grabbed them – but Margaret continued to hold on.

"I've got them," Nadia assured her. "You can let go."

"I'm sorry, Nadia," Margaret said. Nadia squinted. She couldn't see Margaret; the backlight was too bright. "You've been a good friend. But I can't let you ruin this."

Margaret shoved the laptops into Nadia, hard, and Nadia stumbled backwards. Something burst from the top of the spiral staircase. Nadia fumbled for the release on her helmet underneath her trench coat, but she didn't need it. The lights flipped on, the planetarium whirring back to life.

And in front of Nadia stood Margaret.

Dressed *exactly* like the Wasp.

# CHAPTER 18
## CAN'T WE ALL JUST NOT BE EVIL

"I don't want to hurt you," called Nadia from her hiding spot behind one of the planetarium's seats. "You can stop this!"

Margaret shot a Wasp's Sting so powerful it blasted clean through the chair on Nadia's left. She turned her face away from the blast just in time.

"I can't," Margaret yelled back. "You don't understand!"

Nadia took a deep breath and knew she had to do what she did best in these situations: map out her surroundings, consider her entire situation, and then take decisive action. She was going to need to buy herself some time.

She hit the button near her thumb and immediately was

less than a centimetre tall. She ran under the chair, pressed her back up against one of the struts – *Ugh, is that gum? It's always gum* – and tried to figure out what to do next. *Quickly.*

When Margaret had emerged from the stairs Nadia hadn't known whether to laugh or to scream. The idea that Taina and Bobbi and everyone else had been right about Margaret all along – it was too much for Nadia on a day like today. She couldn't reconcile the Margaret in her head, the Margaret she thought she knew, with the woman in front of her. It was cognitive dissonance. It was going to be at *least* four weeks of therapy. She hoped Dr Sinclair was ready.

Nadia had tried to salvage the situation, even as Ying and Priya sprang into defensive positions. "Nice suit," she said, as casually as she could given the circumstances, which were that she was looking directly at Margaret Hoff in a full black-and-green Wasp suit. "From Hank?"

Margaret barked a laugh. "Hank?! Please. You know what he was like. Hank tried to have me *fired*. 'Too driven'. Like he ever told the male interns they were 'too driven'."

"He had some issues," agreed Nadia. "So, Winners, then? T.J. Maxx?"

*"You."* Margaret stepped closer to Nadia, who stood stock-still. "Our VERAs were connected. I had access to

your entire database. Hank never allowed me access to his secrets; this is what I was owed for having to start my career from scratch after that. I made a few modifications after Times Square, though," she said, nodding at Priya. "You have some very interesting friends. And I saw your suit under your clothes. Sloppier than I expected from you, Nadia."

"You were in our *research*?" Priya spat. A wall of vines was beginning to form behind her.

"You're all very good," Margaret said kindly. She held up a palm and the vines behind Priya slowed. "I'm still working out some bugs. But I just want you to listen. Let me explain. Please."

"We're good, actually." Ying sprinted forward and leapt off the ground, swinging her thighs around Margaret's neck. In the next breath, Margaret was gone, shrunk to nothing. Ying's momentum carried her right into a wall. She was back on her feet in an instant.

Nadia felt someone grab her arms from behind. She struggled, but Margaret was strong and fast. She'd caught Nadia off guard, but Nadia held her arm firmly in place, keeping Margaret from shrinking again.

"Server room, *now!*" Nadia yelled at her friends. Priya grabbed her pots and bolted for the spiral staircase, Ying stepping in front of her. As Priya sealed off the top of the stairs with vines, Nadia called after them. "Destroy VERA – I've got Margaret!" She saw the last of the light from below disappear as the plants locked Nadia into the planetarium.

"Please, just *listen*," repeated Margaret. Nadia fired a Wasp's Sting at the ground between them and used the momentum to fly to the other side of the room.

"You used me!" Nadia yelled back, hovering in the air directly in front of Pisces.

"I *need* you!" Margaret countered, swinging her hands in front of her. Plants shot up across the room, gunning for Nadia, who made a mental note to get to the bottom of how she was able to replicate Priya's powers.

Nadia dodged, shooting a plant with a Wasp's Sting and shrinking to avoid another. She ran across its surface, jumping off and grabbing it to swing her legs forward like a gymnast on the parallel bars. As she launched herself off the vine, she popped back to normal size, using her speed and momentum to hurl herself towards Margaret. Her foot connected with Margaret's chin, upending her.

Margaret caught herself on her wings in mid air and fired off two Stings towards Nadia, who easily danced away from them both. "I need you, Nadia," Margaret repeated. "I need you to understand."

"I understand you stole my work and you're *brainwashing* people!" Nadia was livid, and time was running out. She hoped Ying and Priya were well on their way to the server room by now. Dodging another Sting, Nadia zoomed down in size, ducking behind a chair to hide.

Here she was, staring down a giant piece of chewed gum, trying to figure out how her mentor could possibly be responsible for turning her AI evil.

Nadia launched herself into the air and up towards the ceiling. She came to perch on the edge of the planetarium's dome, slowly moving towards the floor. Nadia wanted to take Margaret out. To launch herself across the room and down and place a punch right at the base of her neck and leave her to S.H.I.E.L.D.

But even more than that, she wanted to understand. Nadia wanted to see the best in people, always. But she wasn't a fool. She couldn't believe that she'd been so wrong about this woman. She didn't *want* to believe it. She—

"Nadia, *wait*." She had forgotten that Margaret could also shrink, thereby eliminating her slow-down-time advantage entirely. From the air, Margaret landed gently on the dome with her hands raised. "I want to explain."

Nadia raised a fist, ready to blast Margaret with a Sting. Margaret raised her fist, too. A giant vine slid up across the dome and between the two of them.

She was overpowered. And, more than that, she wanted to *know*.

Nadia dropped her hand. "Fine. Tell me."

"You know VERA has the potential to change the world. You *know*—"

"Spare me the marketing." Nadia crossed her arms.

"Fine," Margaret said bluntly. She dropped her fist. "HoffTech was running out of money. I had the vision for VERA; I knew how important she was. But my father cut me off. He didn't see the potential. First Hank; then my own father. I turned to venture capital, but they started making demands – demands I wasn't comfortable with. I had to find a way to keep this place afloat. It was my *life*."

Nadia counted the exits around her. The vines blocked her escape to the right, but to the left she was free. She could be out of here on her wings in moments. She shifted her stance and continued to listen.

Margaret stepped towards the vine, resting her palms on it and leaning towards Nadia. She spoke quieter. "We had advertisers. Sponsors. The more people buy their products, the more kickback we get. A few small... suggestions... never hurt. Subliminal messaging really only works on people who are already thinking about doing the thing in the message. Didn't you love your white tennis shoes?"

Nadia gritted her teeth. She did love those shoes. They looked so *fresh*.

"Free will is *not* a toy," Nadia said through her teeth. "You don't get to mess with people's brains because you need *money*."

"It was harmless!" Margaret pushed back off the vine, throwing her hands in the air. "No one was hurt."

"And Crédit France?"

"A glitch." Margaret shook her head, pacing back and forth behind the vine. "Not our code."

"And Times Square?"

"A bug!"

"And the countdown?"

Margaret froze. "What countdown?"

Nadia squinted. Was Margaret being obtuse on purpose? Was this part of her trick? "The countdown. Embedded in VERA's subliminal code. Terminating at midnight. Tonight?" Every time Nadia added a statement, she expected to see recognition dawn on Margaret's face. But it never came.

Instead, Margaret sat down on her vine.

"That's the bug. The same bug we saw before Crédit France, and before Times Square." Margaret looked up at Nadia. "And it's happening again? Tonight?"

"System-wide," Nadia confirmed. "We assumed it was VERA herself. Or you."

Margaret shook her head. "VERA's incapable of that, even after you added the CodePhage in our office. We made certain of it. We're not trying to be Ultron."

Nadia stepped forward, cautiously. "Can you shut VERA down while we figure this out?"

"No!" Margaret leapt up again, and the vine vibrated. "No. We can't. We'll lose millions if we shut our network down, even for an hour."

Nadia launched herself into the air, Margaret a moment behind her, ready to fire a Wasp Sting. "There won't be anything left to lose if we don't stop it, whatever this is. There's no user base if they're all hurt." Nadia zoomed towards Margaret, grabbing her by the arms before she had any idea what was going on. The two tumbled to the floor. Nadia hit the button on both of their suits – same place on each, Margaret hadn't bothered to redesign – and they hit the floor hard, full-size.

Both of them sat up gingerly, rubbing their spines where they'd slammed against the hard floor of the planetarium.

"If it's not you," Nadia said, wincing, "and it's not VERA… then who?"

Margaret looked… devastated. "I told you, we were

forced to take venture capital." It was more of a statement than a question. Nadia bobbed her head. "There was one firm that offered more than the rest. *Substantially* more. Enough to keep us going for the rest of the year, at least. But they asked for access to our code. And our servers."

Nadia slid back from Margaret. She knew what was coming – and she didn't want to believe it.

"Thanks for that, by the way," came a man's voice from behind them.

They both turned to find a man in a non-descript grey suit walking towards them. The remains of Priya's plant blockade hung from the top of the stairwell. Nadia squinted, and realised she recognised him; it was the same dour, middle-aged white man from Margaret's finance meeting, the first day they'd met. The one with the hair and beard so black it shone almost blue in the light.

And behind him trailed Monica Rappaccini, her pupils so wide Nadia could no longer tell the colour of her eyes.

"Roger Bain," Margaret spat, standing up. "What are you doing here?"

"A.I.M. has come to collect on its investment," the man said. He offered Nadia a hand. "Nice suit."

Nadia stood up without taking the assist, piecing

it together. "You've been altering people's brains using Margaret's subliminal code."

The man Margaret called Bain shrugged and dropped his hand. "She's a genius, isn't she?" Three more A.I.M. lackeys in their black hazmat suits filed up the staircase.

*The Goth Devo reunion no one asked for,* Nadia thought bitterly.

"We barely had to touch VERA's systems at all," said Bain. "She was already in thousands of homes; after tonight, we'll be able to make people do whatever we ask of them."

"Like fight your wars," Nadia said disdainfully. To her shock, Bain laughed in her face.

"No, my little bug." Bain looked at her the way a father looks at a child he thinks is incompetent. Pitying and condescending. Nadia's least-favourite combination. "We don't need a zombie army. We're not in a movie. We play to people's *strengths*. We need money, we have the employees at a credit union give us money. We need power, we have Monica here build us a test Teleforce."

"Death ray," Nadia said under her breath.

"We need access to the quantum realm," he continued calmly, "we enlist the folks at Pym Labs. It's that simple."

"You do seem simple," Nadia shot back.

Bain tutted. "Too bad. You would have been good little

agents. Monica?" He waved to the woman, and passed his men on the way down the staircase. "I'm going to make sure this is finished. Hoff Tech and VERA are *ours*." Margaret seethed.

"Nice to see you again, Nadia," Monica said, stepping in front of the two women with wings.

"Wish I could say the same," replied Nadia. And she really did. But unfortunately, Monica was still evil. Now more evil than usual. Double evil! The worst kind.

"Are you getting this?" Nadia said, seemingly at random.

"Yeah, I'm getting it," Margaret answered next to her.

"Oh, you *bet*," Taina said in Nadia's ear at the exact same time. "Priya and Ying are hitting A.I.M. agents near the servers, Shay's reporting more outside. They're gonna need an assist."

"Then let's do this," Nadia said, balling her hands into fists. Out of the corner of her eye, she saw Margaret do the same. In perfect sync, they leapt from the ground – and disappeared.

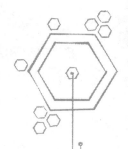

# CHAPTER 19
## PUNCH UP

"You allowed them to do this!" Nadia shouted as she and Margaret pushed an A.I.M agent down the spiral staircase together. He toppled backwards, his idiotic bucket hat popping off as it hit the ground. Pretty useless as a helmet, then, huh?

"I didn't know they were going to brainwash my entire client base!" Margaret waved her hands and vines shot through the air, wrapping the other two A.I.M. agents up and tossing them out of the girls' way. Nadia and Margaret leapt down the centre of the staircase, using their wings to slow their fall.

"What did you expect from *A.I.M.*?!" Nadia shouted up

at her former mentor. "They literally want to overthrow *all governments!*"

"Most governments are terrible!" Margaret landed next to Nadia and began sprinting through the office. "Servers this way!"

"More agents incoming," Shay's voice warned Nadia.

"Monica's on the comms, searching for you," added Taina.

"Got it," she confirmed. Nadia sprinted after the older woman. "That still doesn't mean you should take money from techno-anarchists, Margaret!" They were running through Margaret's aesthetically bland white-and-birch cubicles, right towards another wall of A.I.M. agents.

"I know!" Margaret's voice cut off as she shrank. "I know," she said again, popping back to full size and using her momentum to clothesline two of the agents. They dropped like bricks. "As soon as we started working together – talking about your lists and Hank and your dreams – I knew I'd made a mistake!"

Nadia hit her button and shrank. She waited a moment and Margaret appeared next to her. Nadia grasped Margaret's hands in hers and used her wings to spin the two of them in a circle, faster and faster and faster, until—

"Now!" she yelled over the rushing air. Both Nadia and Margaret hit their buttons and sprang back to full size, a devastating *pas de deux* whirlwind in the middle of the office. Plants went flying. Files and phones were upended. A.I.M. agents went crashing through floor-to-ceiling windows. Not too bad, if Nadia did say so herself.

"Down one more floor!" Margaret yelled, bolting for the emergency exit. Nadia followed, and Margaret sealed the door behind them with plants – just like Priya.

She stopped inside the door and grabbed Nadia by the shoulder. Nadia stopped to look Margaret in the eye, through their helmets. "I'm sorry, Nadia," Margaret said. She sounded sincere. "I tried to get too big too fast and do too much at once, and I think you know how that feels."

Nadia didn't move. She didn't want to admit it, even though they both knew it was true. "You were still using VERA to trick people into buying things they didn't need. You still partnered with A.I.M." Nadia shrugged off Margaret's hand.

"I know." Margaret retracted her helmet. "I left the door wide open for Bain." Someone started pounding on the emergency exit behind them, but Margaret's plants held true. "I just wanted to tell you that I know I screwed up."

Nadia looked at the straining plants and back at Margaret. The truth was that she wasn't entirely certain that Margaret was apologising for the right reasons. Sure, Margaret was obviously upset that A.I.M. used an exploit in her own code to gain access to her system. But she didn't seem that remorseful about including the subliminal messaging in the first place. VERA could do a lot of good, it was true; but nothing was worth robbing people of their free will. *Nothing.*

Nadia grew up in a place where freedom was a joke, a story Americans told themselves so they could sleep at night. And she knew this country wasn't perfect. But the people here had provided her with a second chance. No matter how much she wanted to change the world, she would never ever *ever* sacrifice her values or the free will of those around her in order to effect that change. That would make her just as bad as A.I.M.

Or the Krasnaya Komnata.

Margaret wanted so badly to prove to Hank, and to her father, and even to Robert Bain that she knew what she was doing. That she didn't need their approval. That she was going to change the world. But, for once, it looked like Hank's instincts were right. Margaret's motives were suspect. You couldn't prove anything to the people who'd doubted you in your past; they would never be able to give you the validation you were searching for. You could never know how someone long-gone would feel about *Attack of the Clones.*

And it didn't really matter. Your past was your past. The

only thing you could control was how you reacted to it, and what you did next. But Margaret hadn't realised that; she had been so focused on the big picture that she'd lost sight of the people she was going to have to step on in order to make it. She had been willing to hurt people on her way to the top. And that was unacceptable.

The slamming was getting louder. They had to go. *Now.*

"You did screw up," Nadia agreed. "You can start making up for it now, by destroying VERA's servers and helping me save my friends."

Margaret was already running down the stairs.

⊶————————

"Next left!" shouted Margaret, taking the corner at breakneck speed. She and Nadia were almost at the server room – almost able to shut VERA down once and for all. They were running out of time; only fifteen minutes stood between them and A.I.M.'s brainwashing signal. It was now or never.

Nadia skidded round the corner and immediately shot two Stings into the ceiling. Drywall rained down around them, clouding the air with dust. It bought Nadia just enough time to hit her trusty button, shrink to Wasp size and assess the situation. She flew forward through the dust and scanned the area.

The door to the server room was open in front of her, cold air pouring out of it and chilling the hall. Inside, Monica and her A.I.M. agents were trying desperately to keep the system running, despite interference from Ying and Priya. Vines spilled in tangles over the entire corridor, stemming from Priya's two pots and backlit by a chorus of blinking red lights that caught the dust and made for a deeply eerie haze. The vines held the door open, pinning several A.I.M. agents to the walls.

Ying was standing with one foot each on two downed agents, tossing a third into the air and towards a wall as Nadia approached. Nadia zipped through the open door and directly into the cold room, a cacophony of whirring fans and buzzing servers greeting her tiny ears. In the centre of the room, Priya was trying to dash round Monica to flip the main circuit breaker.

This – this is what happened when the G.I.R.L.s worked together. Nothing could stand in their way.

Nadia flew straight for Monica's head, catching herself in her hair – *Eugh, giant dandruff, eugh* – and swinging forward to land on Monica's nose. Nadia could see Monica's hand swinging up in slow motion to swat at her.

Nadia slammed her fist into the bridge of Monica's nose. Monica went flying back into a bank of servers, sparks and wires flying. Nadia pushed off and flipped backwards through the air, landing sideways on one of the server blocks. She ran towards her friends, leaping from server to server, careful to avoid any wiring that could trip her up. As Nadia raced forward, as if in slow motion, she saw something familiar attached to a server on her left – a quantum oscillator. Modelled exactly after the ones she'd been working with Shay to perfect in Pym Labs.

She'd been frustrated before. Now Nadia was *mad*.

Nadia took to the air and kicked her legs out in front of her just as another A.I.M. agent ran through the door, making a beeline for Priya. In an instant, Nadia expanded to her usual size, her feet ramming directly into the agent. Hit by the girl equivalent of a speeding car, the bucket-head slammed into the nearest block of servers and slumped to the floor.

Nadia looked at Priya – and found herself yanked backwards, a gloved arm tight around her neck. She went to shrink, but found her button-pushing hand restrained by the agent's other arm. Letting out a frustrated yell, Nadia pushed her weight back onto the A.I.M. agent and ran her feet up the wall in front of her, using the momentum to flip over his head, breaking the agent's grip. She landed behind him and used her fists to punch out the backs of both of his knees. The man hit the ground with a groan. Nadia hit him with a Sting just to be sure he wasn't getting up again.

Nadia spun towards the door to see Ying blocking three agents from entering at the same time. She watched Ying jab a man in the throat, and he dropped like a brick – but there were still two to go. Her hand now free, Nadia released her Pym Particles with a press of her thumb and zoomed towards the A.I.M. lackey nearest her. They weren't wearing their flamethrowers – Monica must have told them not to endanger the servers more than was absolutely necessary.

That worked very well for Nadia.

Dodging both bucket-heads, Nadia landed on her friend's shoulder. "Ying," Nadia said, using her comms to make up for the sound-wave distortion. "Love Duet?"

Ying's dry chuckle came through loud and clear through Nadia's helmet. "Why the heck not?"

Nadia grinned. She didn't like hurting people. But she *did* love saving the day. "You go left, I'll go right." She felt her friend nod.

In the Red Room, fighting and ballet were two halves of the same whole. They had a lot more in common than one might assume. Ying had told Nadia 'dance fighting' was a thing in some movies, which did make sense. But it was a very literal correlation in the Red Room. The Love Duet was always Nadia's favourite number in Tchaikovsky's *Swan Lake*. She and Ying had been particularly good at it, especially when she was allowed to be Odette to Ying's Siegfried. Nadia had always been better at the turns and the leaps; Ying preferred the supporting role, holding Nadia steady as she flew up into the air in lifts and holds.

The same applied in battle.

Nadia leapt off Ying's shoulder, exploding into the air directly next to the A.I.M. agent on her right, sending him stumbling back as Ying ducked, spun and kicked, relieving the other agent of his connection to the ground. Ying held out her arms and Nadia tucked her waist between them. At the exact same moment Nadia jumped from the floor, Ying hoisted her friend upwards. Nadia fanned her legs out, kicking in a circle – hitting the right agent on the way up, and bashing the left agent on the way down. Both agents both dropped, unconscious. A perfect pas de deux.

Ying set Nadia down gently. The two spared a second for a high-five as Nadia checked out the door. Clear – for the moment.

Worried for her other friend, Nadia rushed over and grabbed Priya. She could feel how weak her friend already was.

"Are you okay?!" Nadia asked Priya. "You have a lot of plants going—"

"Can't for much longer," Priya said through gritted teeth. She slouched to a seated position. "Brain melting."

"Okay," Nadia said, though she did not in that moment feel okay. "Okay. We can do this. Take Ying and Margaret—" *Wait.* Nadia's head snapped up. Margaret. Where was Margaret?

"Looking for this?" asked a voice behind her. Nadia spun. Monica had come round after Nadia's face punch and was pulling herself out of the mess of servers, looking a little worse for wear.

She had something in her hand. Pinched between two fingers, in fact. And if Nadia just squinted, she could see a tiny, struggling figure.

Margaret.

"Waiting for your backup?" Monica taunted. She shook Margaret a little too hard for it to be a joke. Five more A.I.M. agents marched into the server room, Ying among them in cuffs. Nadia smiled. It *would* take five grown men to hold back one Ying.

Monica laughed. "VERA belongs to A.I.M. And so do her users, in just a few minutes. You tried," she said with a shrug, "but you failed. There's no one coming for you now."

Nadia looked everywhere she could for an exit, a strategy, a plan of any kind – but she was outnumbered. Inside the building and out. She had no other options. Her friends were captured; even Margaret had been bested.

That's what you get for using your super suit as a newbie. Nabbed by Monica Rappaccini. So embarrassing. So frustrating. So *buzzing*.

So... buzzing?

But there *was* buzzing. Lots of it. Loud, and getting louder. Nadia looked around the room in a panic. Were the servers about to blow? Monica and the A.I.M. agents looked just as confused. But it wasn't coming from inside the room. It got louder, and louder, and—

"Sorry, were you saying something about backup?" Dedushka stepped through the door to the server room. Nadia was so shocked to see Jarvis in a combat situation that she almost missed Janet and Bobbi following in their full Super Hero attire. Janet flipped out her wings; Bobbi whipped out her battle staves; Jarvis tightened his ascot. Behind them, a swirling portal yawned, projected from a miniaturised teleportation device on the floor – Ying must have dropped it from her hidden pocket intentionally before being cuffed. As Nadia watched in surprise, Shay crossed the portal's event horizon, pushing Tai in her chair. Tai's hands were too busy to push herself, manipulating a hand-held remote control.

Monica stared for a moment – but a moment was all they needed.

Tai grinned. She pushed a joystick forward on her

controller. From behind her, through the portal, an entire colony of Bee-Boi drones flooded the room, buzzing loudly.

And strapped to each one of their backs was a Wasp's Stinger.

Monica's mouth dropped open.

"Aim for the quantum oscillators!" yelled Nadia.

The Bees opened fire.

Nadia jumped on top of Priya, pushing her flat against the ground and shielding her from the debris as the Bee-Bois annihilated every inch of the room's servers. The electric blasts destroyed row after row, decimating VERA's brain from the inside out. They spared a few blasts for Monica and her agents, too, of course; Nadia hoped that other colony members were able to find Roger Bain before he escaped. But destroying VERA was the primary concern right now, and they were taking care of that effortlessly.

The blasting stopped; the buzzing went silent. Nadia lifted her head, coughing even through her helmet. There were sparks and small electrical fires and dust and twisted metal everywhere. Janet helped Ying to her feet while Bobbi and Jarvis checked to ensure all A.I.M. agents were sufficiently unconscious and zip-tied.

"Did they work?" came Alexis's voice over the radio.

Nadia looked around the room at the total and complete carnage where VERA's servers and core used to stand.

"Yes," Nadia responded. "I would say they did. Nice one, Taina."

Tai shrugged, trying to play it cool, but Nadia knew she was proud. "Just glad Wasp Senior and the Golden Oldies were able to show up with us in time," she said.

"Watch it, kid," Bobbi muttered, but Nadia saw her smiling, too.

With a *pop*, Margaret materialised next to Nadia – full size again. She opened her mouth to speak, but Nadia grabbed a zip tie from her dedushka and had it around Margaret's wrists before she even knew what was happening.

"Wait, I just—" Margaret began to protest, tugging her wrists away – but it was too late. S.H.I.E.L.D. agents were already pouring into the room, examining the decimated servers, dragging incapacitated A.I.M. agents out by their buckets – and coming for Margaret.

"This her?" the suit that approached Nadia asked.

"It is," Nadia confirmed. "But she's not entirely at fault. A.I.M. – Roger Bain—"

"On the lam," said the suit. "But we'll find him."

Nadia sighed. "Or *we* will."

Margaret looked at Nadia – and stopped struggling. Her helmet retracted, and Nadia did the same. She looked into Margaret's eyes, and against all odds, still saw her friend.

A friend who had screwed up really, *really* badly.

But a friend nonetheless.

"Thank you," Margaret said to Nadia.

Nadia was surprised. "Thank me? For what?"

"For understanding me," Margaret said simply.

It was the right thing to say, the one thing Nadia could relate to most.

Nadia squeezed Margaret's hands one more time – and tore off Margaret's Wasp gloves, including the access to her Pym Particles. "Limits are important." Nadia gave a signal to the S.H.I.E.L.D. agent, who took over Margaret's restraints. "I hope you learn to respect that. I know I will. So thank *you*, for that lesson."

"Think they'll let me use my powers for good?" Margaret joked. The S.H.I.E.L.D. agent didn't smile.

"I think VERA should stay buried," said Nadia. "But there are rehabilitation programmes. If you could learn to use your brain to help instead of harm…"

The S.H.I.E.L.D. agent turned. "Let's go."

Margaret looked behind her one last time before walking out the door. She left the remains of her life's work around Nadia's feet. She looked, suddenly, very small.

Nadia turned away from the door to find Ying, Priya, Tai, Shay, Janet, Jarvis and Bobbi waiting for her.

"Well," said Janet. "That was very good work, everyone."

"Sorry we were late," offered Bobbi. "Just glad that Alexis texted us all. About eighty-seven times."

"I did break several speed limits on the way here," Jarvis added.

"I won't tell." Nadia gave him a smile. "Is everyone okay?"

Everyone nodded.

"All good here," Alexis said over the comms. "S.H.I.E.L.D.'s clearing out the last of the walking Hefty bags." She paused. "Everyone good there? Is Tai—"

"We're all okay," Ying cut in. "Decidedly *not* terminated."

From behind them, Shay's portal flashed – and suddenly expelled a massive and completely unexpected pile of socks. On top of the pile, a pair of woollen cat ears pointed straight up at the sky.

"My socks!" Priya blurted out. They all laughed, tension slowly dissipating.

The gang was safe.

"So." Bobbi nudged Nadia with a stick. "Think you can take the rest of the night off work?"

Nadia laughed. It would be her first night off in ages.

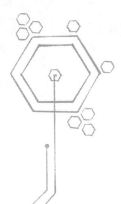

# CHAPTER 20
## THINK SMALL

"Cheers!" Nadia grinned and held up her soda. She was sitting in the G.I.R.L. kitchen – now with a nice new table and chairs, big enough to fit the whole gang! – and celebrating their great success at the Like Minds showcase.

The table was littered with leftovers: turkey, cranberry sauce (the canned kind with the weird indents, obviously), gravy, mashed potatoes, stuffing. Now that Hank Pym's house had been sold, Nadia was officially moved into her room at the lab – and what better way to celebrate her new home than with a real American Thanksgiving dinner?

Which also featured plates of veggie sambusas, atakilt and gomen; Nadia had been craving Ethiopian for *weeks*.

"Can someone pass the salad?" asked Ying, reaching her hands out.

"I can't believe you wanted *salad* at Thanksgiving dinner." Shay shook her head.

"What?" Ying looked at her girlfriend incredulously.

Shay laughed and gave Ying the dish. "You're killin' me, Smalls."

"*The Sandlot!*" Ying said excitedly. "You remembered one!"

"At least she's not seeing dead people," Bobbi sniggered.

Shay shushed her quickly. "We haven't done that one yet!"

Bobbi shoved a giant forkful of potatoes into her mouth by way of shutting up. Once the G.I.R.L. squad had returned to Pym Labs in the aftermath of the whole HoffTech situation, Janet and Bobbi had pulled Nadia aside. Of course Nadia had been grateful they'd arrived to help handle Margaret, but she couldn't help but still be hurt, especially by Bobbi's earlier actions.

"Listen, Nadia," Bobbi said gently, grasping Nadia by the shoulder. "I'm sorry. About before. I hope you know my intentions were good, even if I went about things in the wrong way."

"And I'm sorry if I ever made you feel like you couldn't

come to me with something like Maria's journal," added Janet.

Nadia shook her head. "It wasn't that. I just... didn't want to hurt you."

Surprising Nadia, Bobbi threw her head back and cackled. "Amazing. We were all trying so hard to be nice to each other, we ended up hurting each other. Really solid stuff."

"Next time," suggested Janet, "honesty? Even if it hurts a little upfront?"

Nadia smiled, and threw herself forward, embracing both women in a hug simultaneously. Janet and Bobbi laughed, trying not to bang heads as Nadia's impressive strength dragged them together.

And so they were all back together in the Lab, and things were going to be okay. Things always ended up okay, as far as Nadia was concerned. That was one of the many upsides of having chosen her own family. They always had to keep choosing each other. And they always did.

"So the reception was good?" Janet asked, grabbing some empty dishes off the table and taking them to the sink.

"Definitely," said Priya. "We were also the best-dressed team by a wide margin."

Janet waved a thank-you in acknowledgment of her

skills. She had made sure the team looked impeccable for their presentation on the Like Minds show floor.

"It sounds like Stark Industries is going to pick up the Bee-Bois for further R and D," Taina said excitedly around a mouthful of sambusa.

"They should!" Nadia added enthusiastically. After the debacle at HoffTech, Nadia, Taina, Priya, Shay and Ying had spent the rest of the week together in the lab, working on improving Taina's Bee-Bois. After they removed the weaponised Stingers (naturally), Priya had helped develop a bio-agent that would help make flowers more receptive to the drones, delivered with Ying's sewage-treatment agent. Shay and Taina had made the drones more nimble, and Nadia had linked them all with the quantum-speed connection she'd been working on with VERA. It was the perfect team project, and they'd absolutely nailed it.

"Doesn't seem too small-time to you, still?" Taina asked Nadia, a smirk on her face.

Nadia speared a potato. She deserved that.

"You were all right," she admitted. "There's nothing wrong with starting small." She touched the Crystal Lab charm, safely around her neck once again. She knew she had the strength not to use it. She didn't need to. And it was nice to have it on, as a reminder.

Suddenly, Nadia recalled something she'd been

meaning to do today. "Hold on," she said, jumping up and running to her room. It was all unpacked; a riot of reds and oranges and fairy lights and notebooks and corkboards full of pictures of her family and friends. It was small and cluttered and entirely hers. She loved it. A home. Finally.

On the desk where VERA used to live sat Maria's journal — and a bright pink notebook. Nadia grabbed the notebook and ran back to the kitchen, holding it aloft.

"I have this now!" she said excitedly.

"Please tell me it's not another mind-controlling robo-mom," Taina groaned.

"No." Nadia shook her head. "My *own* journal. Look!"

Nadia opened the book and flipped through it, showing her friends all the different pages. "Here's my current project list — only two to three things at a time, I promise — and here's my ideas for future projects, and here… here's my *own* to-do list."

"That's great, kid," said Bobbi. "What's on it?"

Nadia sat back down in her chair and passed Bobbi the journal. She was happy to share this now, with everyone — no more secrets. Nadia had been clinging to the idea that doing the things Maria wanted to do with her might somehow reveal something more about Maria *beyond* the list — who she was, what she liked, what made her laugh. But with each item completed, Nadia never learned more about

312

Maria – she knew exactly as much about her mother *after* watching *A New Hope* as she did beforehand: that Maria liked Star Wars.

But she knew more about *herself.* She knew that her favourite ABBA song was 'S.O.S.' because it was a bop but it was also kind of melancholy, and that was sometimes how Nadia thought of herself. She knew that she could walk on water and that palacsinta was easier to make than she thought it would be. She knew that she had friends who loved her and wanted to share in these moments with her.

And she knew that Maria and Hank would always live on in her mind. She would never forget them. But she had a family. Right here. A way forward. And she was going to figure out every single item she'd want to put on her *own* list of favourite things.

There was only one way to do that.

"I took some things from Maria's list – like the Insectarium," Nadia explained, "but I added my own things, too. I have a lot to catch up on after the Red Room, but *I* wanted to be the one to decide what was important to me. So 'Thanksgiving dinner in my own home' can be the first item we check off!"

Bobbi passed the journal to Janet with a smile. "I love it. Are you taking suggestions?"

Nadia bobbed her head enthusiastically. *"Absolutely."*

"I notice you kept Star Wars on here," Ying said approvingly.

"'Go shopping with Shay' and 'Learn how to do hair with Priya' are numbers four and five." Shay grinned. "Nice."

"And there's our hockey game." Janet smiled. "Ah, and 'weekly therapy for life'." Janet ruffled Nadia's hair. "Strong choice."

"Is there anything on there about learning to drive a car?" Nadia's dedushka suggested primly. "I sincerely hope so, because you are about to be late for your lesson."

Nadia jumped out of her chair. "Oh no. She's scary when I'm late."

"She's not *that* scary," Bobbi said, rolling her eyes. "Trust me."

"No, she really is." Nadia grabbed her jacket and phone and ran for the door. "See you! Happy Thanksgiving!"

The G.I.R.L.s and A.D.U.L.T.s called their goodbyes to Nadia as she ran out the door, leaving the delicious food smells behind her. She jetted down the elevator and out through the lobby, the Wasp charm on her phone swinging wildly beside her. Nadia ran through the sliding glass doors into glorious rays of the golden-hour sunshine – and sure enough, there was her instructor, leaning against her bright blue ride.

"'Sup, Buzzer?" The blonde woman tipped her chin in greeting. She tossed Nadia her car keys. "You're late."

"I know, I know!" Nadia winced, catching the keys and rushing to the driver's-side door. "Sorry, Captain. Won't happen again."

Carol Danvers slid into the passenger side of her 1971 Mustang and watched Nadia fumble with the keys. "Am I really that scary?"

"Yes." Nadia finally got the car going. She turned to smile at her instructor. "But it's what I like about you."

Carol laughed. "All right. Why don't we head over to my place? Got a certain Flerken that's been missing you."

Nadia's eyes lit up. "I'm ready." She smiled.

Carol nodded and Nadia peeled away from the curb. She was still busy, and she still had a lot to learn about herself – and about being a Cool American Teen. She felt the void left by Margaret in her heart; she hated being disappointed by people she trusted. And she had a long way to go before G.I.R.L. changed the world. But she had her friends, her family, her therapist and the coolest, scariest driving instructor on the planet. Probably on several planets, actually.

Nadia was feeling good about starting small. She knew if she was patient and she worked hard, it would, one day, lead to something big. And that was worth waiting for.

# ACKNOWLEDGEMENTS

I owe a massive debt of gratitude to so many people for this, my actual, real-life YA debut novel that somehow exists in reality: Maria Vicente, my incredible agent and friend, without whom I would be nowhere; Megan Logan and Nachie Marsham, who took a chance on me and helped shape Nadia's prose voice; Lyssa Hurvitz, who got the book into your hands; Laura Bifano, who made the world's most beautiful cover; Dr Matthew Conner and Chris Ceary, MS, who ensured that Nadia's mental health journey was represented as compassionately and accurately as possible; Sarah Sloat, who double-checked my science; Jeremy Whitley, for trusting me with his children; my parents, who showed me what it means to truly prioritise a work-life balance; and Blair, who continues to support me as I try to find that very thing in my own life (slowly). Thanks for waking up with Eevee so often.